THE DEVEREAUX FILE

ROSS H. SPENCER

DIVERSIONBOOKS

Also by Ross H. Spencer

Kirby's Last Circus
Death Wore Gloves

The Lacey Lockington Series
The Fifth Script
The Fedorovich File

The Chance Purdue Series
The Dada Caper
The Reggis Arms Caper
The Stranger City Caper
The Abu Wahab Caper
The Radish River Caper

Diversion Books
A Division of Diversion Publishing Corp.
443 Park Avenue South, Suite 1008
New York, New York 10016
www.DiversionBooks.com

For more information, email info@diversionbooks.com

First Diversion Books edition March 2015.
Print ISBN: 978-1-62681-959-7
eBook ISBN: 978-1-62681-648-0

The Devereaux File is dedicated to John Sebulsky,
world's greatest carpenter,
To Vicky Sebulsky, world's greatest artist,
And to Shirley Spencer, world's greatest wife.

The Devereaux File is dedicated to John Sebulsky,
world's greatest carpenter,
To Vicky Sebulsky, world's greatest artist,
And to Shirley Spencer, world's greatest wife.

When I stop to think
Of the good friends I've had,
My very worst enemies
Don't seem so bad.

—*Monroe D. Underwood*

1

Lacey Lockington eased the balding tires of his road-weary Pontiac Catalina onto the Barry Avenue curbing, thereby granting an additional few inches of clearance to westbound traffic. Not that it'd make a helluva lot of difference on Barry Avenue. On Barry Avenue you could get totaled out while parked in your garage. Still he found consolation in the knowledge that he'd taken the precaution.

He departed the decrepit vehicle, slammed its door, turned his ankle when he stepped on a crumpled Budweiser can, mumbled a few one-syllable words, kicked the offending can into the middle of the street, and limped through the sticky late afternoon toward the vestibule of his apartment building.

The neighborhood was deteriorating rapidly, keeping pace with the rest of the city. Ten more years, Lockington figured—only ten more, and Chicago would be the world's largest ghetto, 250 square miles of slums, Lake Michigan to Elmwood Park, Evanston to Blue Island. He'd given brooding thought to the matter but he'd been unable to pinpoint the origin of a once-great city's decline—there'd been no single event to presage the avalanche, but it was on and there'd be no stopping it, now or ever. Just a few months earlier, Lockington had been forced to shoot two Hispanics who'd attempted to mug him less than three blocks from his own front door. Well, that wasn't entirely accurate—he hadn't been *forced* to shoot them—he might have squeaked out of the predicament because a pair of fancy switchblade knives constitute a poor match for a .38 police special, but he'd killed the bastards anyway, and with considerable gusto. The incident had cost him his job as a Chicago police detective, but what the hell, you win a few, you lose a few.

It'd been another long day at Classic Investigations on West Randolph Street. Boring days are always long. Lockington checked his vestibule mailbox. Empty. That was fine—no news is good news. He unlocked his door, pushed it to find his night-chain hooked. Edna Garson appeared at the narrow aperture, peered through it, detached the chain, and said, "Why, Mr. Lockington, won't you please come in?"

Lockington said, "Thanks a bunch—don't mind if I do." He pitched his crumpled, sweat-stained hat onto his overstuffed chair and flopped on the sofa, watching Edna splash Heublein's double-strength vodka martini mix into a water glass brimming with ice. Edna was in her stocking feet, a certain indication that she was a visitor who felt completely at home. She handed the drink to him and Lockington took a tentative sip of it before settling back and lighting a cigarette. He growled, "What's the occasion?" From their beginning, he'd always played it a shade on the gruff side with Edna and she'd taken it in good-natured stride—it'd become an intrinsic part of their relationship.

Edna said, "Since when do I need an *occasion?*" She wasn't a strikingly beautiful woman, but her big, sincere, smoky blue eyes, a slightly out-of-line ski-jump nose, a wide-mouthed, chipped-tooth smile, and a dazzling mop of honey blonde hair had convinced Lockington that she was mighty close. Then, of course, there was the matter of that long-stemmed, instantly responsive, panther-graceful body. Edna Garson was flat-out bonkers over Lacey Lockington and although the feeling may not have been mutual, it wasn't far from it. Lockington had attempted to avoid dwelling on that question because he was afraid of learning the answer. Edna was saying, "You gave me a *key,* didn't you?"

Lockington nodded, grinning, winking at her, taking a long pull at his vodka martini, half-draining the glass, finding the drink to be excellent. He said, "You brought in my mail?"

"Uh-huh, it's in the trash can—just a flyer from Crossman Brothers Furniture. Crossman's is running a big sale on Chippendale. I didn't think you'd be interested."

Lockington was squinting at her. He said, "Chippendale?"

"Eighteenth century-style furniture—lots of swoops and swirls—heavy on rococo."

"Rococo?"

"Wooden scrollwork, sort of—intricate—excessively ornate."

Lockington shrugged, returning to his vodka martini. He said, "We learn something every day."

Edna withdrew briefly to the kitchen, reappearing with her own martini. She said, "I bought two quarts of the stuff—I figured they'd get us as far as dinner." She shifted Lockington's hat to an end table and sat in the overstuffed chair across from him, wiggling her toes in her nylons. Edna never painted her toenails. Lockington was grateful for that. He suspected women who painted their toenails. He didn't know what he suspected them of, but he suspected them nevertheless. Edna said, "I brought pork chops and delicatessen cole slaw. Okay?"

Lockington said, "Beats hell out of a can of vegetable soup."

"Glad to see me, Locky?"

"Sure."

"Try to control your enthusiasm. Why?"

"Why what?"

"Why are you glad to see me?"

"Because you brought pork chops and delicatessen cole slaw."

Edna reached for his cigarette, lighting her own from it. She returned it and said, "Anything new at Classic Investigations?"

"Oh, sure—a fat woman came in to use my washroom. She got stuck on the john and when I pulled her off she threatened to sue me for invasion of privacy."

Edna shook her head perplexedly. "Locky, what *is* it with you and fat women?"

"I wish to Christ I knew."

"It may have something to do with your horoscope."

"Also, a guy called this afternoon—told me that he'll be in at ten tomorrow morning."

"Regarding?"

"God knows."

"Hungry?"

"If he was, he didn't mention it."

"*You*—are *you* hungry?"

"Probably."

Edna left the room to get the chops started. Their sizzle and the sounds of her clattering around in his kitchen were comforting to Lockington.

She came back into the living room to spruce up his martini and perch on a sofa arm, peeking at him over the rim of her glass. She said, "Would you believe that for two cents I'd move in with you?"

Lockington said, "I'd believe it."

"So?"

"So suit yourself, you have a key."

Edna frowned, considering it. "Well-l-l, probably not immediately, but one of these days."

The pork chops were superb, golden brown, crispy around the edges. Lockington liked his pork chops crispy around the edges. The golden brown part wasn't all that important.

2

TRANSCRIPT: TELEPHONE CALL CLEVELAND-CHICAGO 2017 EDT 5/23/88
FILE # 284-14-8241

CLEVELAND: Blaine?

CHICAGO: Yeah—Horner? Recognized your voice.

CLEVELAND: Look, Blaine, let me have Carruthers in a hurry.

CHICAGO: Stan's on a priority call, you'll have to hold.

CLEVELAND: Hold, my ass! This is hot!

CHICAGO: Carruthers here, Horner. You're in Youngstown?

CLEVELAND: Negative. Cleveland.

CHICAGO: Solo?

CLEVELAND: Negative—I got Phillips.

CHICAGO: What's in Cleveland?

CLEVELAND: Hopkins Airport. Turkey's booked on next United to Chicago under name of J. A. Pfiester.

CHICAGO: What's the sweat? Buy tickets. Have a nice trip.

CLEVELAND: No way. Flight's sold out. You'll have to tag him from your end.

CHICAGO: Damned short notice! He's alone?

CLEVELAND: Negative—female companion. They took a cab from Youngstown. Must have cost a bundle.

CHICAGO: She's seeing him off?

CLEVELAND: Negative—traveling light, but she's booked.

CHICAGO: Under what name?

CLEVELAND: Belle Starr.

CHICAGO: Attire?

CLEVELAND: Turkey in brown hat, brown plaid sports jacket, gray slacks, brown loafers—companion in blue-on-white flowered dress, blue leather pumps, carrying blue leather handbag, white cardigan. Some dish!

CHICAGO: Describe.

CLEVELAND: Young—twenty or so, blue-eyed brunette, five-five, one-fifteen—stacked like hail fucking Columbia!

CHICAGO: Caught that first time around. Turkey's banging it?

CLEVELAND: Looks that way.

CHICAGO: But Turkey's in his fifties!

CLEVELAND: You haven't seen this cupcake.

CHICAGO: They're living together?

CLEVELAND: We located him late last night—we have no pattern, but she spent the evening.

CHICAGO: Code companion "Godiva."

CLEVELAND: I think Godiva was a blonde.

CHICAGO: What's Phillips doing?

CLEVELAND: Watching them getting ready to board.

CHICAGO: Watching them getting ready to *board?* How much time we got?

CLEVELAND: Scheduled arrival at O'Hare 2049 Central.

CHICAGO: Hour and a half—okay, we can hack that. Turkey has what we're looking for?

CLEVELAND: Maybe—he's carrying an attaché case.

CHICAGO: Stay close—phone if they abort.

CLEVELAND: Will do.

Contact terminated Chicago 1920 CDT 5/23/88

3

Edna had busied herself with the dinner dishes, drying them, putting them away before pouring Galliano over ice. They sat at the kitchen table, smoking, sipping Galliano, not saying much. Edna studied Lockington, then winked a calculating, smoky blue eye. She said, "Okay?"

Lockington said, "I think so."

Edna snapped her fingers, craps-shooter-style. "Oh, damn you, Lacey Lockington, you've seduced me *again!*" She popped to her feet, making for the bedroom without looking back, unbuttoning her blouse, unzipping her skirt on the way. Edna had wasted precious little time. She lay on her back, naked, knees cocked, feet flat on the bed, legs spread.

Lockington sat on the edge of the bed, kicking off his scuffed loafers. He said, "Y'know, I'd take an oath that it winked at me."

Edna's smile was dreamy. She said, "I have no control over who it winks at." She rolled onto her right side, reaching for him. She murmured, "Come here, you big bastard—it's been a *century!*"

Actually, it hadn't been a century—it'd been less than forty-eight hours. On Saturday evening Edna had brought ribeye steaks and delicatessen potato salad.

Later, considerably later, shortly after midnight, Edna sat up in bed. She said, "Oh, golly, Locky, I just remembered something!"

Lockington stirred, half-asleep. He mumbled, "Well, whatever it was, we did all right without it."

"Not *that!* You had a telephone call just before you got home. Are you acquainted with a man named—damn, I'm not sure—it could have been Devlin or Deverino—*something* like that."

Lockington opened one sex-blurred eye. "Could it have been Devereaux—Rufe Devereaux?"

"Yes, *that's* it—Rufe *Devereaux*—you know him?"

"Used to. He called?"

"Uh-huh—he's coming into town later tonight."

"From where?"

"I think he said Ohio, but it might have been Oregon."

"Yeah, seeing as how they're so close together and everything."

Edna spun on the bed, jackknifing forward to seize him by the hair of his head, kissing him ferociously. She hissed, "Get smart with me and I'll bite your balls off!"

"So tell me about Rufe Devereaux coming into town tonight."

"That was about all—he said that he'll be staying at the International Arms on Michigan Avenue and that he'd like to have lunch with you tomorrow. He said that he'll call you at the agency in the morning."

"How did he know that I have an agency?"

"I don't believe he did. I gave him the Classic Investigations number. Was that all right?"

"Sure, thanks—I've been wondering what happened to Rufe."

Edna put an inquisitive hand on Lockington's chest. "Locky, by the way, now that we're awake—well, why don't we—?"

"We just *did*."

"We just *didn't*—my God, that was six *hours* ago!"

"We *started* six hours ago—we *finished* less than *two* hours ago!"

Edna said, "Well, yes, if you want to look at it *that* way, but we still have five and a half before daybreak."

"Somehow you always manage to see the bright side, don't you, Edna?"

"Locky, I *invented* optimism!"

"Uh-huh, and you didn't *really* forget about Rufe Devereaux's call."

"Uhh-h-h, well, Locky, you see—that is—okay, you're right, I didn't forget about it!"

"You saved it for now—extra innings wasn't enough—you wanted a double header."

Edna Garson nestled close to Lockington, giggling softly in the darkness. She whispered, "Batter up."

4

Lockington came into the kitchen, yawning, buttoning his shirt, squinting into an eight o'clock sun that blazed through the window like a Viet Cong rocket attack. Edna Garson was buttering toast. She was wearing yesterday's white blouse and navy blue skirt. There was a small grease splotch on the front of the skirt—from the pork chops, Lockington figured. On Edna it looked good. He seated himself at the table as she poured coffee. He said, "Your hair's a mess."

Edna nodded. "A passion perm—you've seen a few." She sat across from him, sipping at her coffee. "Say, could I hustle you for a lift downtown?"

"Sure, if we can get out of here in twenty minutes. I'll be going it alone today. Moose won't be in."

"He's sick?"

"No, he has a bunch of loose ends to attend to—insurance, funeral expenses, grave maintainence—that sort of thing."

Edna frowned into her coffee. "I'm barely acquainted

with Moose, but I can feel for him—he's had a rough row to hoe. You knew his wife well?"

Lockington nodded. "She was like a sister—Helen baked apple pies for me when Moose was my partner on the force."

"Well, you're partners again, sort of."

Lockington nodded, munching toast.

Edna said, "You were at the funeral?"

"Uh-huh."

"How was it?"

"How *was* it? You ever been to a happy funeral?"

"Yes, a couple."

"So have I, come to think of it." Lockington slurped coffee and lit a cigarette. "What's going on downtown?"

"I'm gonna buy a sheer teddy with sequins."

"Why?"

"Why not?"

"What color?"

"What color do you prefer?"

Lockington gave the question some thought. "Black, I guess. Where are you gonna wear this thing?"

Edna winked. Edna had the most provocative wink in all of Cook County, Lockington thought—it promised a great many things, every one of which Edna was capable of delivering in abundance. She said, "Oh, hither and thither, I suppose."

Lockington said, "Hither and thither are okay, but stay the hell out of yon—you could get arrested in yon."

Edna stuck out the tip of her tongue, wiggling it.

Lockington didn't say anything. Neither did Edna until they were on Belmont Avenue, thumping toward the Outer

Drive. Then she wanted to know about Rufe Devereaux. Who was he?

Lockington said, "CIA—Cajun guy from the Baton Rouge area—worked out of the Chicago office until winter before last."

"How did you ever manage to get hooked up with a CIA man?"

"I was a Chicago cop. You don't remember that?"

"Oh, God, who *doesn't?* You just *got* to be in the *Guinness Book of Records!*"

"Well, the Chicago police force has cooperated with the CIA on occasion."

"On what—looking for Russian spies?"

"Not really. Anyway, I drank a lot of beer with Rufe Devereaux."

"And chased a lot of pussy."

"No, I watched Devereaux chase pussy." Which was one-half wrong.

Edna said, "Horse manure." Which was one-half right.

Lockington said, "Hey, Rufe Devereaux got around! He had his first heart attack when he was in the hay with a Clark Street hooker—he was fifty-three at the time."

"He's had more than one?"

"Hookers? Oh, sure, *dozens!*"

"*Heart* attacks!"

"Two that I know of. His second came with a Wilson Avenue pro."

"How old was he then?"

"Fifty-four."

"Whatever happened to him?"

"He recovered, obviously."

"I mean, where did he go?"

"Up to Sheridan Road. Sheridan Road got *hundreds* of hookers."

Edna was glaring at him.

Lockington shrugged. "Hell, I don't know—CIA people won't tell you where they're going—you're lucky if they tell you where they've *been*. With that bum ticker, maybe he retired."

On the southbound Outer Drive Edna said, "What did you two talk about?"

"Baseball, mostly—Rufe was a walking baseball encyclopedia."

"So are you."

"I know some baseball but I wasn't in Rufe's league—he knew baseball *history*. He claimed that the nineteen-oh-six Chicago Cubs were the greatest team ever."

"Were they?"

"Not a chance! The 'twenty-seven Yankees were the best. We'd argue about that."

"Maybe that's why you got along—because you could argue about baseball."

"I suppose so."

"You said baseball *mostly*. What else—pussy?" Edna Garson had the unflagging curiosity of a kitten when it came to matters having to do with Lacey Lockington, and once she'd gotten onto a subject, getting her off it was extremely difficult.

Lockington said, "Men talk about things other than baseball and pussy."

"Okay, *name* one."

"Football."

"Football's a *sport!*"

"So is pussy."

"Oh *shit!*"

"Well, there was one other thing—we listened to country music."

"Where?"

"Honky-tonks—joints on Milwaukee Avenue, usually."

"The Club Howdy?"

"Yeah, there, and that dive a couple of doors south."

"Nashville Corners. I've been in both of 'em—badass places. You like country music?"

"Not as well as Rufe liked it—he was crazy about it—what the hell, he was from Louisiana. I prefer ragtime." This was better—he'd managed to get her switched from his private life to music.

They'd turned into Michigan Avenue, then swung west to the Randolph Street parking lot. Edna walked east with him, holding his hand. They paused at the entrance to the vestibule housing the steps leading down to the Classic Investigations office. Lockington said, "Luck on your teddy."

Edna said, "I have a few other things to do—I'll pop for lunch. How's eleven-thirty?"

Lockington shook his head. "I gotta meet Rufe Devereaux."

"Oh, damn, that's right! Well, I'll see you around, stud." She stood on tiptoe to kiss him on the cheek. Then she headed for State Street. Lockington watched her until she'd vanished into the 9:00 Randolph Street maelstrom. Edna Garson's walk would have busted up a eunuchs' convention.

5

LANGLEY-CHICAGO/ ATTN CARRUTHERS/ 1101 EDT/ 5/24/88
BEGIN TEXT: **AVERY REPORTS UNFAVORABLE
DEVELOPMENTS CHICAGO/ CONFIRM OR DENY**/ END
TEXT/ MASSEY

CHICAGO-LANGLEY/ ATTN MASSEY/ 1003 CDT/ 5/24/88
BEGIN TEXT/ **CONFIRMED/ SERIOUS COMPLICATIONS
THIS STATION**/ END TEXT/ CARRUTHERS

LANGLEY-CHICAGO/ ATTN CARRUTHERS/ 1104 EDT/ 5/24/88
BEGIN TEXT: **TRAIL?**/ END TEXT/ MASSEY

CHICAGO-LANGLEY/ ATTN MASSEY/ 1005 CDT / 5/24/88
BEGIN TEXT: **NONE VISIBLE/ CHECKING**/ END TEXT/
CARRUTHERS

LANGLEY-CHICAGO/ ATTN CARRUTHERS/ 1106 EDT/ 5/24/88
BEGIN TEXT: **LUGGAGE?/** END TEXT/ MASSEY

CHICAGO-LANGLEY/ ATTN MASSEY/ 1007 CDT/ 5/24/88
BEGIN TEXT: **GONE**/ END TEXT/ CARRUTHERS

LANGLEY-CHICAGO/ ATTN CARRUTHERS/ 1108 EDT/ 5/24/88
BEGIN TEXT: **GODIVA?**/ END TEXT/ MASSEY

CHICAGO-LANGLEY/ ATTN MASSEY/ 1008 CDT/ 5/24/88
BEGIN TEXT: **LIKEWISE**/ END TEXT/ CARRUTHERS

LANGLEY-CHICAGO/ ATTN CARRUTHERS/ 1108 EDT/ 5/24/88
BEGIN TEXT: **EXIT ROUTE?**/ END TEXT/ MASSEY

CHICAGO-LANGLEY/ ATTN MASSEY/ 1009 CDT/ 5/24/88
BEGIN TEXT: **FIRE ESCAPE LIKELY**/ END TEXT/ CARRUTHERS

LANGLEY-CHICAGO/ ATTN CARRUTHERS/ 1110 EDT/ 5/24/88
BEGIN TEXT: **YOUR STATION INCOGNIZANT POSSIBILITIES
AFFORDED BY FIRE ESCAPE**/ END TEXT/ MASSEY

CHICAGO-LANGLEY/ ATTN MASSEY/ 1011 CDT/ 5/24/88
BEGIN TEXT: **ASSIGNMENT ROOM 333 UNANTICIPATED/
ORIGINAL RESERVATION ROOM 206/ NO FIRE ESCAPE
ROOM 206**/ END TEXT/ CARRUTHERS

LANGLEY-CHICAGO/ ATTN CARRUTHERS/ 1112 EDT/ 5/24/88
BEGIN TEXT: **LAST MINUTE CHANGE?**/ END TEXT/ MASSEY

CHICAGO-LANGLEY/ ATTN MASSEY/ 1013 CDT/ 5/24/88
BEGIN TEXT: **AFFIRMATIVE**/ END TEXT/ CARRUTHERS

LANGLEY-CHICAGO/ ATTN CARRUTHERS/ 1113 EDT/ 5/24/88
BEGIN TEXT: **SWITCH BY TURKEY OR MANAGEMENT?**/
END TEXT/ MASSEY

CHICAGO-LANGLEY/ ATTN MASSEY/ 1014 CDT/ 5/24/88
BEGIN TEXT: **MANAGEMENT/ 206 SHOWER ON FRITZ/
STORY CHECKS/ MAINTAINENCE CREW QUESTIONED**/
END TEXT/ CARRUTHERS

LANGLEY-CHICAGO/ ATTN CARRUTHERS/ 1115 EDT/ 5/24/88

BEGIN TEXT: **FIRE ESCAPE CERTAIN WAY OUT?**/ END TEXT/ MASSEY

CHICAGO-LANGLEY/ ATTN MASSEY/ 1016 CDT/ 5/24/88
BEGIN TEXT: **NOT CERTAIN/ PROBABLE**/ END TEXT/ CARRUTHERS

LANGLEY-CHICAGO/ ATTN CARRUTHERS/ 1117 EDT/ 5/24/88
BEGIN TEXT: **HOW ELSE IF HALLWAY MONITORED?/ HALLWAY MONITORED OF COURSE**/ END TEXT/ MASSEY

CHICAGO-LANGLEY/ ATTN MASSEY/ 1019 CDT/ 5/24/88
BEGIN TEXT: **NEGATIVE/ PRIMARY CONCENTRATION LOBBY/ HAD UNDER 2 HRS LOCATE HOTEL RESERVATION J. PFIESTER/ SHORT TIME ORGANIZE HOTEL DETAIL/ REACHED INTERNATIONAL ARMS BARELY PRIOR TURKEY ARRIVAL/ SUBJECT GAVE NO INDICATION AWARE SURVEILLANCE INTERNATIONAL ARMS**/ END TEXT/ CARRUTHERS

LANGLEY-CHICAGO/ ATTN CARRUTHERS/ 1121 EDT/ 5/24/88
BEGIN TEXT: **TURKEY TOP FLIGHT PROFESSIONAL/ TOP FLIGHT PROFESSIONALS GIVE NO INDICATIONS**/ END TEXT/MASSEY

CHICAGO-LANGLEY/ ATTN MASSEY/ 1022 CDT/ 5/24/88
BEGIN TEXT: **RECOMMENDED COURSE OF ACTION?**/ END TEXT/ CARRUTHERS

LANGLEY-CHICAGO/ ATTN CARRUTHERS/ 1123 EDT/ 5/24/88
BEGIN TEXT: **NOTHING FOR SITUATION BUT SHELL GAME**/ END TEXT/ MASSEY

CHICAGO-LANGLEY/ ATTN MASSEY/ 1024 CDT/ 5/24/88
BEGIN TEXT: **AGREED/ SHELL GAME**/ END TEXT/ CARRUTHERS

LANGLEY-CHICAGO/ ATTN CARRUTHERS/ 1124 EDT/ 5/24/88
BEGIN TEXT: **LAW HANDLES CORRIDORS AND LOBBY ONLY/ ABSOLUTELY NO POLICE ADMITTANCE 333/** END TEXT/ MASSEY

CHICAGO-LANGLEY/ ATTN MASSEY/ 1026 CDT/ 5/24/88
BEGIN TEXT: **UNDERSTOOD**/ END TEXT/ CARRUTHERS

LANGLEY-CHICAGO/ ATTN CARRUTHERS/ 1126 EDT/ 5/24/88
BEGIN TEXT: **MUNICIPAL AUTHORITIES GET MINIMUM INFORMATION/ NEWS MEDIA NONE/ REPEAT NONE/ THIS NATIONAL SECURITY MATTER/ YOU KNOW ROUTE**/ END TEXT/ MASSEY

CHICAGO-LANGLEY/ ATTN MASSEY/ 1027 CDT/ 5/24/88
BEGIN TEXT: **UNDERSTOOD**/ END TEXT/ CARRUTHERS

LANGLEY-CHICAGO/ ATTN CARRUTHERS/ 1128 EDT/ 5/24/88
BEGIN TEXT: **POSSIBLE COLLUSION HERE?**/ END TEXT/ MASSEY

CHICAGO-LANGLEY/ ATTN MASSEY/ 1029 CDT/ 5/24/88
BEGIN TEXT: **BETWEEN WHOM?**/ END TEXT/ CARRUTHERS

LANGLEY-CHICAGO/ ATTN CARRUTHERS/ 1129 EDT/ 5/24/88
BEGIN TEXT: **BETWEEN ANYBODY AND ANYBODY**/ END TEXT/ MASSEY

CHICAGO-LANGLEY/ ATTN MASSEY/ 1030 CDT/ 5/24/88
BEGIN TEXT: **NOTHING POINTS COLLUSION**/ END TEXT/ CARRUTHERS

LANGLEY-CHICAGO/ ATTN CARRUTHERS/ 1131 EDT/ 5/24/88
BEGIN TEXT: **TURKEY DIRECT O'HARE FIELD TO HOTEL?**/ END TEXT/ MASSEY

CHICAGO-LANGLEY/ ATTN MASSEY/ 1032 CDT/ 5/24/88

BEGIN TEXT: **NEGATIVE/ OVER 2 HR LAPSE**/ END TEXT/
CARRUTHERS

LANGLEY-CHICAGO/ ATTN CARRUTHERS/ 1132 EDT/ 5/24/88
BEGIN TEXT: **EXPLAIN**/ END TEXT/ MASSEY

CHICAGO-LANGLEY/ ATTN MASSEY/ 1033 CDT/ 5/24/88
BEGIN TEXT: **TURKEY DEPARTED O'HARE RENTED
JAGUAR V–12/ LOST JAGUAR KENNEDY EXPRESSWAY
VICINITY HARLEM AVENUE**/ END TEXT/ CARRUTHERS

LANGLEY-CHICAGO/ ATTN CARRUTHERS/ 1134 EDT/ 5/24/88
BEGIN TEXT: **HOW DOES ONE LOSE JAGUAR V–12?**/ END
TEXT/ MASSEY

CHICAGO-LANGLEY/ ATTN MASSEY/ 1035 CDT/ 5/24/88
BEGIN TEXT: **FORD ESCORTS GO 85 MPH/ V–12 JAGUARS
GO 140 MPH/ THAT IS HOW**/ END TEXT/ CARRUTHERS

LANGLEY-CHICAGO/ ATTN CARRUTHERS/ 1136 EDT/ 5/24/88
BEGIN TEXT: **TURKEY DROVE JAG?**/ END TEXT/ MASSEY

CHICAGO-LANGLEY/ ATTN MASSEY/ 1036 CDT/ 5/24/88
BEGIN TEXT: **VRROOOOOM**/ END TEXT/ CARRUTHERS

LANGLEY-CHICAGO/ ATTN CARRUTHERS/ 1137 EDT/ 5/24/88
BEGIN TEXT: **PRESENT LOCATION JAG?**/ END TEXT/ MASSEY

CHICAGO-LANGLEY/ ATTN MASSEY/ 1037 CDT/5/24/88
BEGIN TEXT: **RETURNED HAPPIDAY MOTORS ROSE-
MONT ILL/ TURKEY AND GODIVA ARRIVED
INTERNATIONAL ARMS YELLOW CAB #1609/ JAG
CHECKED/ NO LEADS**/ END TEXT/ CARRUTHERS

LANGLEY-CHICAGO/ ATTN CARRUTHERS/ 1138 EDT/ 5/24/88
BEGIN TEXT: **NO KNOWLEDGE INTERIM?**/ END TEXT/ MASSEY

CHICAGO-LANGLEY/ ATTN MASSEY/ 1038 CDT/ 5/24/88
BEGIN TEXT: **NONE**/ END TEXT/ CARRUTHERS

LANGLEY-CHICAGO/ ATTN CARRUTHERS/1139 EDT/ 5/24/88
BEGIN TEXT: **SHIT**/ END TEXT/ MASSEY

LINE CLEARED LANGLEY 1139 EDT 5/24/88

6

At 9:15 on that Tuesday morning the temperature in Chicago's Loop was a flat eighty degrees, this promising an early afternoon peak of low to mid-nineties. By 11:00 it was ninety and climbing.

When Moose Katzenbach came down the stairs and into the Classic Investigations office, he found Lacey Lockington dozing in the creaky swivel chair behind the desk. Moose Katzenbach was a big man, six-five plus a fraction, weighing upwards of 260, and although he walked with a splay-footed gait, it was a virtually silent splay-footed gait. He eased the office door shut behind him and he reached Lockington's desk undetected, an unholy smile creasing his hound-dog features. He stepped back and delivered a swift kick to the base of the swivel chair. Lockington's head snapped up. Moose said, "Wake up and piss, the world's on fire!"

Lockington wiped his mouth with the back of his hand. He said, "For lesser offenses I have torn men to shreds and fed them to whippoorwills."

Around a yawn, Moose said, "You wouldn't know a whippoorwill from a fucking ostrich."

Lockington said, "The hell I wouldn't. Ostriches don't go 'tweet-tweet.'"

Moose said, "Neither do whippoorwills—whippoorwills go 'too-wit-too-woo.'"

Lockington said, "Any whippoorwill that goes 'too-wit-too-woo' got to be a fag whippoorwill. What color are whippoorwills?"

Moose lowered his bulk onto the client's chair at the side of the desk, inserting a cigarette in a corner of his mouth and giving one to Lockington. He said, "Why should I tell *you*?"

Lockington held a match for them. "You're the fucking bird expert, ain't you?"

"Well, sure, but us bird experts can't go around passing out free information." Moose sucked on his cigarette, speaking through a swirling gray veil of smoke. "What's happening?"

Lockington shrugged. "Our ten o'clock appointment was on time. Name's Hector—Hector Godwin."

"What's Hector's problem?"

"Hector's under twenty-four-hour surveillance."

"Who's watching him?"

"Creatures from another galaxy."

Moose thought about it. He said, "What galaxy? That's important, what galaxy."

"Hector ain't sure—he wants us to find out."

"We better get on that first thing in the morning."

Lockington glanced at his watch. "Eleven-fifteen—I thought you were gonna be tied up all day."

"So did I, but the insurance company paid up quick

and it took that fucking undertaker less than ten minutes to screw me out of an extra three hundred dollars. I already had lunch, so if there's something you want to attend to, go ahead."

"Nothing really pressing, but now that you're here, I'm gonna ankle over to the International Arms a bit earlier than I planned."

"What's the attraction at the International?"

"I'm supposed to have lunch with Rufe Devereaux— he's back in town."

"Never knew he left. You're talking about the CIA cat you used to get soused with?"

"Yeah, he phoned Edna yesterday afternoon."

"Edna? How come Edna—why didn't he phone *you?*"

"I wasn't home yet, so he got Edna."

"Uh-huh—so Edna moved in."

"No, but she's working on it—using the gradual approach. She doesn't want me to panic."

Moose nodded, making the sign of the cross. "What's with Devereaux?"

"No idea. I haven't seen him in a blue moon."

"Yeah, well, maybe you better call him before you hike clear the hell to South Michigan Avenue. It's hotter than a virgin's crotch out there."

"I've already called three times. The desk tells me he isn't registered, but you know these fucking computerized systems."

"Maybe he's there under another name."

"If he's working on something, that's likely. I'll find him— probably in the lounge, drinking peppermint schnapps."

"Lacey, you shoulda been a detective."

"I know it, Moose, but it's too late now."

Lockington located his hat and went out, thinking about the old Greek philosophers. They too had indulged in profound dialogues.

7

The noonday heat was stifling. Lockington plodded toward State Street, perspiring like a Bourbon Street whore, waving to Information Brown, who leaned against the wall of his newsstand, talking to a pair of nattily attired young men. Brown's return wave was a perfunctory thing—he seemed deeply immersed in the discussion. Whatever the conversation concerned, Lockington knew that its pertinent points were being filed into the voluminous computer-bank recesses of Information Brown's phenomenal memory.

Information Brown knew more about the city of Chicago and its people than any man on the face of planet Earth and he bartered his knowledge for Walker's Deluxe whiskey at the bar of the Squirrel's Cage on West Randolph Street. He was in demand, policemen sought him out, so did gossip columnists, and so did private investigators— Lockington had used him to great advantage during the previous summer. Anyone who'd spring for a few hookers of Walker's could acquire an education—he could learn who was sleeping with whom and where and when and why, he could find out who was at the top of the Mafia hit parade and who'd been hired to handle the job, and who the Chicago Bears were willing to give up in return for what. For so long as the Walker's did flow, so would Information Brown's stream of enlightenment regarding the blighted city of Chicago, Illinois.

Lockington made his way across North State Street, continuing east on Randolph, repeatedly buffeted and battered by women with bulging shopping bags and purposefully glinting eyes, the slitted eyes of leopards closing on a crippled antelope—hard eyes, merciless. Lockington's myriad experiences with the fat women of Chicago had carried him beyond respect for that breed, transporting him to consternation, and thence to a state of salivating, twitching terror. As a callow lad, he'd been lured into the bed of one of them, an ordeal he'd since likened to a night spent under intense naval bombardment, an odd parallel because Lockington had never spent a night under intense naval bombardment.

He turned south on Michigan Avenue, walking leisurely, pausing briefly at intersections to peer through heat rivulets at Lake Michigan—blue, serene, thoroughly polluted—remembering it for what it'd been before Chicago defiled it. And he considered the matter of Rufe Devereaux who'd dropped from sight as though he'd stepped into an uncovered manhole, then surfaced just as suddenly—Rufe Devereaux, a man with insatiable yens for baseball discussion, country music, ladies of the night and peppermint schnapps, a fellow who'd kept his own counsel, rarely mentioning the ins and outs of his profession. There'd been times when

Lockington had wondered about Devereaux's experiences, how many brushes he'd had with the KGB and its affiliates, how many attempts had been made on the life of the quiet man from Louisiana. He'd wondered but he hadn't asked, and Devereaux had volunteered a minimum of information. On one occasion he'd referred to a man known as the Copperhead, calling him "the Babe Ruth of assassins," but he'd taken the subject no further and Lockington hadn't pursued it. Devereaux had been well-traveled, he'd possessed impressive knowledge of global politics, he'd rattled off the names of those in power and those next in power, Argentina to Uganda, but this had come as casual comment, and their conversation had always drifted back to baseball and Devereaux's beloved 1906 Chicago Cubs. "That wasn't a baseball team," he'd said, "it was a *machine!*" He'd never seen the 1906 Chicago Cubs, of course, and Lockington had never seen the 1927 New York Yankees, but they'd gone at it, sometimes heatedly, Lockington's argument having been that a team that could whip the Philadelphia Athletics and Dykes and Cobb and Cochrane and Simmons and Foxx and Grove by nineteen games just *had* to be the finest in history, and Rufe Devereaux had smiled a vastly superior smile, reminding Lockington that the 1906 Chicago Cubs had beaten the New York Giants of Devlin and Seymour and McGinty and Matthewson by *twenty* games. They'd been locked into a no-win situation, as baseball fanatics usually are, and they'd enjoyed every minute of it, as baseball fanatics usually do.

Lockington had no knowledge of what the wily Cajun had been up to over the span of the previous fifteen or so months. He might have resigned from the Agency as he'd occasionally intimated during their non-baseball chats, or he might have been barging around in the hell of Lebanon, attending to whatever designs the CIA had in that area. If he'd withdrawn from government service, Lockington would find that out quickly enough. If he hadn't, the subject probably wouldn't come up. But one thing was certain—if Rufe Devereaux wasn't back in Chicago on a liberal expense account, he was earning a respectable dollar on his own, because the International Arms wasn't a hostelry for traveling housewares salesmen. It towered seventeen haughty white-stone stories above the lakefront, looking for all the world like what it was—simply the finest hotel in Chicago.

Lockington pulled to a sweaty halt under its blue canvas sidewalk canopy, sensing the magnificent texture of the establishment, awed as is the bootblack about to enter Buckingham Palace. Then he took a deep breath, squared his shoulders and went in, an oarsman riding the rim of a whirlpool, diligently rowing in the wrong fucking direction.

8

The lobby of the International Arms Hotel sprawled spacious and reservedly elegant—pearl gray sculptured carpeting three inches deep, pecan-paneled walls studded with copper-framed seascape oils—exquisite originals, every one. There were low-hanging crystal chandeliers the size of beach umbrellas, thick-cushioned blue velour sofas and chairs, highly polished leather-topped genuine Philippine mahogany tables strewn with copies of *Fortune* and the *Wall Street Journal*, huge beige-shaded brass lamps, and heavy bronze pedestal-type ashtrays. And there was silence, the silence of reverence—the International Arms and its trappings demanded it.

Lockington spotted the desk, a massive hand-tooled expanse of hardwood half the size of a river barge. It was manned by a complement of five: a quartet of slim, dark-haired young ladies, all attractive, all clad in bluish gray tailored business suits and crisp pink blouses, all sporting white chrysanthemums on their left-hand lapels, all wearing plastic smiles, all under the command of a portly, balding man with haunted eyes and a nervous tic in his right cheek. He was fifty or so, he wore a brass-buttoned powder blue coat and his chrysanthemum was red—the badge of authority, Lockington figured. He lumbered back and forth behind the counter, riffling through sheafs of paper, answering telephones, issuing instructions, an impressive figure who reminded Lockington of a uniformed circus bear.

Lockington, approaching the desk, suddenly remembered that his walk had been a hot and thirsty ordeal. He changed course, veering sharply to port and through the swinging louvered doors of the lobby lounge, the Never-Never Room, according to the discreetly recessed blue neon sign above its entrance. It was a dim, quiet, cozy cove with a large horseshoe bar, three white-jacketed bartenders, and music—distant whispering strings playing "Santa Lucia." He slid onto a comfortable high-backed leatherette bar stool, waiting for his eyes to adjust to the toned-down lighting of the place. Rufe Devereaux might be present, Lockington thought. Bars had been like magnets to Rufe—he'd never been able to pass one.

A bartender approached and Lockington ordered a Martell's cognac with a water wash, scanning the Never-Never Room with a practised eye. There were fifteen or more customers scattered around the bar and none of them was Rufe Devereaux. The cognac arrived, the bartender swooping up Lockington's five-dollar bill, nodding curtly, spinning on a heel, and marching away, never to return. Lockington registered the Never-Never Room as a place not conducive to the art of serious drinking, estimating that a man could run through upwards of fifty dollars before getting a buzz. There were those who had that kind of money and there were those who didn't. Lockington was one of those who didn't.

He polished off his five-dollar Martell's at a gulp, leaving his seat to return to the lobby and the desk. One of the trim, prim young ladies breezed to the counter, her smile frozen in place, her dulcet voice devoid of inflection. "May I be of assistance, sir?" She reeked of efficiency.

Lockington said, "Yes, ma'am, I've been calling to reach a friend who was scheduled to register here last night, but you have no record of him. Would you run a check on that, please?

She stepped to a computer. "Certainly, sir. The name of the party?"

"Devereaux—Rufus Devereaux. That's D-E-V—" Lockington pulled up short. She was staring at him as if he'd crawled from under a flat, mossy rock, her eyes widening perceptibly. Instinctively, Lockington glanced down at his fly. It was zipped. When he looked up, the girl was gone, having scurried to the far end of the desk to confer with Rear Admiral Fluttervalve. The conversation was brief and subdued, the admiral throwing a furtive squint in Lockington's direction before picking up a white telephone to punch a single button and speak tersely. Lockington shuffled around for a time, lighting a cigarette, soaking up the plush atmosphere of the International Arms, wondering what the hell the delay was all about. He felt a hand clamp down on his shoulder and he turned to see a horse-faced, lantern-jawed man in a baggy tweed suit. The man grinned, shoving out his hand. "Lacey Lockington, you beat-up old wardog, how've you been?"

Lockington's Devereaux-welcoming smile was fading. He knew this one from up the road a piece—Webb Pritchard, an eager-beaver cop who'd brown-nosed his way from traffic detail to detective rank. They'd never been close or anywhere near it. Lockington hadn't liked Pritchard. He couldn't recall his reason for that but he still didn't like him. They shook hands. Pritchard's grip was a clammy, limp-wristed thing. He said, "I understand that you're trying to locate Rufus Devereaux."

Lockington nodded. "You know Rufe?"

Pritchard shook his head. "I wouldn't know Devereaux from Mahatma Gandhi." He snickered, indicating that he'd appreciated his own line.

Lockington said, "Well, Devereaux will be the one who ain't wearing a bed sheet."

Pritchard said, "Devereaux—he was with the Agency, wasn't he?"

"Yeah, last I heard. What's with the past-tense stuff—did he quit?"

Pritchard took Lockington by the arm, leaning toward him, lowering his voice to a hoarse whisper. "Uhh-h-h, Lacey—Devereaux's dead."

9

The shock wave rolled over him like an Andes landslide over a sapling. There was a surging roar in his ears and the lobby lights seemed to dim for a moment. A great gray net had engulfed Lockington but his reflex questions wriggled through it. "Dead—*when?*"

Pritchard said, "Couple hours ago—nine, nine-thirty, they figure."

"Where?"

"Room Three thirty-three."

"How?"

"Heavy caliber weapon—silencer, probably. Soft-nosed slug—took off half of his head, as I understand it."

"*Who*, for Christ's sake—*why?*"

"They ain't saying much, but money wasn't the motive—there was over a grand in his wallet when they found him."

Lockington was steadying. "Hold it! *They*—who's *they?*"

"The Agency—the Agency phoned us for assistance. Seems that they happened onto this thing through an anonymous telephone call."

Lockington said, "Look, why don't we sit down for a few minutes?"

Pritchard said, "Sure thing—ain't no law against sitting down." He snickered and Lockington wanted to whack him in the mouth for it. Pritchard was one of those people who take pleasure in delivering bad news—the role carries a sense of importance.

They parked on a blue velour sofa. Lockington put out his cigarette and lit another, noting a slight tremor in his hands. He said, "The Agency's running this circus?"

"Wire-to-wire. They're using the Chicago police department to secure the third-floor hallway and to intercept Devereaux's visitors. Those are our only functions."

"How many visitors so far?"

"So far, just you."

Lockington shook his head emphatically. "It doesn't rhyme. This is a Chicago murder—it's a Chicago police matter."

Pritchard said, "Don't you believe it. National security transcends all that municipality stuff—we're on the outside looking in."

Lockington sat in silence, watching his personal fog dissipate a wisp at a time. Webb Pritchard was saying, "What was Devereaux working on the last time you saw him?"

Lockington snorted. "C'mon, Pritchard, you know better than that! CIA people don't talk shop. He rarely touched on his job."

"Well, all I know is what I've heard, but I've picked up a few items. The CIA thinks that maybe somebody turned the tables on Devereaux."

"All right, go on."

"They got a hunch it was a guy Devereaux was looking for—the Copperhead. You ever hear of the Copperhead?"

Rufe had mentioned the Copperhead once, but Lockington lied. "No. Who's the Copperhead?"

Pritchard shook his head. "They know what he does but they don't know who he *is*."

"What does he do?"

"He kills people for money—it's his trade."

"And Devereaux was on the prowl for the Copperhead?"

"That's my impression. He must have been working on something. He was traveling under an assumed name—J. A. Pfiester."

"Jesus, I wonder where he got *that* one. What was in his luggage?"

"All he carried was an attaché case. It's gone. So is the woman."

"*What* woman?"

Pritchard spread his hands. "Who knows? She had no reservation, she didn't register, Devereaux didn't account for her at the desk, but she was *with* him, no doubt about it. And that ain't all—one of the night crew guys said that she's stayed at the International before—he remembers her."

"When did she stay here—who did she stay with?"

"It was about a month ago—he doesn't recall the guy she came in with, but they were in Room Four-seventeen. They looked up the registration—fella named Frank Schulte."

"They're sure of that?"

"Yeah, it was the only time Four-seventeen was occupied that week."

Lockington shrugged. "She may have been an O'Hare

field hooker—some of 'em are getting five hundred a night."

"Devereaux would have paid five hundred?"

"Devereaux would have paid five *thousand* if he had it."

"Could be she shot him and hauled ass with the attaché case."

"And left his billfold with a grand in it? No way. Maybe she was kidnapped by the killer."

Pritchard made a deprecatory gesture. "The CIA had three men in the lobby."

"Three men in the lobby and nobody in the Three thirty-three hallway."

Pritchard's head snapped up. "How did you know that?"

"I didn't, but it figures. They saw Devereaux and the woman go up, but they didn't see 'em come down?"

"Guess so."

"What was in the attaché case?"

"Whatever it was, the CIA certainly wants it. Look, Lacey, off the record, just what was your business with Devereaux?"

"That'll be off the record for about ten minutes, and you know it."

Pritchard snickered. "Yeah—it's a question they told me to ask."

"Okay, Rufe called me late yesterday afternoon—said he'd be in last night, that he'd be staying at the International. He was supposed to contact me at my office this morning but he didn't. I tried to phone him and they told me that he wasn't registered here. I got curious and walked over from Randolph Street. Tell the CIA to make something sinister out of *that*."

"Why did he want to see you—was it important, did

he say?"

"No—I gathered that it'd amount to no more than a get-together. I hadn't seen him in fifteen months, give or take."

"You knew him well?"

"Well enough to like him. We did some drinking, talked some baseball—hell, what else *is* there?"

Pritchard winked a man-to-man wink, snickering. "Broads?"

"Hundreds—movie starlets, fashion models. You're a man of the world, Pritchard—you know how it goes with gigolos." He'd just remembered why he'd never liked Pritchard. It'd been that abominable snicker.

"Where did Devereaux call from?"

Lockington said, "I was foggy on that—Ohio, I think."

"That's what they were saying upstairs—he flew in from Ohio."

"What about the woman—a good-looker?"

"A phenom, according to the night clerks—young, brunette, fabulous blue eyes, leggy."

"Maybe she wasn't a pro—maybe she flew in with him."

Pritchard shrugged. "There were sixty-seven women on that flight from Cleveland. It'll take time to sort 'em out."

"It was Cleveland?"

"Yeah, they have that nailed down. Where did Devereaux go when he left Chicago?"

"Ohio, apparently."

"That's where he *came* from, not necessarily where he *went*."

Lockington yawned. "It isn't my problem, Pritchard. Any information on his wake?"

"Nothing."

They lapsed into silence, listening to music drifting from

the Never-Never Room, a tango, "Orchids in the Moonlight." Lockington recognized the melody. So did Webb Pritchard. He said, "Damn, Lacey, ain't it funny the way a song can take a man back?"

Lockington said, "Yeah."

Pritchard said, "In 'fifty-eight, my family lived on the southside, and we had a mailman who always whistled 'Orchids in the Moonlight.'"

"Remember his name?"

"Naw, kids don't pay much attention to names. We could hear him coming, soon as he turned the corner, whistling 'Orchids in the Moonlight.' Geez, those were wonderful days, Lacey." Pritchard's voice trailed off.

Lockington nodded. "In 'fifty-eight, we lived on the northside. My uncle was staying with us, and every morning he'd run across the street and hop in bed with Sam Holterhofer's wife."

Pritchard said, "Where was Sam Holterhofer when all this was going on?"

Lockington said, "On the southside, delivering mail."

Pritchard said, "Did Sam Holterhofer go around whistling 'Orchids in the Moonlight?'"

Lockington said, "I never noticed, but the sonofabitch shot my uncle."

10

He emerged from the International Arms and drew back as four huge women approached, walking abreast. He pinned himself against the International's white stone wall, watching them rumble by, one thousand pounds of bad news, resembling a southbound tidal wave. When they were gone he heaved a sigh of relief and made his way back to the corners of State and Randolph, weighing the murder of Rufe Devereaux, trying to contain the thunderbolt and minimize its damage. He was without a sense of direction and, lacking one, he had no course of action. He wasn't certain that a course of action was called for—this was the CIA's ball game, certainly not Lacey Lockington's.

Information Brown wasn't at his newsstand, which indicated that Information Brown was either dead or at the Squirrel's Cage. Lockington took a chance on the latter, slipping unobtrusively into the shabby saloon, running a glance down the stretch of battered mahogany to spot Information Brown at its far end, hunched over, head down, staring sorrowfully into an empty shot glass. He was a graying, fragile man with bloodshot hazel eyes, thinning hair, a three-day silver stubble on his chin, and traces of egg at the right-hand corner of his thin-lipped mouth, a burnt-out case seemingly dedicated to drinking himself into the Great Hereafter. Lockington eased past the jutting rumps of the career drinkers to slide onto a rickety stool next to Brown's. He said, "Walker's Deluxe?"

Information Brown said, "I can think of no reason that would prompt a negative response."

Lockington flipped a twenty onto the bar, motioning to a wide-shouldered, ham-handed barkeep named Avalanche MacPherson who claimed to have gone five with Marciano back in fifty-one. Lockington believed that he'd gone five. He'd have believed ten. Avalanche MacPherson's face looked like the target area of a howitzer range. MacPherson located a bottle of Walker's, and Lockington turned to Information Brown. He said, "Whatcha got on the festivities at the International Arms?"

Brown frowned, watching the amber elixir stream into his glass. He jolted it down, shoving the glass to the inner rim of the bar, nodding to Avalanche MacPherson's questioning stare. MacPherson poured the encore and Information Brown said, "Very little at the moment, Lacey, but it'll get here."

Lockington said, "I want to be the first to know."

"An Agency guy got scragged. Why the concern?"

"He was a friend of mine."

Brown shook his head. "You were Devereaux's friend, Devereaux wasn't *any*body's. Devereaux *used* people."

"Hell, he was CIA—he *had* to use people."

Brown shrugged. "I've heard nothing but bad on him."

"Maybe you listened to the wrong people."

"They don't *come* any wronger than Rufe Devereaux."

"Whatever—just keep me in mind, will you?"

Brown nodded. "I could have something this afternoon or in the morning. A pair of his stablemates had me cornered when you went by earlier."

"Yeah, I saw that you had company. What'd they want?"

"Anything they could get. Better leave this one alone, Lacey—it rings out of key."

"I'll be listening." Lockington picked up ten dollars of his change, leaving the remainder on the bar. He said, "Drink it up."

Information Brown said, "Sir, you are a gentleman of quality and great understanding."

Lockington said, "I'm aware of that, but don't let it get around."

11

CHICAGO-LANGLEY/ ATTN MASSEY/ 1301 CDT/ 5/24/88
BEGIN TEXT: **POTENTIAL PROBLEM HERE**/ END TEXT/
CARRUTHERS

LANGLEY-CHICAGO/ ATTN CARRUTHERS/ 1402 EDT/ 5/24/88
BEGIN TEXT: **CLARIFY**/ END TEXT/ MASSEY

CHICAGO-LANGLEY/ ATTN MASSEY/ 1303 CDT/ 5/24/88
BEGIN TEXT: **MAN NAMED LOCKINGTON IN PICTURE**/
END TEXT/ CARRUTHERS

LANGLEY-CHICAGO/ ATTN CARRUTHERS/ 1404 EDT/ 5/24/88
BEGIN TEXT: **LOCKINGTON NOT HOUSEHOLD NAME**/
END TEXT/ MASSEY

CHICAGO-LANGLEY/ ATTN MASSEY/ 1304 CDT/ 5/24/88
BEGIN TEXT: **OPERATES SMALL PRIVATE INVESTIGATIONS
AGENCY/ EX-CHICAGO COP**/ END TEXT/ CARRUTHERS

LANGLEY-CHICAGO/ ATTN CARRUTHERS/ 1405 EDT/ 5/24/88
BEGIN TEXT: **WHY EX?**/ END TEXT/ MASSEY

CHICAGO-LANGLEY/ ATTN MASSEY/ 1306 CDT/ 5/24/88
BEGIN TEXT: **KILLED FOUR IN WEEK/ PRESS CRUSADE
FORCED DISMISSAL**/ END TEXT/ CARRUTHERS

LANGLEY-CHICAGO/ ATTN CARRUTHERS/ 1408 EDT/ 5/24/88
BEGIN TEXT: **HAS CONNECTION WITH TURKEY?**/ END
TEXT/ MASSEY

CHICAGO-LANGLEY/ ATTN MASSEY/ 1309 CDT/ 5/24/88
BEGIN TEXT: **AFFIRMATIVE/ DRINKING BUDDY**/ END
TEXT/ CARRUTHERS

LANGLEY-CHICAGO/ ATTN CARRUTHERS/ 1410 EDT/ 5/24/88
BEGIN TEXT: **SOURCE INFORMATION?**/ END TEXT/ MASSEY

CHICAGO-LANGLEY/ ATTN MASSEY/ 1311 CDT/ 5/24/88
BEGIN TEXT: **LOBBY DETAIL PLAINCLOTHES COP
NAMED WEBB PRITCHARD/ ACQUAINTED LOCKINGTON
CHICAGO FORCE**/ END TEXT/ CARRUTHERS

LANGLEY-CHICAGO/ ATTN CARRUTHERS/ 1412 EDT/ 5/24/88
BEGIN TEXT: **LOCKINGTON INQUISITIVE?**/ END TEXT/
MASSEY

CHICAGO-LANGLEY/ ATTN MASSEY/ 1313 CDT/ 5/24/88
BEGIN TEXT: **COULD GET THAT WAY**/ END TEXT/
CARRUTHERS

LANGLEY-CHICAGO/ ATTN CARRUTHERS/ 1414 EDT/ 5/24/88
BEGIN TEXT: **LOCKINGTON GOOD?**/ END TEXT/ MASSEY

CHICAGO-LANGLEY/ ATTN MASSEY/ 1315 CDT/ 5/24/88
BEGIN TEXT: **PRITCHARD SAYS DYNAMITE**/ END TEXT/
CARRUTHERS

LANGLEY-CHICAGO/ ATTN CARRUTHERS/ 1415 EDT/ 5/24/88
BEGIN TEXT: **TAIL ON LOCKINGTON?**/ END TEXT/ MASSEY

CHICAGO-LANGLEY/ ATTN MASSEY/ 1316 CDT/ 5/24/88
BEGIN TEXT: **AFFIRMATIVE/ DELLICK**/ END TEXT/
CARRUTHERS

LANGLEY-CHICAGO/ ATTN CARRUTHERS/ 1416 EDT/ 5/24/88
BEGIN TEXT: **BUY LOCKINGTON**/ END TEXT/ MASSEY

CHICAGO-LANGLEY/ ATTN MASSEY/ 1317 CDT/ 5/24/88
BEGIN TEXT: **GET IN OR STAY OUT?**/ END TEXT/
CARRUTHERS

LANGLEY-CHICAGO/ ATTN CARRUTHERS/ 1418 EDT/ 5/24/88
BEGIN TEXT: **STAY OUT**/ END TEXT/ MASSEY

CHICAGO-LANGLEY/ ATTN MASSEY/ 1319 CDT/ 5/24/88
BEGIN TEXT: **QUESTION WISDOM THAT MOVE/ WILL MAKE
LOCKINGTON MORE CURIOUS**/ END TEXT/ CARRUTHERS

LANGLEY-CHICAGO/ ATTN CARRUTHERS/ 1420 EDT/ 5/24/88
BEGIN TEXT: **PRECISELY**/ END TEXT/ MASSEY

CHICAGO-LANGLEY/ ATTN MASSEY/ 1321 CDT/ 5/24/88
BEGIN TEXT: **UNDERSTOOD/ LIMIT?**/ END TEXT/
CARRUTHERS

LANGLEY-CHICAGO/ ATTN CARRUTHERS/ 1422 EDT/ 5/24/88
BEGIN TEXT: **FIVE FOR NOW**/ END TEXT/ MASSEY

CHICAGO-LANGLEY/ ATTN MASSEY/ 1322 CDT/ 5/24/88
BEGIN TEXT: **WHAT IF NO DICE?**/ END TEXT/ CARRUTHERS

LANGLEY-CHICAGO/ ATTN CARRUTHERS/ 1423 EDT/ 5/24/88
BEGIN TEXT: **EXCELLENT/ WE CAN USE HIM**/ END
TEXT/ MASSEY

LINE CLEARED LANGLEY 1423 EDT 5/24/88

12

It'd been before Edna Garson and before Julie Masters. It'd been before the Morning Sentinel had drummed Lockington out of Chicago police force service. It'd been in the early spring of '84. The Billy Mac Davis for President bandwagon had swept out of the south and into Chicago, a gala caravan of red, white and blue chartered buses. SUDDENLY, A CHOICE! the placards had proclaimed. There'd been a rally at the Chicago Stadium on West Madison Street and Lockington had been there, heading up a five-man plainclothes pickpocket detail. Rufe Devereaux had attended for whatever reasons CIA operatives attend such functions—possibly the apprehension of subversives, Lockington had figured.

It'd been a rip-snorting Sunday afternoon affair replete with satin- and sequin-attired country singers and denim-clad guitar pickers. It'd packed all the fervent, feverish vibrancy of an old-fashioned, fire-and-brimstone Dixie revival meeting. The stage had been awash in American flags, the Chicago Stadium pipe organ had boomed and blasted, fifteen thousand people had joined in the singing of "America the Beautiful," and Lockington had come down with a severe case of goose-bumps, *because if there'd have been anything that he'd have appreciated more than fifteen thousand people singing "America the Beautiful," it'd have been fifteen million people singing "America the Beautiful." Lockington was a hard-nosed, two-fisted, dyed-in-the-wool patriot.*

The Sunshine Brothers Quartet had sung "Church in the Wildwood" and "If I Could Hear My Mother Pray Again." Then Bobbie Jo Pickens had been introduced. Bobbie Jo Pickens had been a tall, middle-aging, hoarse-voiced, blonde vocalist in a tight-fitting gold lamé gown. She'd strode confidently to centerstage to grab a microphone stand, straddle it, roll her hips, twitch her groin, and belt out "Sleepwalkin' Mama" to the accompaniment of a wailing electric guitar and a slow bluesy piano. She'd brought the house down. The switch from gospel to honky-tonk had been abrupt, but Billy Mac Davis had been touching all bases. Following a rambling prayer by a cadaverous Pentecostal preacher, Davis had stepped to the lectern to tear into the Loyal Order of Moose, the Citrus Growers' Association, the Mystery Writers of America, and similarly dangerous organizations. He'd been a chunky, silver-haired, wild-eyed, arm-waving foot-stomper, one step short of full swastika rank and mere inches removed from an insane asylum. He'd spouted a venom-marinated doctrine calling for the immediate deportation of all blacks to Africa, the return of every last Mexican to Mexico, and "trial by the people" for white liberals.

Through it all, Rufe Devereaux had been studying Lockington, seeing in him, perhaps, the quintessential subversive, and Lockington had been keeping a suspicious eye on Rufe Devereaux, waiting for him to dip into somebody's hip pocket. Eventually they'd run out of patience, approaching each other to demand identification. Identification produced, they'd laughed about the incident, shaking hands to slip across West Madison Street and into a skid-row ginmill for a few belts, and while they'd been drinking, two black men had set fire to one of Billy Mac Davis's red, white and blue buses, and a Mexican had picked Lockington's pocket.

13

Moose Katzenbach was slumped in the client's chair, hat tilted to the back of his head, elbows on the desk, face buried between his forearms. His snoring rattled the picture of Wrigley Field on the wall. Lockington dropped into the swivel chair and Moose grunted, raising his head. "Back so soon?"

Lockington said, "Rufe Devereaux got shot in the head."

Moose yawned. "Well, in Rufe Devereaux's racket, you gotta expect getting shot in the head every once in a while." Like Lockington, Moose Katzenbach was no stranger to violence.

Lockington said, "In Rufe's case it ain't gonna happen every once in a while."

"Dead?"

Lockington nodded.

Moose said, "Sorry to hear that. Devereaux cut a few corners, I've been told."

Lockington shrugged. "I suppose he did—in a dirty

game you gotta shoot dirty pool. Go on home, Moose, and catch up on your sleep."

Moose lurched to his feet, straightened his hat, and said, "Thanks, Lacey—I think it just caught up with me. See you in the morning."

Lockington watched his friend go out, a big man who'd been chewed up in an emotional meat-grinder for years.

He leaned back in the spavined swivel chair, smoking, feeling the pressure of the mounting afternoon heat, attempting to martial his thoughts. According to Webb Pritchard, Rufe had been last seen in the company of a good-looking female. Given the man and his lecherous leanings, that figured. According to Pritchard, he'd been last seen carrying an attaché case. Depending on what Rufe had been up to, maybe *that* figured. Both the woman and the attaché case had vanished, also according to Pritchard, which underlined the possibility that the woman had blown Devereaux's brains out and made off with the attaché case. That *didn't* figure. A woman in Devereaux's good graces would have had countless opportunities to steal an attaché case without firing a shot. The telephone was ringing and Lockington clambered from the depths of his brown study to grab it. He said, "Classic Investigations."

The voice was coarse, grating against Lockington's raw nerve ends. "You're Lockington."

Lockington said, "I know it."

"I have a few questions for you."

Lockington said, "If nominated, I will not run."

The caller chuckled, sounding like a four-cylinder engine firing on three. He said, "Sergeant Joe Delvano here, Lockington—Chicago Police Superintendent's office calling."

Lockington said, "Delvano, Delvano—I don't recognize the name."

"Well, hell, you've been gone nine months—there've been changes."

"My God, I hope so."

"You were at the International Arms a couple hours ago." It was a statement, not a query.

Lockington said, "Yeah, I was gonna buy the joint but I came up thirty-seven dollars short."

"You were a friend of Rufe Devereaux's." Again, no question mark.

"True. We sang together at the Met—*Barber of Seville*."

"Spare me the cute lines, Lockington—this is a serious matter."

"Okay, Joe, sorry. By the way, how's Terry Scott doing? I heard he had surgery."

"Scott's fine."

"Harry Jamieson—he take the pension yet?"

"He's thinking about it. I'm just back from vacation, Lockington—I'm not quite up to date. Now, about Devereaux—we're trying to track his activities after he reached Chicago last night. Did he contact you when he got in?"

"No. Tell me, is it true that Buck Sarno bought a race horse?"

"I've heard nothing of it. Devereaux had a woman with him and there was a rental Jaguar waiting for him at O'Hare. He outran a Ford on the Kennedy but our guys kept him in sight. He was a foxy bastard—he stopped at Mike's Tavern at Belmont and Kimball, called a cab, instructed that it wait in the alley, left the broad at the bar, and ducked out the back door. He was gone before we got the drift."

"I see. Is there anything to the story that Rip Tilman may get married? That'd make four times for Rip."

"I don't see much of Tilman. We figure that Devereaux was gone from Mike's Tavern over a couple hours. Since Mike's is just a few blocks from your apartment, we wondered if he might have dropped in for a visit, seeing as how you were such a good friend of his."

"Never laid eyes on him. How's Ace Hopkins—did he ever get cleared on that rape case?"

"I think he got a postponement on that. When Devereaux got back, he picked up the quiff, returned the Jag to the agency in Rosemont, called another cab, and went to the International Arms Hotel. Our problem is with those couple hours he was missing. They're critical."

"Yes, well, my understanding of this thing is that the Chicago police are locked out of it, and if that's the case, how come you're digging into it?"

"We're just nibbling around the edges, Lockington, finding out what we can. It's going to spill into the open eventually, and we want to be ready."

"Your people were tagging Devereaux from the time he got to O'Hare?"

"You got it."

"How did you know he was coming in, and why the surveillance—was he on a wanted list?"

"Uhh-h-h, look, Lockington, that's police business and I can't discuss it with you. You aren't a cop now."

Lockington said, "No, and *you* never *were!* There ain't no Terry Scott, there ain't no Harry Jamieson, Buck Sarno's been dead for ten years, Rip Tilman quit the force in 'sixty-three, and Ace Hopkins is a gay piano player at Mario's Lounge in Arlington Heights. You're tying up my phone line."

There was a short intermission while Delvano regrouped. Then he said, "Hey, tell me about Devereaux's attaché case and you get a pass. I'm trying to save your ass."

"From what?"

"From getting it blown off."

"By whom?"

"You'll never know—not in *this* world."

"Joe, you're boring me."

"Don't get in over your head, asshole! You'll be hearing from me!"

Lockington hung up, no more puzzled than before the call. Certainly no less.

14

Lockington's final hour with Rufe Devereaux had come in early '87 during the vacuum between Julie Masters and Edna Garson. It'd been a cold, wet evening, the kind that penetrates to the marrow, a good night to have gone home and stayed there. Instead, Lockington had stopped at the Shamrock Pub on West Diversey Avenue to stretch his legs and try to forget a long and unproductive afternoon spent trying to run down a chop shop reported to be operating in the Jefferson Park neighborhood. He'd put away a few belts of Martell's before deciding that it was high time he found Rufe Devereaux and established once and for all the '27 Yankees' superiority over the '06 Cubs. When Devereaux attempted to locate Lockington he'd usually find him at the Shamrock Pub. When Lockington looked for Devereaux he'd start at the Club Howdy on Milwaukee Avenue. These hadn't been certain points of contact, but they'd been good three times in four.

It'd been six weeks since Lockington had been in the Club Howdy. There'd been no changes for the better—the lights were still dim, the barstools ripped, the booths and tables lopsided, the paint peeling from the walls, the tiles peeling from the floor. Lockington had wondered if the men's washroom was the same. Not possessed of a strong stomach, he'd opted not to find out. Cockroaches had been conducting a track-and-field meet along the footrail of the bar, the pungent odor of urine had been held to a draw by the generous application of sweet-smelling disinfectant, the old status quo had prevailed, and Lockington had spotted Rufe Devereaux sitting in a rear booth, talking to a blonde woman. There'd been something vaguely familiar about her but Lockington hadn't been able to put his finger on it. Devereaux had observed Lockington's entrance, waving to him, motioning him to take a seat at the bar, then holding up a be-with-you-in-a-moment finger.

Club Howdy attendance had been sparse—a few scruffy-looking characters had been clustered in a dark corner of the place, there'd been a pair of elderly men at the end of the bar, but the tables had been deserted, and Lockington had discounted the threat of being crushed in a rush. A four-piece string band had been mauling "Clayton's Ridge" when Lockington had seated himself. "Clayton's Ridge" came under the heading of bluegrass, and Lockington had never been convinced that bluegrass came under the heading of music. Bluegrass had always reminded Lockington of a midnight cat fight in a trash heap, but he'd ordered a Martell's and waited. The musical mayhem had subsided before Rufe Devereaux had occupied the barstool next to Lockington's, growling, "Lacey, where the hell you been? I was at the Shamrock last week and somebody said that you'd joined the fucking Foreign Legion."

Lockington had said, "I tried, but they've stopped taking misfits."

Devereaux had slapped him on the shoulder. "Hang on, Lacey— you'll get over this!" He was referring, of course, to the death of Julie Masters. Lockington had shrugged, saying nothing, watching Rufe Devereaux's booth companion mount the steps to the tiny elevated stage behind the bar. Devereaux had grinned at Lockington. "Recognize her?"

Lockington had nodded. "Sure—she's the gal who sang with

that Billy Mac Davis political carnival a few years back—Bobbie Jo Pickens."

"Right! She bought the joint a month ago—she thinks that she can make something of it."

Lockington had frowned. "If she's gonna make something of this place, she'd better start with fifty gallons of gasoline and a match."

Three men had followed Bobbie Jo Pickens onto the stage, one seating himself at the drums, the others plugging guitars into amplifiers. Bobbie Jo Pickens waited, a commanding on-stage presence, a hard-faced woman probably in her mid- to upper-forties, with long, wavy peroxide-blonde hair, wary brown eyes, a slim-bridged nose, flaring nostrils, a full-lipped sensuous mouth. There'd been no gold lamé gown this time around. Approximately one hundred twenty pounds of Bobbie Jo Pickens had been stuffed into a faded denim outfit that'd been geared for one-oh-five, and every important crease in her well-preserved body had shown to excellent advantage. When her musicians were ready, she'd plucked a microphone from a stand, smiling into a smattering of applause and murmuring, "Hello, there, you good ole boys an' good ole gals—partickellary you good ole boys!" She'd flashed white bridgework when one of the good ole boys had howled like a brokenhearted timber wolf. Then she'd nodded to the band and lit into "Stand On It," snapping and jerking to the rapid boogie background. When she'd lowered the mike, the small turnout had sent up a roar that could have been heard in Highland Park. She'd winked, gasping, "Whew-e-e-e— why, my gracious, that was almos' as tirin' as somethin' else I enjoy doin', only nowheres near as much fun!" That'd prompted another roar. Then her smile had faded, the stage lights had dimmed, a blue spotlight had clicked on, and Bobbie Jo Pickens had sung "Too Many Rivers to Cross," "Send Me the Pillow that You Dream On," and "When the Echo of Your Footsteps Died Away." On these selections she'd been very good—she'd known how to handle her big, throaty voice, how to milk the last tear from a song concerning love lost, stolen or abandoned.

Lockington had given Devereaux a sidelong glance, noting that the big Cajun had been mesmerized. Bobbie Jo had closed out her set with "Fool Number One" and she'd bowed, waving a temporary bye-bye before stepping down to sit at the bar with a cork-tipped cigarette and a double hooker of Chivas Regal, flicking a few glances in Devereaux's direction. The lights had come up, the bluegrass group had piled noisily onto the stage, shattering the spell, cutting loose with "Black Mountain Rag." Lockington had turned to Devereaux. "Sounds like brain surgery with no anesthetic."

Rufe had said, "Yeah, but can't that Pickens woman sing up a storm?"

"She can, and that ain't all. She's giving you the eye."

Devereaux had nodded. "I just struck up an acquaintance with her. She's friendly people."

"Maybe you can score."

Rufe's smile had been enigmatic. "A man doesn't know if a man doesn't try."

Lockington had said, "Well, far be it from me to foul the wheels of progress."

They'd shaken hands and Lockington had driven back to the Shamrock Pub, feeling slightly brushed off. Baseball hadn't been mentioned.

That'd been how they'd closed out.

When Lockington had entered the Shamrock Pub, there'd been a fat woman in a bright yellow coat parked at the bar. She'd borne a strong resemblance to a school bus. Lockington had taken a seat a dozen barstools to her north. She'd glared at him. She'd snarled, "Get away from me, you slavering beast!"

Lockington had said, "Ma'am, if I get any further away from you, I'll be out in the parking lot."

The fat woman had said, "Oh, dear God, is there no peace?" She'd stormed out of the Shamrock Pub, slamming the door. Vic Zileski had been working the bar. Vic hadn't said anything.

Neither had Lockington.

15

It was Wednesday, cloudy, still unseasonably warm, late May by the calendar, mid-August according to the thermometer. Edna Garson hadn't come around on Tuesday evening, and Lockington had experienced no profound regrets on that score. Not that he didn't think the world of Edna—she'd provided solutions to more than one of his problems, but the problem she'd solved first was the problem she'd solved with alarming frequency, and Lockington was closing in on forty-nine years of age. He'd enjoyed their passionate interludes, he'd indulged with reckless abandon, but the piper must be paid, and on mornings following such sessions he was listless and aching from stem to stern. It wasn't one of those mornings.

Moose came in at nine. Lockington said, "You look better."

Moose said, "Yeah? Than *what?*"

"Than you looked yesterday."

"I *feel* better than I did yesterday—there ain't much that

fifteen hours in bed won't cure."

Lockington said, "If you're *sleeping,* that is." It was an unfortunate remark. Moose Katzenbach's bed was empty now.

They sat around the office, Lockington pondering recent events, Moose struggling with the *Chicago Chronicle* chess problem. After a while, Moose closed the newspaper. He said, "Chess is for the fucking Bolsheviks."

Lockington said, "It's their game. In Russia they teach chess to third-grade kids."

"And we don't."

"Of course we don't—we don't even teach our kids to read and write."

"That's true, but why *don't* we?"

"Because we'd be infringing on their civil rights."

"The Bolsheviks don't got no civil rights."

"Which is why their kids can read and write."

The office door banged open and Information Brown was standing on the threshold. Lockington motioned him into the office but Brown shook him off. "No time, Lacey. So far, all I got is that Devereaux's wake is gonna be at Olenick's on North Clark—eight o'clock tonight. Closed casket—cremation tomorrow morning."

"Who's paying the freight?"

"Christ, I dunno—the Agency, I suppose."

Lockington nodded. "Anything else?"

Brown said, "Yeah—no hoopla, no flowers, no ceremony." He closed the door, heading up the steps to Randolph Street.

Lockington's half-smile was tight. That's the way Rufe would have wanted it—no hoopla, no flowers, no ceremony.

Someone had said that the greatest knowledge man can hope to acquire is that life is utterly meaningless, and Lockington was certain that Rufe Devereaux had subscribed to that theory.

They drifted back into silence, Lockington welcoming the respite, considering the phone call from Sgt. Joe Delvano—wondering who was behind the shabby attempt at trickery. Had the press gotten into the Devereaux murder? Lockington didn't think so. The press would've handled it differently, charging into the affair like a herd of stampeding buffalo, trampling everything in its path. Then who—the CIA? Probably not, but he had a hunch that he'd be hearing from those fellows shortly—they worked slowly but they worked thoroughly.

Lockington dredged up what little he knew of the past, looking for a link to what little he knew of the present. He found a maybe—Rufe Devereaux had seemed reasonably confident that he could take Bobbie Jo Pickens to bed. When Rufe had blended a few drinks with an attack of hot drawers, he was usually entertaining delusions of grandeur, but there was a possibility that he'd made out, and any old possibility beat hell out of no possibility at all. Lockington said, "Moose, do you know where the Club Howdy's located?"

Moose squinted. "I've heard of it—northside somewhere, I think."

"Yeah, it's a hog trough on the east side of Milwaukee Avenue just south of Diversey."

"Shitkickers' joint, ain't it?"

"Country music, yes."

"What about it?"

"Take a run up that way—see if you can talk to a

Bobbie Jo Pickens. Tall, blonde woman—she probably owns the place."

"Okay, what should I talk about?"

"Rufe Devereaux—find out how well she knew him. Tell her he's gone west, and that his wake will be held at Olenick's tonight. Get her reaction, if any."

Moose nodded, finding his hat, going out, coming right back in. He dropped an envelope on the desk. "Mail for the day." The phone rang. Moose grabbed it and handed it to Lockington. He said, "It's for you."

Lockington said, "You didn't answer the sonofabitch—how do you *know* it's for me?"

Moose said, "Gotta be for you. Who'd be calling *me?*"

Lockington said, "You got a lousy attitude."

Moose went out.

Hector Godwin was on the line. Hector said, "Mr. Lockington, I visited your office yesterday morning, remember?"

Lockington sighed. "Vividly."

"Are you armed, Mr. Lockington?"

"Occasionally."

"How quickly can you get here?"

Lockington said, "Well, that would depend on just where 'here' is."

Hector said, "I live at Seven twenty-eight Laurel Lane in Batavia."

Lockington said, "I might locate Laurel Lane if I knew how to find Batavia."

"It's just forty or so miles southwest of Chicago. This is of the utmost urgency, Mr. Lockington!"

"You'll have to take that just a step further."

"You'll recall that I've been under observation by outer-galactic beings."

"Uhh-h-h, yes, I believe you mentioned that."

"They're *here*, Mr. Lockington!"

"They are?"

"Yes, there's a spaceship in front of my house!"

"What color?"

"Silver gray. Most of them are silver gray."

"*Most* of them?"

"I haven't seen *all* of them, Mr. Lockington."

"Have you contacted the Batavia police?"

"I have, and they've informed me that parking on Laurel Lane is perfectly permissible!"

"Well, Hector, I don't know exactly how to advise you on this. I'm at least an hour from Batavia—probably longer."

"My *God*, they're leaving the ship!" Hector's voice had risen a couple of octaves. "They're crossing my lawn—the bastards are walking on my *geraniums*—!" The line went dead.

Lockington never heard from Hector Godwin again.

There'd be times when he'd wonder about that.

16

The envelope on Lockington's desk was a cheap manila three-by-five-inch with a shiny tin clasp—nothing distinctive about it, it was of a type readily available in office supply shops and drugstores. It'd been addressed in sprawling black ballpoint, its upper left-hand corner blank. Lockington studied the postmark. It was smudged, but he could make out *Chicago, Illinois*. He balanced the envelope on the palm of his hand, then shook it briskly. It didn't rattle, jingle or tick, and it weighed no more than an ounce. He pinched the flaps of the clasp together, opened it, and tilted it over the desk. A depleted book of matches skidded out to tumble on the green blotter pad. The envelope wasn't empty and he freed its remaining contents—a slim sheaf of United States currency. He riffled rapidly through the money, his eyes widening. Ten one-hundred-dollar bills—probably more money than he'd handled at one time since the day of his birth.

He counted again. He'd been right the first time—one

grand. He folded it, placing it under the baseball encyclopedia in his bottom desk drawer. Then he concentrated on the empty matchbook. It was glossy white with bold red-block lettering: CLUB CROSSROADS—AUSTINTOWN, OHIO. There was a telephone number in smaller print.

He sat at the desk, frowning, tugging at an ear, staring into space. Apparently something was expected of him, a service had been paid for in advance. Prepayment by whom, and for what? And Austintown was in Ohio, obviously, but *where* in Ohio?

He picked up the telephone, signaling for an operator. The area code for Austintown, Ohio, please. *I'll give you the number of Ohio information, sir.* She gave him the number and he rang it. *What city, sir?* Austintown—I'd like to have the area code number for Austintown. *One moment, pleeyuz— Austintown is listed in the Youngstown directory. The Youngstown area code number is two-one-six—do you have the number of your Austintown party, sir?* Lockington said yes, thanking her.

Youngstown, Ohio—Lockington had heard of it. He'd known a bartender who'd been from Youngstown—Whitey Greb, who'd worked at Imogene's Interlude on North Cicero Avenue until Imogene had been busted for peddling her ass. Whitey had been homesick and he'd talked incessantly about Youngstown. It'd produced steel and lots of it, a prosperous city. Then, almost overnight, the steel mills had moved or folded. Union demands had become insatiable, driving the cost of making steel higher than the stuff could be sold for, and Detroit's automobile manufacturers had turned to Denmark, Sweden and Japan, washing fifteen thousand Youngstown jobs down the drain. A city with a diversified industrial base might have handled such a kick in the economic groin, but Youngstown had been founded on steel, it'd made steel and steel only, and the area was still in a state of paralysis, according to Whitey Greb.

Lockington shrugged, turning to the telephone, dialing 1–216, then the number on the Club Crossroads matchbook. He heard one ring before a recording cut in, a sultry female voice. "Hel-lo, there! Club Crossroads opens at six pee-yem, seven days a week! You'll just *love* our headline attraction, Pecos Peggy and the Barnburners! Come visit us soon, won't you?" The answering device snapped off and Lockington hung up to lean back in the swivel chair, certain of one thing—the envelope had been mailed by Rufe Devereaux.

It'd been established that Rufe had flown into Chicago from Cleveland, and Whitey Greb had mentioned that Cleveland was just sixty-eight miles from Youngstown—an hour's drive, give or take. For reasons as yet unknown, Rufe Devereaux had gotten his ass in a sling in Youngstown or its environs, he'd been tracked to Cleveland and intercepted in Chicago. He'd been in danger and he'd known it, otherwise why the Keystone Cops chase on the Kennedy Expressway and why the peek-a-boo routine prior to his arrival at the International Arms Hotel? If the Club Crossroads matchbook hadn't been a cry for help, it'd certainly been a plea for vengeance, indicating a starting point—square one: the Club Crossroads in Austintown, Ohio.

Pecos Peggy and the Barnburners—the names smacked of country entertainment, and Rufe Devereaux, a Louisiana man, would have gravitated toward it. He'd thrived on the stuff and the knock-down, drag-out places where it could be found—the atmosphere had been an elixir. Not so in Lockington's case—country music joints spooked him. He had no objections to the average two-fisted workingman's taverns—these were predictable to an extent, but the country dives were explosive without cause. One midnight in a Chicago cesspool called Dixie Central, he'd watched a big hillbilly rip a toilet from the floor of the men's room, then heave it through a plateglass window into the middle of North Austin Boulevard. When the police had arrived and subdued the miscreant, they'd inquired as to why he'd done it. The big guy had thought it over and said, "Wall, goldang iffen I *know* why—it juss seemed lak th' thing to do at th' time."

Lockington checked his watch—going on four o'clock. He kicked off his shoes and hoisted his feet onto the desk, tilting his head to a comfortable angle, permitting his eyelids to droop and close. "Sleep that knits up the ravelled sleeve of care"...Shakespeare. Lockington dozed off, wondering how Shakespeare would have fared in Chicago, deciding that he'd have despised it.

So did Lockington.

17

The harsh jangle of the telephone startled Lockington. Moose Katzenbach said, "Hey, Lacey, that Club Howdy ain't no roach ranch! It's a swanky-tonk!"

Lockington said, "The last time I saw it, it looked like the south end of a northbound gut wagon."

"Not now! Paneling, chrome, red leather, white tile floors, clean as a pin—strictly top drawer!"

"You get hold of the Pickens woman?"

"Yeah, but I had to wait to do it. This one sleeps *late!*"

"Sorry, I should have thought of that. She stays up half the night—the place is open till three in the morning. What'd she have to say?"

"About what?"

"About Devereaux."

"Nothing."

"You didn't *ask* her?"

"Sure, I asked her, but she never heard of Devereaux."

"The hell she didn't."

"Seemed level—she just gave me one of them long, blank stares. There's a fine-looking woman, Lacey—tough, but she got class."

"Don't get class confused with poise. She's in show business—she *gotta* have poise. Same thing goes for Siamese cats."

"Okay, so it's poise—ain't no way I'd kick her outta bed!"

Lockington yawned. "Well, what the hell, it was worth a shot."

"We talked for maybe an hour. Like you said, she probably owns the place. She bought me a couple drinks, and when she raised a finger, that bartender jumped about forty feet!"

"Didn't she want to know who you were?"

"Yeah, and I showed her my old police badge—told her that I was a cop, checking Devereaux's background. I said that we'd heard that he'd been a regular at the Club Howdy."

"Did it fly?"

"I think so. She told me that she'd had a phone call from the police—a Sergeant Delvano in the superintendent's office. I never knew no Sergeant Delvano, did you?"

"No. What'd Delvano want?"

"She didn't say."

"Okay, Moose, thanks. Call it a day—no reason to come back here—the fucking Martians already got Hector Godwin."

Lockington dropped the phone into its cradle. So much for his missing link. He'd leave it in the water. An open link could double as a hook.

18

At 6:45 on that cloudy and rapidly darkening evening, Lockington drove north on Clark Street. Wrigley Field loomed on his right and he stared glumly at the gaunt floodlight towers that were being erected on the grandstand roofs, far from operational now, but they'd be functioning in August. Night baseball in Wrigley Field—a sacrilege of unthinkable proportions, like a dice game smack dab in the middle of Vatican Square.

Olenick's Funeral Home was located a few blocks north of Wrigley Field, up toward Irving Park Road. Lockington knew the place and a swatch of its history. In the good old days, Scarface Al Capone's loyal hoodlums had been laid out in grand style at Olenick's. Al's disloyals had been buried along the eastern banks of the Fox River—not all of them deceased at the time of interment, it'd been rumored.

He swung west across southbound Clark Street traffic to pull into Olenick's blacktopped parking lot, this maneuver arousing the ire of a creature in a maroon Cadillac. She clamped down on her horn and shook a fist in Lockington's direction. He shrugged it off. Rare had been the day when he hadn't had some sort of run-in with a Chicago fat woman. He parked his car, pausing to study the Olenick building before getting out—red brick desperately in need of tuckpointing, cracked stained-glass windows, cobwebbed concrete walks bordered by untended densiformis, much of it browning with blight, dying. He counted a dozen or so automobiles in the Olenick lot, most being older models, but none within five years of Lockington's wobbly Pontiac Catalina.

Being a detective, and gifted with the excellent peripheral vision demanded by his profession, Lockington had spotted a tavern half a block to the south, a dingy, ramshackle, gray-shingled structure, Helga's Place, wedged into a row of small shops, the majority of these having been vacant for years. The neighborhood had gone completely to hell, and to walk its streets was to invite sudden disaster of one sort or another, but Lockington had time, he had a thirst, and he had a .38 police special, so he hiked the few doors to Helga's Place. Under normal conditions it was a joint he wouldn't have been caught dead in, but circumstances have a knack for altering cases. The dilapidated tavern was all but deserted, its bar splintered, its stools teetery, the woman on duty two or three sheets to the wind. He took a seat and ordered Martell's with a water wash. The barmaid, an aging, bony female in a baggy green jumpsuit, studied him with suspicious bloodshot eyes. She said, "Martell's? Martell's *what?*"

Lockington said, "Cognac—Martell's cognac."

The barmaid said, "*Cognac?* Looky, buster, this ain't no fag joint!"

Lockington spread his hands. He said, "All right, booze will do."

"What kinda booze?"

"The kind you're pushing."

"Thass better!"

She popped a murky shot glass onto the formica and poured from a bottle of Nolan's Bourbon Supreme. By way of relieving the tension, Lockington said, "Are you Helga?"

"No, I'm the fucking Countess Maritza!" She broke into a hoarse staccato cackle, sounding a great deal like a motorboat hung up on the sandbar, Lockington thought, although he was unfamiliar with motorboats and he wouldn't have known a sandbar from a butterscotch sundae. He said, "Well, maybe you ain't the Countess Maritza, but I'll bet you were a hummer in your day." It was one of Lockington's very best lines.

The acid seeped out of her. She took his ten-dollar bill, rang up a dollar, and fanned out nine singles on the bar. There was a wistfulness about her. She said, "Hey, mister, I wasn't too shabby—no guys never objected to *me* dropping my panties!" She lit a cigarette and broke into a series of racking consumptive coughs. She spat into the bar sink. "Yeah, I'm Helga. You from around here someplace?"

"Sort of."

"Uh-huh. Going to a wake?"

"Right—old friend of mine."

Helga thought about it. "Old friends' wakes ain't all that much fun."

Lockington nodded agreement, saying nothing.

Helga said, "I get the biggest chunk of my action from Olenick's—sometimes six, eight people at a time, but they don't never stay long."

"You probably pull some ball-game trade."

"Not much—I'm too far north."

"You oughta do pretty good when they start playing night ball."

She shook her head. "Doubtful. Nobody in his right mind would walk clear the hell up here from Wrigley after dark."

A young man had come in, seating himself on the first stool inside the entrance. He was a hatless, sturdily built fellow, sandy-haired, clean-cut, with quick gray eyes and neatly dressed. Helga looked his way and he mumbled, "Just a bottle of Old Washensachs, please." He seemed ill at ease, his knuckles rat-ta-tat-tatting on the countertop. Lockington's experienced gaze noted the shoulder-holster bulge in his powder-blue sports jacket. He avoided Lockington's eyes, turning self-consciously away to watch the Clark Street traffic crawl by.

Lockington gulped his Nolan's Bourbon Supreme, understanding why the stuff wasn't famous. He left a dollar on the bar, waved to Helga, and went out to head north. He didn't look back. Looking back wasn't necessary. He'd picked up a tail. He shouldered his way through the thickening dusk, wondering why.

19

The scent of carnations hit him in the face like a moist blanket, it permeated the interior of the decaying brick building on North Clark Street. It'd never go away, Lockington figured—over the decades, the pores of the place had become clogged with the odor. He made his way up a long, narrow hallway, hat in hand, feeling the hush. The walls were dark-paneled, the floors dark-carpeted, the lamps on little black tables were amber-shaded and dim. Somewhere an organ and chimes recording was playing. Lockington was acquainted with the number—"Abide With Me." An old woman with a fractured voice had sung it at his grandmother's funeral. Lockington's grandmother had been run over by a Budweiser truck just ten days after she'd quit drinking. There'd been a moral there, Lockington was certain, but he'd never been able to locate the damned thing.

Olenick's Funeral Home was silent—death reigned there, death was the force, death was the reason for living. Some reason. Lockington detested all fucking undertakers.

Like the stem of a flower, the hallway terminated at its blossom, an oblong room that featured an enormous reproduction of an oil painting of Jesus Christ. To its black wooden frame a wag had taped a crudely lettered white filing card—WOULD YOU BUY A USED CAR FROM THIS MAN? If management had noticed it, it hadn't done anything about it. What the hell, this was North Clark Street in Chicago.

There were registration books on tall tables, and to left and right there were small smoking lounges with uncomfortable-looking straight-backed chairs. Dead ahead were two rooms where caskets rested on low, blue velvet-draped biers. Hanging over the entrances to these rooms were chrome-framed white-on-black signs—above the door on the right, LIPSCOMB, JOHN; above the door on the left, DEVEREAUX, RUFUS. The white letters of the signs were interchangeable, lightly secured in the slender grooves of their black backgrounds. Lockington had seen similar displays in greasy-spoon eateries—HAMBURGER & FRIES $1.95. Chicago prices, of course. In New York they said HAMBURGER & FRIES $5.95 ONIONS EXTRA. Lockington had been to New York once, a mistake he had no intention of repeating.

There were half a dozen people in the Lipscomb room, another eight or ten in the Lipscomb smoking lounge. A woman was sobbing softly in the smoking lounge. So was a man. Men will weep now and then—not so readily as women and not so often, but it'll happen. Lockington had cried when he'd lost his mother, he'd cried when he'd lost Julie Masters, and he might cry if he lost Edna Garson, but that would depend on how he lost her. He wasn't sure that he'd *ever* lose Edna Garson, nor that he'd ever want to. Edna was a pillar, propping up his life.

There was no one in the Devereaux room, no one but Rufe. Lockington stood beside the battleship gray casket, gnawing on his lower lip, the gravity of the moment closing in on him like a great vise. The casket lid was down. They didn't bother attempting to reconstruct a man's head unless the man was a helluva lot more important than Rufe Devereaux.

In a corner of the room there was a single magnificent array of flowers contained by a white wicker basket the size of a laundry tub. Lockington appraised it at two hundred dollars—a thousand in New York. He saw no card. Possibly the boys at the Agency—but the Agency had set up the ground rules. No hoopla, no flowers, no ceremony.

A pudgy, cherub-faced little man in a black suit came into the room—probably one of the Olenick family, Lockington thought. The man nodded, smiled, and picked up the flower basket, shifting it to a position at the foot of the casket. He said, "Looks better there, don't you think?"

Lockington said, "That's one helluva bunch of posies."

The little guy said, "Isn't it, though? Reindorff's arrangement—instantly identifiable. Reindorff's does beautiful work—another gentleman commented on it earlier."

Lockington said, "Reindorff's—Reindorff's is on Wabash Avenue."

"No, Reindorff's is in Logan Square."

"Yeah, that's right—I was thinking of Rheingold Jewelry. Rheingold is on Wabash."

The little guy said, "No, Rheingold is on West Monroe." He went out.

Lockington hadn't considered sending flowers.

Flowers don't help.

20

He touched the top of the casket with a gentle hand before withdrawing from the room and crossing to the Devereaux smoking lounge, there to hunch on a straight-backed chair, light a cigarette, and wait, but not for long. A man in a powder blue sports coat hove into view, coming from the hallway at a tentative gait to peer into the room where Rufe Devereaux's casket rested, then turned to check the smoking lounge. His smile was halfhearted. He said, "Ah—Lockington."

Lockington made no reply, watching him come into the lounge and park on a chair. He produced a cork-tipped cigarette, firing it to life with a chrome Zippo lighter. He crossed his legs and leaned back, blowing a gray plume of smoke in Lockington's direction. He said, "I wanted to talk to you at Helga's Place, but—well, you know how it goes."

Lockington said, "No, how does it go?"

"Well, let's just say that at this time, it's a bit hairy." He put out a hand. "I'm Steve Dellick."

Lockington's handshake was unenthusiastic. "I'm

Lockington, but you already know that. What else do you already know?"

Dellick said, "Well, for one thing, you were at the International Arms yesterday, speaking with a Chicago police detective named Webb Pritchard."

"Briefly, yes."

"You know Pritchard?"

"After a fashion."

"You were looking for Rufe Devereaux. What was your business with Devereaux?"

"We were going to overthrow the government, establish a police state, and declare war on Russia. We planned to attack through the northeastern tip of Turkey—saturation bombing, then heavy armor, then—"

Steve Dellick's audible sigh was of the monumentally patient variety. He said, "Please, Lockington—we're trying to bust a murder case. Rufe Devereaux was one of ours."

Lockington said, "We—Knights of Columbus, San Diego Chargers—who's we?"

"Central Intelligence Agency." Dellick dug for his wallet. "Identification?"

Lockington waved the offer away. "Okay, I'll buy it. I hadn't seen Rufe Devereaux in more than a year. We'd probably have gotten drunk. We used to do that on occasion."

"'On occasion'—what would 'on occasion' amount to?"

"Once a week, once a month—it varied. Why?"

"I'm trying to determine if you two were close—were you friends or merely acquaintances?"

"I can't say—probably a bit of both."

"Tavern pals?"

"I suppose that'd sum it up."

"In your last drinking sessions with Devereaux, did he tell you that he was taking an indefinite leave of absence?"

"No."

"Did he at any time make reference to someone known as the Copperhead?"

"Once—passing mention. An expert assassin, he said."

"Did he speak of a man named Sheckard—Sam Sheckard?"

"No. Who's Sam Sheckard?"

"Probably an alias for the Copperhead."

"You people believe that Devereaux was killed by the Copperhead?"

"We've considered that possibility."

"Because Rufe was on the Copperhead's trail?"

"Was he?"

"You tell *me*."

Dellick shook his head. "Lockington, we just don't know." He studied the carpeting between his feet. "You're an ex-cop, right?"

"Right."

"With an itchy trigger finger?"

"Wrong."

Steve Dellick's knowledgeable smile bordered on a smirk. "And now you're a private investigator?"

"That's what my license says."

"When did you last see Devereaux?"

"Winter before last—February, or thereabouts."

"Any reason why he should contact you after all that time?"

"I didn't know his reason. I assumed that we'd have lunch and a few drinks."

"Did you catch a sense of urgency?"

There'd probably been an urgency, but Rufe had spoken with Edna Garson, and there was no point in dragging Edna into the picture. Lockington said, "No."

"Do you know that Devereaux had in his possession an item of considerable importance?"

"Are you talking about the attaché case or the woman?"

"The attaché case. Webb Pritchard mentioned it?"

"Yes, but he didn't get into details. What was in the attaché case?"

Dellick ignored the question, clearing his throat. Here comes the commercial, Lockington thought—funny how people telegraphed it by clearing their throats. Dellick said, "Uhh-h-h, look, Lockington, the Agency is beginning to wonder if you aren't on the verge of getting involved in something that you have no business getting involved in— you know what I mean."

"No, what do you mean?"

"Well, you see, this Devereaux affair is sticky—it figures to get stickier. Why get your hands dirty?"

"You're jumping to conclusions. I haven't turned a hair."

"You've been asking questions."

"What the hell, I'm *curious*. Any law against asking questions?"

Dellick's gray eyes glittered in the half light of the smoking lounge, but his tone was laid-back—that of a third-grade teacher attempting to reason with the class spitball sharpshooter. "We want you to leave it alone, Lockington— just leave it *alone*." There was a pleading, boyish sincerity about Dellick—the kid was doing his best.

Lockington said, "Is that a request or an order?"

"It's friendly advice. Everything will be attended to."

"By whom?"

"By specialists. We have a few of those."

Lockington sighed. "You followed me here to tell me *that?* You could have picked up a *telephone!*"

Dellick said, "Let me finish, please. You come across straight—I believe we can do business."

"What *kind* of business?"

Dellick dug into a jacket pocket to produce a white business envelope, handing it to Lockington. "There's five thousand dollars there."

"For what—blowing up the fucking Kremlin?"

"For staying out of this thing—for standing clear of it."

Lockington tossed the envelope into Dellick's lap. "I can stand clear of it for nothing."

"Yes, but *will* you?"

"I don't have the slightest idea."

Dellick scowled. "All right, Lockington, it's a free country, but watch your step. This is a major league ball game—in addition to snaffing it, you could get yourself killed."

"By the Copperhead?"

"Doubtful. You're a conservative—the Copperhead kills liberals." He crushed his cigarette butt into a brown glass ashtray. "One more question—have you heard of an organization known as LAON—Law and Order Now?"

Lockington nodded. "Also Robin Hood and Santa Claus and the Tooth Fairy."

"You doubt its existence?"

"Definitely. What's your point?"

"There are threads that may link the Copperhead to LAON. LAON doesn't like liberals, and we've heard that it pays well—something like fifty thousand per job."

"That's hearsay."

"LAON claimed responsibility for torching the *Chicago Morning Sentinel* last summer."

"Anybody can make a crank telephone call—hell, you could claim responsibility for the next airlines disaster."

Steve Dellick shrugged. It was the shrug of a man who's just rolled snake eyes.

Lockington got to his feet, leaning to clamp a hand on Dellick's shoulder, squeezing hard. He said, "Listen, son—you've taken up my time, you've attempted to bribe me, you've made veiled threats, you've inferred this and intimated that, you've cloak-and-daggered it to the hilt, and I know about half as much as I knew before you *got* here! Now, if we're gonna talk, we're gonna talk *English!* What's behind the fucking curtain?"

Dellick ran stubby fingers through sandy hair. Tiny beads of perspiration glittered on his forehead. He stared up at Lockington with frustrated gray eyes. He said, "Rufe Devereaux was a man out of control—you didn't know Devereaux, not *really*."

Lockington released Dellick's shoulder. He said, "Y'know, that's been a problem of mine—I've never known *any*body, not *really*." He left the building. A misty rain was falling.

21

"A man out of control"—a strange remark, but then Dellick
had been vague throughout. Lockington walked the cracked
blacktop driveway toward the parking lot, avoiding puddles.
Without the rain it'd have been a depressing evening—
with it, it was little short of crushing. His mood was black,
his thoughts revolved around the battleship gray casket in
Olenick's Funeral Home—what sort of hornet's nest had
Rufe Devereaux stumbled into? He'd taken a leave of absence,
Dellick had said. Leave of absence for what purpose—to
engage adversaries or to avoid them? Had there really *been* a
leave of absence, or had Dellick's story been a red herring
intended to divorce the Central Intelligence Agency from a
fatal mission it'd handed to Devereaux? Lockington harked
back to early '87 and his last contacts with Rufe, digging
for words or actions that might have indicated involvement
in a dangerous project, finding nothing that he could hang
his hat on.

He'd been offered one thousand dollars to get in, five

thousand to stay out. The first was in his bottom desk drawer, he'd refused the second—apparently he was in. In over his head, chances were.

There'd been an attaché case and a woman, both missing. What'd been in the attaché case, where was the woman, and who was the Copperhead—*was* there a Copperhead? Dellick had hinted that the Copperhead was employed by LAON—a shadowy figure working for a shadowy organization, and Lockington leaned toward discounting both. He'd seen no proof that either existed. For openers he had a blurred equation of ifs and maybes, half factors of undetermined values—one helluva way to start a ball game.

The flower arrangement at Rufe Devereaux's casket— from whom? The phony Sergeant Delvano who'd called Classic Investigations and the Club Howdy—what was *that* sonofabitch up to? And why was Lacey Lockington suddenly a focal point in the murder of a man he hadn't seen since Christ was a corporal? Assembling the scattered and unverified pieces available, Lockington came up with a disjointed and bewildering scenario—Rufe Devereaux had flown into O'Hare, leaving there in a rented automobile to drive at breakneck speeds to a Chicago tavern, sneak out the back door, hop into a waiting cab, disappear for a couple of hours, double back to the tavern, return the rented car to its agency, then summon another cab for the trip to the International Arms Hotel—a circuitous route serving what purpose? Whatever the intent, it'd availed him nothing— somebody had been ahead of him or not far behind.

Devereaux's cold-blooded murder appeared to be running a distant second to the fact that his attaché case had vanished, and the whole cockeyed world seemed to be laboring under the impression that Lockington had knowledge of its whereabouts. He reached the Pontiac in the drenched, poorly lighted expanse behind Olenick's Funeral Home, fumbling for the ignition key in a gusty west wind and a rain that was turning nasty. He didn't hear the footsteps behind him, he *sensed* them, and he turned to look down the barrel of what appeared to be a Colt .45 automatic pistol, a close-range weapon that can decapitate a man. It was held unwaveringly by a lean, hook-nosed fellow with an Errol Flynn mustache and a receding chin. The newcomer said, "Get in the car, hotshot—you and me gonna have us a little chat about Rufe Devereaux." Lockington recognized the raspy voice of Sgt. Joe Delvano. He also recognized a big man who'd materialized silently from the shadows to stand behind Delvano. The big man growled, "Drop the gun or I'll blow your fucking head off."

Delvano froze, the Colt .45 clattering on the blacktop. The big man kicked it across the parking lot. He placed his left hand on Delvano's right shoulder, turning him clockwise, busting him on the jaw with a whistling right haymaker. Delvano, suddenly airborne, arched to crash-land face-down on the hood of a white Chevrolet, adhering to its surface with the animation of that much raw liver. Moose Katzenbach turned to Lockington. He said, "Lacey, this is a piss-poor neighborhood."

• • •

Driving west on Irving Park Road, Lockington whistled tunelessly to the beat of his frayed windshield wipers. After a while he said, "Thanks, Moose."

Moose said, "My pleasure. I stopped to gargle a few beers and I got to thinking maybe you might need some help, so I grabbed a cab."

Lockington said, "Who was the cat with the howitzer?"

Moose said, "Bugsy Delvano—third-rate syndicate monkey. I didn't recognize the other one."

"The *other* one?"

"Yeah, there was a guy who followed you out of Olenick's. Any damn fool coulda seen he was on your trail, so I stopped him and asked who he was. I might of let him go if he hadn't been a wiseass."

"What did he say?"

"He told me he was with the CIA. That pissed me off."

"Uh-huh—where is he now?"

"I whacked him one and I stuffed him in a garbage can on the north side of the building."

Lockington groaned a bowel-wrenching groan. "Jeezus *Christ!*"

Moose shook his head. "Naw, Lacey—impossible. No beard, no robe, no sandals, and he was packing a heater."

22

CHICAGO-LANGLEY/ ATTN MASSEY/ 0803 CDT/ 5/26/88
BEGIN TEXT: **LOCKINGTON APPROACHED BY DELLICK/
NO SOAP**/ END TEXT/ CARRUTHERS

LANGLEY-CHICAGO/ ATTN CARRUTHERS/ 0904 EDT/ 5/26/88
BEGIN TEXT: **FIVE THOUSAND NOT ENOUGH?**/ END
TEXT/ MASSEY

CHICAGO-LANGLEY/ ATTN MASSEY/ 0805 CDT/ 5/26/88
BEGIN TEXT: **MONEY APPARENTLY NO OBJECT/
DELLICK SLUGGED**/ END TEXT/ CARRUTHERS

LANGLEY-CHICAGO/ ATTN CARRUTHERS/ 0906 EDT/ 5/26/88
BEGIN TEXT: **LOCKINGTON?**/ END TEXT/ MASSEY

CHICAGO-LANGLEY/ ATTN MASSEY/ 0806 CDT/ 5/26/88
BEGIN TEXT: **NEGATIVE/ DELLICK**/ END TEXT/
CARRUTHERS

LANGLEY-CHICAGO/ ATTN CARRUTHERS/ 0907 EDT/ 5/26/88
BEGIN TEXT: **WILL REPHRASE/ DID LOCKINGTON SLUG**

DELLICK?/ END TEXT/ MASSEY

CHICAGO-LANGLEY/ ATTN MASSEY/ 0808 CDT/ 5/26/88
BEGIN TEXT: **NEGATIVE/ SOMEBODY ELSE**/ END TEXT/
CARRUTHERS

LANGLEY-CHICAGO/ ATTN CARRUTHERS/ 0909 EDT/ 5/26/88
BEGIN TEXT: **WHERE DELLICK SLUGGED?**/ END TEXT/
MASSEY

CHICAGO-LANGLEY/ ATTN MASSEY/ 0810 CDT/ 5/26/88
BEGIN TEXT: **BETWEEN EYES**/ END TEXT/ CARRUTHERS

LANGLEY-CHICAGO/ ATTN CARRUTHERS/ 0910 EDT/ 5/26/88
BEGIN TEXT: **WILL REPHRASE/ WHERE DELLICK WHEN
SLUGGED?**/ END TEXT/ MASSEY

CHICAGO-LANGLEY/ ATTN MASSEY/ 0811 CDT/ 5/26/88
BEGIN TEXT: **DRIVEWAY OLENICK FUNERAL HOME
NORTH CLARK STREET CHICAGO**/ END TEXT/
CARRUTHERS

LANGLEY-CHICAGO/ ATTN CARRUTHERS/ 0912 EDT/ 5/26/88
BEGIN TEXT: **MONEY LIFTED?**/ END TEXT/ MASSEY

CHICAGO-LANGLEY/ ATTN MASSEY/ 0812 CDT/ 5/26/88
BEGIN TEXT: **NEGATIVE**/ END TEXT/ CARRUTHERS

LANGLEY-CHICAGO/ ATTN CARRUTHERS/ 0913 EDT/ 5/26/88
BEGIN TEXT: **GUN?**/ END TEXT/ MASSEY

CHICAGO-LANGLEY/ ATTN MASSEY/ 0813 CDT/ 5/26/88
BEGIN TEXT: **NEGATIVE**/ END TEXT/ CARRUTHERS

LANGLEY-CHICAGO/ ATTN CARRUTHERS/ 0914 EDT/ 5/26/88
BEGIN TEXT: **DELLICK DESCRIBE ASSAILANT?**/ END
TEXT/ MASSEY

CHICAGO-LANGLEY/ ATTN MASSEY/ 0815 CDT/ 5/26/88
BEGIN TEXT: **AFFIRMATIVE/ APPROX HEIGHT 14 FT/ APPROX WEIGHT 600 LBS/ NEEDED SHAVE**/ END TEXT/ CARRUTHERS

LANGLEY-CHICAGO/ ATTN CARRUTHERS/ 0916 EDT/ 5/26/88
BEGIN TEXT: **ODD THAT MONEY AND GUN NOT HEISTED/ MOTIVE FOR ATTACK?**/ END TEXT/ MASSEY

CHICAGO-LANGLEY/ ATTN MASSEY/ 0817 CDT/ 5/26/88
BEGIN TEXT: **PROBABLY PSYCHOPATH/ PSYCHOPATHS DONT NEED MOTIVES**/ END TEXT/ CARRUTHERS

LANGLEY-CHICAGO/ ATTN CARRUTHERS/ 0918 EDT/ 5/26/88
BEGIN TEXT: **WHERE LOCKINGTON NOW?**/ END TEXT/ MASSEY

CHICAGO-LANGLEY/ ATTN MASSEY/ 0818 CDT/ 5/26/88
BEGIN TEXT: **UNKNOWN/ DELLICK FOLLOWING LOCKINGTON WHEN SLUGGED/ WILL RENEW CONTACT SHORTLY**/ END TEXT/ CARRUTHERS

LANGLEY-CHICAGO/ ATTN CARRUTHERS/ 0919 EDT/ 5/26/88
BEGIN TEXT: **IMPERATIVE NOT LOSE LOCKINGTON/ CODE LOCKINGTON BIRD DOG EFFECTIVE IMMEDIATELY**/ END TEXT/ MASSEY

CHICAGO-LANGLEY/ ATTN MASSEY/ 0820 CDT/ 5/26/88
BEGIN TEXT: **UNDERSTOOD**/ END TEXT/ CARRUTHERS

LINE CLEARED LANGLEY 0920 EDT/ 5/26/88

23

Chicago, Illinois is a city of gross excesses, its weather not excluded. On that May Thursday morning the heat was stifling, coiling around the throat boa constrictor-style, boiling from the blistered asphalt of Kimball Avenue to cascade into Reindorff's Gift and Flower Shop with Lockington's entrance. He closed the door behind him hurriedly, luxuriating in the coolness of the place. The woman at the counter was rather attractive for her probable fifty years, Lockington thought—she had neatly groomed, slightly wavy, gray-streaked dark hair, a pug nose, a soft mouth, and she wore a loose, open brown smock over a starchy white blouse and sharply pressed beige slacks. She was arranging red silk tulips in a white ceramic vase and she glanced up, her green eyes sparkling inquisitively behind the thick lenses of her spectacles. "Yes, sir—may I be of assistance?" This puzzled Lockington. In Chicago they hardly ever ask.

He said, "I hope so, ma'am." He took out his billfold

to flash the tarnished badge he'd neglected to turn in. There were times when it came in handy. "Chicago Police, ma'am—we're backtracking a floral piece sent yesterday from Reindorff's to Olenick's Funeral Home on North Clark Street. The name of the deceased was Devereaux—Rufus Devereaux."

The lady in the brown smock squinted, reaching for a thick blue ledger on the countertop, pulling it to her, then pushing it away. "No need for that. I remember it now—our Imperial grouping. Lovely thing. You've seen it?"

"Yes, ma'am, yesterday evening—exquisite. Who was the sender, do you recall?"

"Certainly—a woman named Pickens. She's well known in the Logan Square neighborhood. She operates a country music tavern on Milwaukee Avenue, just around the corner, practically." She jammed red silk tulips into the vase with savage thrusts. "Oh, I could tell you a few things about *that* one, if you're interested."

She was hopeful that he'd be interested, Lockington could tell. He said, "Every bit of information helps, ma'am. Are you acquainted with Miss Pickens on a personal basis?"

"I wouldn't be caught on the same side of the street with her! I'm aware of the things she does!"

Lockington lit a cigarette, saying nothing but nodding a green light.

She was in high gear now, gathering momentum. "You know about the country music element, I suppose."

"Not really. What about the country music element?"

"Why, these people have sex *indiscriminately—*like *animals!*"

"Is that a fact?"

"It most assuredly *is*, and they say that this Pickens creature has—er-r-r—would *obliged* be the word I'm looking for?"

"Probably, if you want to use more than four letters."

"No, let's make it *accommodated*—*accommodated* conveys my meaning clearly enough, wouldn't you say?"

"It'll do just dandy, ma'am."

"All right, she's accommodated as many as *four* of those scruffy guitar players in the same bed at the same *time!* Now isn't that downright *revolting?*"

"Not if you're a scruffy guitar player."

"Her first name's Bobbie, but they call her Easy—Easy Pickens. You grasp the significance, I'm certain."

Lockington shrugged comprehension of the significance, studying the ash of his cigarette.

She said, "What's she done? *Nothing* will shock me, I *guarantee!*"

"It's a police matter, ma'am—I'm not at liberty to discuss it."

"But it'll be in the newspapers, won't it—I mean *eventually?*"

"*Eventually* is a long word, ma'am."

She was silent for a moment. Then she giggled. "*My*, but you're *interesting!* I've always labored under the impression that policemen were—were—oh, *damn*, what *is* the word?"

"Scruffy, ma'am?"

"No, *doltish*—I've already used *scruffy* and I simply *detest* repetition!"

Lockington said, "'Use not vain repetitions as the heathen do, for they think they shall be heard for their much speaking.'"

She clapped her hands. "Oh, that's *excellent!* Who said it?"

"My father—he used it twenty times a day."

"It sounds almost *biblical.*"

"It *is* biblical—it's the only verse my old man ever memorized."

"I could tell you more about this Pickens female, if it'll aid in your investigation."

"I believe I have all I'll need at this time. You've been extremely helpful, ma'am—I want to thank you for your cooperation."

"You're entirely welcome! You're much nicer than Sergeant Delvano—Sergeant Delvano was—well, *scruffy.*"

"Joe? When was Joe in?"

"Yesterday afternoon, three or so. I'm a widow—my name's Martha Merriam. I don't believe I caught yours."

Lockington said, "Voltaire—Sergeant Voltaire."

"Any relation to the French playwright?"

Lockington turned to go. "No, but my cousin pitched for the Toledo Mudhens." He went out. The heat was clamping down on Chicago, there wasn't a cloud in the sky. He crossed the street to his car and a gray Buick missed running him down by three-quarters of an inch. There was a heavy-set woman at the wheel. Lockington shrugged. Some things never change.

24

Lockington drove south on Milwaukee Avenue, southeast, really—Milwaukee Avenue runs on a diagonal. The Club Howdy was on his left, and Moose Katzenbach's report had been accurate—it was a different Club Howdy now. Its shabby gray shingles had been replaced by neat beige brick veneer. Its gaudy flashing red neon sign was gone. The new sign was smaller, pale blue, reserved. Throw in Moose's description of the Club Howdy's interior and it stood to reason that Bobbie Jo Pickens was cutting a hefty buck belting out country ballads. Or she was sleeping with the right people. Or both.

Lockington was entertaining a host of second thoughts. Second thoughts were new to him—he'd never had time for them. Although rarely a player of sudden hunches, he'd been given to responding to first impulses, often rashly, sometimes violently. Procrastination and Lacey Lockington were virtual strangers, this providing the reason for Lockington being alive and reasonably well in Chicago. As a police detective he'd prowled the dark corners of the city, and spontaneous action had become a habit. There'd been moments when it'd been all that'd stood between him and a cemetery plot.

At this stage of the ball game, he found himself in a position to empathize with Mrs. O'Leary's much maligned cow. The hapless bovine had done no more than kick over a lantern. She'd burned Chicago to the ground. Lockington was no less innocent. He'd dropped into a local hotel to hoist a few with an old friend. He'd wound up smack dab in the middle of a red-hot homicide case.

He should have walked away from it forty-eight hours earlier—he knew that now. He should have left the International Arms, stopped at the nearest ginmill, gotten quietly crocked, and forgotten the whole confusing mess. He should have, but he hadn't. Instead he'd managed to get himself grilled by Webb Pritchard, receive an intimidating telephone call, reject an unusual five-thousand-dollar offer from the Central Intelligence Agency, and be threatened by a Colt .45 automatic in a funeral home parking lot. On the plus side, if there *was* a plus side, he'd learned a bit more than he'd known earlier concerning a matter that'd been none of his affair in the first place—there'd been something between Rufe Devereaux and Bobbie Jo Pickens. Just how serious it'd been, Lockington didn't know, but there'd been a relationship. A woman who isn't acquainted with a man hardly ever dispatches a wagonload of flowers to his bier—a line of reasoning probably shared by the ubiquitous Sgt. Joe Delvano, if Moose Katzenbach's booming right hand hadn't scrambled Delvano's brains.

Lockington hadn't seen Rufe Devereaux since the evening he'd left him at the bar of the Club Howdy, apparently convinced that he could take Bobbie Jo Pickens to bed. According to Martha Merriam at Reindorff's Flower Shop, taking Bobbie Jo Pickens to bed wouldn't have qualified Rufe for anybody's Hall of Fame, but, directly or indirectly, it might have been an action that'd put him in a northside crematorium. His interest in Bobbie Jo could have been a pivot point—at the time it'd blossomed, or shortly afterward, Rufe had taken an unexplained leave of absence from the Central Intelligence Agency, disappearing over Lockington's horizon to surface scant hours before he'd been shot to death. Had Rufe rung Bobbie Jo's bell and been run off the Club Howdy range by a jealous hillbilly guitar-picker, and had he been blown away because he hadn't stayed gone? Lockington junked that line of thought instantly because Rufe had returned to Chicago with a different woman in tow, one who'd make Bobbie Jo Pickens look like a busted bale of alfalfa, if Webb Pritchard's second-hand description was to be granted credence.

Lockington had a thousand dollars in his desk drawer, and he'd have returned it to its sender if he'd known the sender's identity. If it was Rufe Devereaux's money, as Lockington believed, he *couldn't* return it. If it'd belonged to somebody else, they'd have to show up and ask for it. Well, so much for the sudden and untimely demise of Rufe Devereaux—Lockington was washing his hands of the whole tragic business. Aside from the loss of a dear friend, he had but one regret—he should have accepted the CIA's offer of five thousand dollars to stay out of the picture. Making that kind of money for doing nothing is excellent work if you can get it. But, what the hell, it hadn't been his first mistake and it certainly wouldn't be his last. He nosed the Pontiac into the Randolph Street parking lot, his thoughts veering to verdant pastures—this evening he'd stop at the Shamrock Pub, and if Edna Garson was there, perhaps something could be arranged. It'd been a while.

He piled out of his car, turning it over to a scowling attendant—ancient, rusted-out vehicles such as Lockington's fail to promise a great deal in the way of customer gratuities. There were several automobiles behind the smoking old dragon, all awaiting parking accommodations, and at the curb was a sparkling '88 white Cadillac sedan driven by a portly, red-faced, silver-haired fellow wearing wire-framed, amber-lensed sunglasses, the type usually seen under the brim of a Georgia deputy's Stetson. The man's gaze hooked up with Lockington's for a moment, then shifted to Randolph Street traffic. Lockington had seen him before, he thought. He shrugged the possible recognition off. He might have sat next to him in one of Chicago's multitudinous northside taverns. He might have discussed the Cubs or the Sox or the Hawks with him. It'd happened on countless occasions—brief sports chatter with men he'd never seen before or since.

Lockington shouldered his way through the oppressive late spring heat. By noon the office would be untenable. If nobody laid claim to that thousand dollars, he'd have an air conditioner installed, a big mother, one that'd freeze the balls off a penguin. He smiled wryly. There was a line he'd damned well better keep to himself. If Moose got hold of it, it'd become an issue, Moose voicing doubts that penguins have balls, Lockington assuring him that they do—it had a time potential of hours, and the thought of becoming involved in such a discussion with Moose Katzenbach was enough to send a chill rippling up Lockington's back.

Randolph Street clanged and clattered, a woman caught Lockington with her shoulder, spinning him into the path of another who knocked him against a utility pole, and he was less than half a block from the Classic Investigations office when the man in the '88 white Caddy flashed onto the screen of his memory. There he was, silver hair flashing in the footlights, red face beaded with sweat, eyes glaring, pacing back and forth like a short-leashed Bengal tiger, waving a hand mike with one hand, a Bible with the other, exhorting a crowd of fifteen thousand people to wake up and join the noble cause of America for whites only, to stamp out the gross permissiveness that was sweeping the country, to return to the old values, to an era of law and order, to vote for Billy Mac Davis in the 1984 presidential election.

That campaign had busted out before November of '84, and Lockington wondered what Billy Mac Davis had been doing on West Randolph Street. Maybe he'd gone straight and taken a job. Politicians have been known to do that. Even in Chicago.

25

When Lockington entered the Classic Investigations office, Moose Katzenbach was pacing the floor, snapping his fingers. Lockington said, "How's about a chorus of 'Rose of Washington Square?'"

Moose said, "Lacey, I got up late this morning and I didn't have time for coffee. Coffee! I gotta have *coffee!*"

Lockington slid into the swivel chair. He said, "So go get coffee."

Moose said, "May Allah attend your steps and grant your every lecherous desire!" He left the office as if the seat of his pants were on fire, and Lockington settled back, yawning. His mind was at ease. He'd faced the facts, which were: Rufe Devereaux was gone, he wouldn't be back, nothing could be done to change that, and Lockington was out of it.

The door crashed open and a man came reeling into the office. His left eye was swollen shut, his prominent nose was bent out of shape, the right-hand side of his Errol Flynn mustache was missing, and there was a large bluish lump on his receding chin. He wobbled to the client's chair, collapsing onto it to teeter precariously there. Lockington recognized him—the Colt .45 menace from Olenick's parking lot, Sgt. Joe Delvano. Two men had followed Delvano into the office. The first was a hulking creature in a baggy brown suit. He had an expressionless simian face, the chest of a bull gorilla, and the hairy paws of a grizzly bear. His companion was a slender man attired in a lemon-hued sharkskin leisure suit, a forest green silk shirt, and oxblood alligator-skin loafers. He had the smoky eyes of a pissed-off king cobra, and his thin-lipped smile was devoid of humor. He said, "You're Lacey Lockington?"

Lockington said, "Well, at the moment, that would depend on factors too numerous to mention."

The shambles in the client's chair mumbled, "Yeah, he's Lockington."

The man in the lemon-colored leisure suit said, "Hi, Lockington, I'm Vince Calabrese."

Lockington said, "Vince, I'm hanging on your every word."

Vince Calabrese said, "My friend, today you find yourself in the presence of the dumbest cocksucker God ever put on the face of this fucked-up planet!"

Lockington's eyes flicked between the wreck in the client's chair and the animal in the baggy brown suit. He said, "Which one?"

Calabrese said, "The one what got trouble walking straight."

Lockington said, "Oh, *him*."

Calabrese gestured vehemently. He said, "Get him outta here, Angelo, before I blow his fucking liver out!"

The monster in the brown suit reached for the casualty in the client's chair, hauling him to standing position, pushing him in the direction of the exit, hastening his departure with a swift kick.

Calabrese had occupied the client's chair, shaking his head. He said, "You give a fucking imbecile a job, and you get a fucking imbecilic performance—right?"

Lockington shrugged. "I dunno—I never gave a fucking imbecile a job."

Calabrese said, "Dom told him, 'See what you can find out about where Devereaux went when he sneaked outta that tavern on Monday night.' Dom told him, 'Check with this guy Lockington—maybe he can help you.' That's what Dom told him."

Lockington didn't say anything.

Calabrese went on. "So what does this jackoff do? He makes like some kind of fucking secret agent, *that's* what he does! Instead of walking in here and asking you a couple straight-up questions, the sonofabitch gets on the fucking telephone and pretends he's a fucking Chicago police sergeant, and when that don't work, he goes around waving a fucking cannon like a fucking banana republic revolutionary! That's *bush* league, Lockington—this ain't fucking nineteen twenty-eight no more!"

Lockington said, "What's on your mind, Vince?"

Calabrese said, "Well, so now you see what happens to assholes who take matters into their own hands! Can I use your telephone?"

"Local call, or Sicily?"

Calabrese reached for the phone, laughing. It was a shrill cackle, the midnight laugh of a foggy river loon, Lockington thought, but he'd never heard the midnight laugh of a foggy river loon, so it was probably a lousy metaphor. Calabrese had dialed a number. In a moment he whistled into the mouthpiece and hung up, winking at Lockington. He said, "Marvelous things, them fucking cellular phones—you can talk to a guy parked right outside the door."

Within a minute the vestibule door had opened and a man with a cane had made his way down the stairs and into the office. He was a very old man, white-haired, dressed in a dark blue suit. His shirt collar was high and stiff, his blue-striped gray necktie was perfectly knotted, his highly polished black oxfords sparkled in the dimness of the office. Calabrese strode across the room to take the old fellow's arm, escorting him to the client's chair, seating him there. He said, "I'll leave you gentlemen alone." With that he went into the vestibule to stand ramrod-straight at the bottom of the stairs, like a sentry at a castle drawbridge. The old man extended a limp hand. He said, "Mr. Lockington, this is a distinct pleasure."

Lockington shook hands with him, just a single pump. He said, "I'm afraid you have me at a disadvantage."

The old man smiled wanly, placing his cane between his knees, cupping his hands over its crook, hunching to rest his chin on them, studying Lockington with inquisitive brown eyes. His face was gnomelike, wrinkled like a bas-relief map of Tibet. He said, "Spatafora, Mr. Lockington—Dominic Spatafora."

Lockington nodded. This was the big fish, the Don, the honcho of Mafia Midwest, a man who could have your guts ripped out by twitching a finger. Spatafora was saying, "I regret that our first meeting has been prefaced by so ugly an incident." His voice was harsh but he controlled its abrasiveness by speaking softly. "However, every organization has its misfits, its foul balls, if you will—I'm sure that you're aware of that."

Lockington spread his hands, acknowledging that every organization has its misfits, its foul balls.

Dominic Spatafora said, "Unfortunately, one of my—er, associates has waxed, shall we say, overly zealous?"

Lockington said, "Yes, I suppose we could say that."

Spatafora slipped a pale hand into a coat pocket, bringing forth an envelope, placing it on the desk at Lockington's elbow. He said, "Where there's a wrong, there must be a right." He tilted his cane to a forty-five-degree angle, leaning in Lockington's direction. "Mr. Lockington, on Monday evening, an acquaintance of yours slipped through the back door of a tavern at the corners of Belmont and Kimball avenues. He came back shortly, but it's likely that he returned with less than he left with. Do you follow me?"

Lockington said, "Not at all, Mr. Spatafora—I don't know what you're talking about."

Spatafora's smile was slow and genuine—the appreciative smile of a chess enthusiast for a britches move. He said, "Well, Mr. Lockington, so be it for this time, but in the event you should come upon information or material pertinent to this matter, I would appreciate a call. You would be handsomely rewarded, I assure you. You will find my card in the envelope." He struggled to his feet, bowing stiffly, and Vince Calabrese left the vestibule, hustling to the old man's side, and guiding him toward the door.

They went out and Lockington opened the envelope. He found a five-hundred-dollar bill folded around a simple black-on-white business card. He studied the card. STARCREST IMPORTS & EXPORTS. Lockington's smile was sour. Imports translated to cocaine, exports to firearms, probably. There was no name on the card, just a telephone number.

He slipped the cash and the card into a pocket, considering the difference between appearances and realities. Dominic Spatafora had seemed a friendly and courteous fellow, a gentleman by the most demanding standards—there'd been an aura of grandfatherly kindness about him. Lockington lit a cigarette. That old sidewinder had sentenced more men to death than any ten judges in the country.

26

A man may mute his words and tether his actions but his mind remains free to do as it pleases. Lockington had withdrawn his physical capabilities from the Devereaux affair, but his thoughts swarmed to it like bees to a clover patch. The mysterious attaché case constituted the eye of this particular hurricane. He ticked off the sequence of events as he'd understood them—Rufe Devereaux renting a high-performance automobile at O'Hare, barreling down the Kennedy Expressway, peeling off at the Kimball Avenue exit to enter Mike's Tavern with his female companion, leaving the lady at Mike's, scooting through the rear door to a waiting taxi, coming back better than two hours later *with* the attaché case, obviously, because it'd been in his possession when he'd reached the International Arms. Old Dominic Spatafora had seemed convinced that the contents of the attaché case had been disposed of during Devereaux's brief absence. Beyond that, Spatafora was harboring a notion that Lockington had been the recipient thereof, a theory apparently shared by just about everybody.

There was a woman to be accounted for—a lovely, dark-haired, blue-eyed young thing. Where the hell did she figure—had Rufe known her in Ohio, had he met her during the Cleveland-to-Chicago flight, had she been an O'Hare field hustler, one of those five-hundred-dollar overnight conveniences—what was her role? Rufe had never been particular as to where and how he'd gotten his women. If the big Cajun had owned an Achilles heel, it'd worn sheer black lingerie. Such were the meanderings of Lockington's mind when Moose Katzenbach came in to plunk a large white styrofoam cup on the desk top. He said, "Coffee, sahib."

Lockington scowled. He said, "Sahib ain't bad, but in the future you will address me as Your Omnipotence."

Moose said, "Say, I'm feeling better! You still in the market for 'Rose of Washington Square?'"

Lockington said, "That urge has flown."

Moose seated himself, crossing his legs, lighting a cigarette. "That's good—I forgot the fucking words anyway."

Lockington took a noisy slurp of his coffee. He said, "My God, this is *awful* stuff! The Greek joint across the street?"

Moose said, "Yes, Your Omnipotence."

They drifted into a comfortable silence, a sense of normalcy pervading the little office—no place to go, and nothing to do when they got there. Disinvolvement brought a feeling of tranquility, Lockington thought, wondering if there *was* such a word as *disinvolvement*, deciding that there probably wasn't, but that there *ought* to be.

The telephone was ringing. Lockington reached lethargically for it. Edna Garson said, "What time you gonna get home this evening?"

Lockington said, "Same time as usual—when I get there."

Edna said, "Okay." She hung up.

Normalcy indeed.

27

CHICAGO-LANGLEY/ ATTN MASSEY/ 1158 CDT/ 5/26/88
BEGIN TEXT: **BIRD DOG HAD OFFICE VISITOR/ DOMINIC SPATAFORA**/ END TEXT/ CARRUTHERS

LANGLEY-CHICAGO/ ATTN CARRUTHERS/ 1259 EDT/ 5/26/88
BEGIN TEXT: **CHICAGO SYNDICATE WHEEL?**/ END TEXT/ MASSEY

CHICAGO-LANGLEY/ ATTN MASSEY/ 1159 CDT/ 5/26/88
BEGIN TEXT: **AFFIRMATIVE**/ END TEXT/ CARRUTHERS

LANGLEY-CHICAGO/ ATTN CARRUTHERS/ 1300 EDT/ 5/26/88
BEGIN TEXT: **BIRD DOG INVOLVED RACKETS?**/ END TEXT/ MASSEY

CHICAGO-LANGLEY/ ATTN MASSEY/ 1200 CDT/ 5/26/88
BEGIN TEXT: **DOUBTFUL**/ END TEXT/ CARRUTHERS

LANGLEY-CHICAGO/ ATTN CARRUTHERS/ 1301 EDT/ 5/26/88
BEGIN TEXT: **REPORT MANPOWER SITUATION YOUR STATION**/ END TEXT/ MASSEY

CHICAGO-LANGLEY/ ATTN MASSEY/ 1202 CDT/ 5/26/88
BEGIN TEXT: **ADEQUATE**/ END TEXT/ CARRUTHERS

LANGLEY-CHICAGO/ ATTN CARRUTHERS/ 1302 CDT/ 5/26/88
BEGIN TEXT: **ASSIGN ADDITIONAL OPERATIVE BIRD DOG**/ END TEXT/MASSEY

CHICAGO-LANGLEY/ ATTN MASSEY/ 1203 CDT/ 5/26/88
BEGIN TEXT: **WILL BE CROWDED/ HARGAN JUST NOW REPORTS 3 OTHERS FOLLOWING BIRD DOG**/ END TEXT/ CARRUTHERS

LANGLEY-CHICAGO/ ATTN CARRUTHERS/ 1304 EDT/ 5/26/88
BEGIN TEXT: **IDENTIFY**/ END TEXT/ MASSEY

CHICAGO-LANGLEY/ ATTN MASSEY/ 1204 CDT/ 5/26/88
BEGIN TEXT: **UNKNOWNS/ KRAMER SHOOTING PIX/ WILL SEND BLOWUPS FAX**/ END TEXT/ CARRUTHERS

LANGLEY-CHICAGO/ ATTN CARRUTHERS/ 1305 EDT/ 5/26/88
BEGIN TEXT: **DESCRIBE**/ END TEXT/ MASSEY

CHICAGO-LANGLEY/ ATTN MASSEY/ 1205 CDT/ 5/26/88
BEGIN TEXT: **FIRST APPROX 45/ APPROX 5–10/ APPROX 170/ BLACK HAIR/ GASH LEFT CHEEK/ DRIVES 87 GREEN PONTIAC TRANS AM**/END TEXT/ CARRUTHERS

LANGLEY-CHICAGO/ ATTN CARRUTHERS/ 1306 EDT/ 5/26/88
BEGIN TEXT: **SOUNDS B MOVIE MAFIA**/ GO ON/ END TEXT/ MASSEY

CHICAGO-LANGLEY/ ATTN MASSEY/ 1207 CDT/ 5/26/88
BEGIN TEXT: **SECOND APPROX 50/ APPROX 5–7/ APPROX 180/ SILVER HAIR/ FLORID FACE/ WILD GRAY EYES/ DRIVES 88 WHITE CAD DEVILLE/ BUMPER STICKER JESUS SAVES**/ END TEXT/ CARRUTHERS

LANGLEY-CHICAGO/ ATTN CARRUTHERS/ 1308 EDT/ 5/26/88
BEGIN TEXT: **CHECK/ DESCRIBE THIRD**/ END TEXT/
MASSEY

CHICAGO-LANGLEY/ ATTN MASSEY/ 1209 CDT/ 5/26/88
BEGIN TEXT: **THIRD APPROX 30/ APPROX 5-5/ APPROX
115/ RED HAIR/ PALE BLUE EYES/ STUNNING/ DRIVES
88 BLACK MERCEDES SEDAN**/ END TEXT/ CARRUTHERS

LANGLEY-CHICAGO/ ATTN CARRUTHERS/ 1310 EDT/ 5/26/88
BEGIN TEXT: **FEMALE?**/ END TEXT/ MASSEY

CHICAGO-LANGLEY/ ATTN MASSEY/ 1210 CDT / 5/26/88
BEGIN TEXT: **VERY**/ END TEXT/ CARRUTHERS

LANGLEY-CHICAGO/ ATTN CARRUTHERS/ 1311 EDT/ 5/26/88
BEGIN TEXT: **HOW LONG THESE IN PLACE?**/ END TEXT/
MASSEY

CHICAGO-LANGLEY/ ATTN MASSEY/ 1211 CDT/ 5/26/88
BEGIN TEXT: **FIRST NOTICED THIS MORNING**/ END
TEXT/ CARRUTHERS

LANGLEY-CHICAGO/ ATTN CARRUTHERS/ 1312 EDT/ 5/26/88
BEGIN TEXT: **BIRD DOG AWARE?**/ END TEXT/ MASSEY

CHICAGO-LANGLEY/ ATTN MASSEY/ 1212 CDT/ 5/26/88
BEGIN TEXT: **NO SIGN**/ END TEXT/ CARRUTHERS

LANGLEY-CHICAGO/ ATTN CARRUTHERS/ 1313 EDT/ 5/26/88
BEGIN TEXT: **LICENSE PLATE CHECKS?**/ END TEXT/
MASSEY

CHICAGO-LANGLEY/ ATTN MASSEY/ 1213 CDT/ 5/26/88
BEGIN TEXT: **IN MILL/ DUE SHORTLY**/ END TEXT/
CARRUTHERS

THE DEVEREAUX FILE

LANGLEY-CHICAGO/ ATTN CARRUTHERS/ 1314 EDT/ 5/26/88
BEGIN TEXT: **HURRY PHOTOS/ THIS URGENT**/ END
TEXT/ MASSEY

CHICAGO-LANGLEY/ ATTN MASSEY/ 1215 CDT/ 5/26/88
BEGIN TEXT: **WILCO**/ END TEXT/ CARRUTHERS

LINE CLEARED LANGLEY 1315 EDT 5/26/88

28

The morning had ground into early afternoon with all the speed of a glacier. The phone had been silent, nothing of consequence had happened, and this was just fine with Lockington—it was too damned hot for telephones and happenings of consequence. He'd have closed shop and gone to the ball game but the Cubs and Sox were playing an exhibition thing, and exhibition stuff held no appeal for Lockington. Like all-star games, playoffs, and the World Series, they proved absolutely nothing. Lockington liked regular season play when pitching wore thin and injuries piled up and slumps came and went, *that* was baseball, that was when they separated the men from the boys.

Moose had gone out for hamburgers and he stood in the vestibule, chewing thoughtfully on his fourth, staring into West Randolph Street. Lockington was polishing off his second burger at the desk, mopping sweat with a blue bandanna. In the unseasonable heat time was without meaning. He dug the Yellow Pages out of a desk drawer.

He leafed through it briefly before calling Apex Heating and Cooling on West Madison Street. A gruff voice answered. Lockington said, "I'm looking for an estimate on an air-conditioning job."

"Where you located?"

"West Randolph between State and LaSalle."

"What floor?"

"It makes a difference what floor?"

"Sure it makes a difference what floor. If it didn't make a difference what floor, why would I be asking you what floor?"

"Basement."

"Maybe you'll need a window unit."

"We don't got no windows."

"No problem. We'll just knock a hole in your wall."

"You'll just knock a hole in my wall? You just knock a hole in my wall and my landlord will blow your ass clear to fucking Brazil!"

"You serious?"

"Damn right, I'm serious. He's a gun dealer."

The line went dead. Lockington called back. He said, "You got fans."

"What kind of fans?"

"*Big* fans."

"Hey, we got a fan that'll blow the balls off a buzzard. Cost you two eighty-six with tax."

"Okay, I'll send a guy over." Lockington hung up, gesturing Moose into the office. He said, "Go over to Apex at Four-oh-eight West Madison and buy a fan."

"How big?"

"They'll have one waiting. They say it'll blow the—it's a

big one, Moose."

"Okay. Hey, Lacey, I just saw a real jim-dandy fistfight!"

"Where?"

"Right outside the door."

"There'll be a lot of those today—it's the heat."

"It was over a parking space—Slats Mercurio and some fat white-haired character."

"Slats Mercurio?"

"Second-rate syndicate hood."

"Mercurio—he got a scar on his cheek?"

"Yeah. You know Slats?"

"I arrested him a couple times."

"Hey, for a fat man with a Jesus Saves bumper sticker, that old guy could really wing it! He decked Mercurio twice."

"Who got the parking space?"

"A little red-headed broad with a black Mercedes."

Lockington yawned, placing money on the desk top. He said, "Go get the fan."

29

Moose came down the vestibule steps shortly after three o'clock, the fan over his shoulder. It was an ominous-looking chrome thing, over six feet in height and sporting half a dozen thirty-inch transparent blue plastic blades behind its nine-gauge wire screening. With its weighted base, it must have weighed close to two hundred pounds, Lockington figured. Moose eased it to the floor near an electrical outlet. He said, "It's the biggest damn thing they had."

Lockington nodded approval.

Moose said, "The guy told me that it'll blow the balls off a buzzard."

Lockington said, "Plug it in."

Moose said, "Do buzzards got—"

"I don't know, Moose, honest to God, I don't."

"Neither did he."

"Plug it in."

"If they do, they sure ain't visible."

"Plug it in."

"'Course, I ain't seen enough buzzards to qualify as an expert."

"For Christ's sake, plug it *in,* will you?"

Moose plugged it in. There was a menacing low-pitched sound, like the warning growl of a mama lion, Lockington thought. The rumble faded into a whine, the whine mounting in pitch to an almost inaudible whistle. Lockington's cigarette flew from his mouth, a button was ripped from his shirt, the ashtray shot from the desk, the wastebasket capsized and the office was filled with flying papers wheeling like swallows in the gale until they were plastered against the north wall. Lockington was yelling, "Okay, turn it off!"

Moose was behind the fan, looking for the switch. He shouted, "I can't find the little bastard!"

Lockington roared, "The plug! Pull the fucking *plug!*"

Moose lunged for the plug, jerking it from the outlet. The torrent subsided. Lockington said, "Jesus Christ *Almighty!*"

Moose said, "Hey, Lacey, I'll bet this sonofabitch could blow the balls off an *eagle!*"

The phone was ringing. Edna Garson said, "I picked up baby back ribs and delicatessen garden salad and a coconut cream pie."

Lockington said, "Okay."

Edna said, "You like coconut cream pie?"

"Why not?"

"Is your broiler working?"

"I don't know—I've never used it."

"Maybe you better come to my place tonight."

"All right."

"My broiler works like a charm."

"It sure does."

30

When they'd located the switch and adjusted the speed control, when the debris had been picked up and the office restored to order, Lockington said, "You hit it off pretty good with Bobbie Jo Pickens yesterday?"

Moose shrugged. "Well, she didn't proposition me, but she was affable."

"Fair enough. Why don't you take another run up that way?"

"When—and do what?"

"Right now—just sit around the joint, suck up a few beers, talk to Bobbie Jo if she's around."

"And if she ain't?"

"Keep your eyes open, yak with the barkeep and maybe a couple customers—see if you can shake something loose."

"Regarding Devereaux, of course."

"Yeah. Bobbie Jo denied any knowledge of him—then she sent a couple hundred dollars' worth of flowers to his wake. That don't rhyme."

"So they had a relationship. You and Edna got a relationship. A whole bunch of people got relationships."

"A whole bunch of people ain't hiding 'em."

"Depends on their marital status, I'd say."

"Okay, so it's fifty-fifty—take a whack at it anyway."

"I thought you were backing off of this Devereaux thing."

"I *am* backing off. I'm just trying to clear up a point."

"You think she's covering something?"

"I *know* she's covering something. Look, this broad has been in bed with ten trillion guys! Why should she play hide-and-seek where Rufe Devereaux's concerned?"

"Maybe he was married."

"Maybe he was, but I'll lay fifty-to-one that he *wasn't*."

Moose got up and put on his hat. "Well, what the hell, I got nothing better to do with my time."

Lockington said, "We're closing for the day. See you in the morning."

Moose waved and went out, Lockington locked the door and walked west to the Randolph Street parking lot. He drove north to Belmont Avenue, then west to Kimball. There was no point in reporting to Edna Garson at so early an hour—it already figured to be a long and strenuous night. Funny thing, he thought—a man will eat his heart out, hoping that a woman of Edna's caliber will cross his path. Then, when she does, he starts looking for ways to assert his independence—it makes him feel better about himself.

A woman of Edna's caliber knows that.

31

Mike's Tavern was housed in a dismal gray-shingled two-story building on the southwest corner of the Belmont-Kimball junction. Lockington was familiar with the place—he lived less than a mile from it and he'd shot a drug hustler just across the street, the episode having been the beginning of his rapid fall from grace with the City of Chicago Police Department. He'd known Mike Kazman for years and he found him very much as he'd last seen him, leaning against the backbar, arms folded across his chest, staring glumly at a row of unoccupied barstools. Kazman was a big jovial man with an unruly shock of gray hair, a ruddy complexion, a set of keen blue eyes, and a pronounced limp from a Guadalcanal shrapnel wound. He was staring at Lockington. He said, "Oh, my God, ain't it awful the things a man will run into when he ain't got no gun!"

Lockington grinned, straddling a backless barstool. They shook hands and Lockington said, "Been a while, Mike."

"Late last summer—the day you dropped Sapphire

Joe Solano."

"That's right."

Kazman said, "I heard you got your own agency now."

"Less said about that the better. What's new in this corner of the canyon?"

Kazman threw up his hands. "Lacey, in the last few days, I've had more action than you could shake a stick at. You still on Martell's?"

"Yeah, and get in with me." Lockington shoved a twenty onto the bar. "What kind of action?"

Kazman produced a pair of double shot glasses, filling them with Martell's cognac. "Water?"

Lockington shook his head.

They drank and Lockington made the sign for another round, making a series of tight circles above their glasses with his forefinger. Kazman poured and said, "Well, last Monday night some guy come in here and I heard he got shot Tuesday morning at the International Arms Hotel."

Lockington said, "I'll be damned."

Kazman said, "Of course, I ain't even sure he *got* shot—that's just a rumor I picked up—I didn't see nothing about it in the papers. But goddamn it, *something* happened because there's been a regiment of people coming in here asking all sorts of questions, and I can't answer *any* of 'em!"

They drank and Lockington nodded for a repeat. He said, "Who was the guy?"

Kazman poured cognac. "Damned if I know, I never laid eyes on the sonofabitch! George Pollard works Monday nights. George don't know mud from marmalade. You're acquainted with George, ain't you?"

"Yeah, I know George Pollard. How do these

questions run?"

They drank and Kazman sloshed Martell's into their glasses. He said, "Oh, like what time did the guy come in here and was he carrying an attaché case, and what time did he leave and did he take the attaché case with him when he left, and how long was he gone and did he have the attaché case when he got back, and how long was he here the second time? Stuff like that."

"He was here twice?"

"Yeah, according to George. George says he was with some chick what was an absolute showstopper—long-legged brunette, blue-eyed, beautiful—George says he ain't never seen nothing *like* her, but George ain't the world's greatest living authority. So they was at the bar, these two, and the guy called a cab, and he had it wait in the alley out back because I guess he figured somebody was following him or something. He went out the alley door, jumped in the cab and hauled ass. The woman hung around, had a few highballs, played some country music on the jukebox, didn't say much. In a while he come back and collected the tomato. George says they drove off in some high-class foreign car, but George wouldn't know a Ford from a fucking Ferrari."

They drank and Lockington said, "One more time." Kazman poured one more time. The story meshed with what Lockington had heard.

Kazman hoisted his glass. He said, "To the old days, Lacey." Lockington clinked glasses with him and they belted down their double hookers. Kazman was pouring again. He said, "I guess what all these people are trying to find out is where the hell was this guy while he was gone."

They drank and Kazman provided refills. They drank

and Lockington signaled for another. He said, "All these people? What kind of people—how many have been here?"

Kazman tilted the bottle of Martell's, draining it, rummaging in a backbar cabinet for a replacement, finding one, opening it. He said, "Well, a couple of 'em was hoods, that was obvious—hell, I know a hood when I see one. There was a few others what could of been government men—you know the type—clean-cut, well-dressed, polite guys. Then there was an older character, a real asshole—had shiny silver hair and a southern drawl—drove a white Caddy sedan with a Jesus Saves bumper sticker—parked it right out front during rush hour, and Max Murphy gave him a ticket. You know Max Murphy?"

Lockington nodded. "Yeah—old timer—I think he was born in a blue-and-white." They drank and Kazman poured from the new bottle of Martell's. Lockington said, "Interesting group."

"Uh-huh, and there was one more—redheaded heifer—oh, man, Lacey, she was something *special*—I mean *table* pussy!"

They drank and Lockington waved for another. "She asked the same questions?"

"Hell, all I remember is she drank straight vodka with no wash! She stopped my wagon!"

"You catch her name?"

"She never give none and I never asked her, but I'd saddle that one if her name was Rhoda Blunderschitz!"

They drank and Kazman poured again. Lockington said, "I don't think I ever knew anybody named Blunderschitz."

They drank and Kazman dumped Martell's into their glasses, spilling a few drops in the process. He said, "Me neither—I just made that name up. You ever just make a name up, Lacey?"

"Oh, sure, several times."

They bumped glasses and down went the Martell's. Lockington checked his watch. Plenty of time yet. He motioned for another round. Kazman said, "Hey, Lacey, you sill shing harmony on 'Tie Me Your Apurn Shrings Again?'"

Lockington said, "Yeah, but lass time, ole broad upstair call cops. She still up there?"

"Nellie Carshon? Sure, Nellie still up there." They drank the new round and Kazman poured cognac. He said, "We use do 'Apurn Shrings' an' 'I'm Drifting Back Dreamland' an' whole bunch others too alsho."

Lockington's smile was for days long gone, a gentle, pensive thing. He said, "We did 'Let Resh World Go By' an' 'Darrtown Strutters' Balls.'"

They gulped their drinks, banging their glasses to the bar. Kazman filled them. This was hard-nosed, relentless, Chicago-style drinking. Kazman said, "Doan forget 'When Brue Moon Turn Gole.' That probly our very bess nummer—'Brue Moon Turn Gole.'" He threw back his head, staring at the ceiling, humming the pitch. "Okay, Lacey-boy, you ready?"

Lockington cleared his throat. He said, "Let 'er flicker!"

Mike Kazman lit into "When My Blue Moon Turns to Gold Again." Lockington's tenor soared above the melody line. At least Lockington had the impression that it was soaring. Like an eagle, he thought. The cognac was going down like honey, the hour was golden, a magic spell was upon them. He felt his down-in-the-mouth mood release and tumble away like a spent booster rocket. Some days were better than others.

32

LANGLEY-CHICAGO/ ATTN CARRUTHERS/ 1643 EDT/ 5/26/88
BEGIN TEXT: **THANX EXCELLENT PIX/ RUN FOLLOWING AGAINST PLATES CHECKS/ FIRST NICHOLAS SLATS MERCURIO/ CHGO/ HANGERON SPATAFORA ORGANIZATION/ ODD JOBS MAN/ 12 ARRESTS/ 2 CONVICTIONS/ 2 PROBATIONS**/ END TEXT/ MASSEY

CHICAGO-LANGLEY/ ATTN MASSEY/ 1544 CDT/ 5/26/88
BEGIN TEXT: **MERCURIO VEHICLE REGISTERED STARCREST IMPORTS EXPORTS/ PROCEED**/ END TEXT/ CARRUTHERS

LANGLEY-CHICAGO / ATTN CARRUTHERS/ 1645 EDT/ 5/26/88
BEGIN TEXT: **SECOND BILLY MAC DAVIS/ MEMPHIS/ EX-PENTECOSTAL EVANGELIST/ EX-SENATORIAL CANDIDATE TENNESSEE 1980/ EX-PRESIDENTIAL HOPEFUL 1984/ EXTREMIST CONSERVATIVE/ WHITE SUPREMACY ADVOCATE/ PROBABLE MENTAL CASE**/ END TEXT/ MASSEY

CHICAGO-LANGLEY/ ATTN MASSEY/ 1546 CDT/ 5/26/88
BEGIN TEXT: **DAVIS VEHICLE CARRIES ILLINOIS PLATES/ ORRINGTON AVENUE EVANSTON ADDRESS/ PROCEED**/ END TEXT/ CARRUTHERS

LANGLEY-CHICAGO / ATTN CARRUTHERS/ 1647 EDT/ 5/26/88
BEGIN TEXT: **THIRD NATASHA GORKY/ BORN ODESSA/ LINGUIST CHGO POLISH CONSULATE/ IN U.S. POLISH DIPLOMATIC VISA/ SPEAKS FLAWLESS ENGLISH/ LIKELY KGB AFFILIATIONS**/ END TEXT/ MASSEY

CHICAGO-LANGLEY/ ATTN MASSEY/ 1548 CDT/ 5/26/88
BEGIN TEXT: **CHECK/ BLACK MERCEDES REGISTERED CHGO POLISH CONSULATE**/ END TEXT/ CARRUTHERS

LANGLEY-CHICAGO / ATTN CARRUTHERS/ 1649 EDT/ 5/26/88
BEGIN TEXT: **BIRD DOG?**/ END TEXT/ MASSEY

CHICAGO-LANGLEY/ ATTN MASSEY/ 1549 CDT/ 5/26/88
BEGIN TEXT: **MOST RECENT REPORT TAVERN BELMONT-KIMBALL AVENUES**/ END TEXT/ CARRUTHERS

LANGLEY-CHICAGO / ATTN CARRUTHERS/ 1650 EDT/ 5/26/88
BEGIN TEXT: **SAME AREA DEVEREAUX SKIPPED FROM?**/ END TEXT/ MASSEY

CHICAGO-LANGLEY/ ATTN MASSEY/ 1551 CDT / 5/26/88
BEGIN TEXT: **SAME TAVERN**/ END TEXT/ CARRUTHERS

LANGLEY-CHICAGO / ATTN CARRUTHERS/ 1651 EDT/ 5/26/88
BEGIN TEXT: **EXCELLENT**/ END TEXT/ MASSEY

CHICAGO-LANGLEY/ ATTN MASSEY/ 1552 CDT/ 5/26/88
BEGIN TEXT: **WHY EXCELLENT?**/ END TEXT/ CARRUTHERS

LANGLEY-CHICAGO / ATTN CARRUTHERS/ 1652 EDT/ 5/26/88

BEGIN TEXT: **BIRD DOG ABOUT TO MAKE MOVE/ WATCH CLOSELY**/ END TEXT/ MASSEY

CHICAGO-LANGLEY/ ATTN MASSEY/ 1553 CDT/ 5/26/88
BEGIN TEXT: **WILCO**/ END TEXT/ CARRUTHERS

LINED CLEARED LANGLEY 1653 EDT 5/26/88

33

The Thursday evening was warm, moist, and overcast. There was no breeze, there were no stars. When the cab pulled away from the lockup, Edna Garson said, "Who called the police?"

Lockington growled, "Nellie Carson."

Edna said, "Who's Nellie Carson?"

Lockington said, "The witch who got the apartment above Mike's Tavern."

"Where's your car?"

"Across the street from Mike's."

"Where's Mike's?"

"Belmont and Kimball."

Edna gave instructions to the driver, then she turned back to Lockington. "Are you capable of driving?"

"Ever since I was fifteen."

"Yes, but you haven't been drunk ever since you were fifteen."

"Don't bet on it."

"The charge was disturbing the peace. What the hell were you *doing?*"

"Singing."

"Oh, my God! For how long?"

Lockington shrugged. "I dunno—maybe two, three hours. Who bailed Mike Kazman out?"

"His brother-in-law."

"Impossible. Mike ain't married."

"His sister is."

"Oh."

"You're still drunk."

"So is Mike Kazman."

"I got that impression. When they let him out, he was singing 'My Wild Irish Rose.'"

"Yeah, I heard. Who was that lousy tenor?"

"The desk sergeant."

Lockington shook his head. He said, "They were downright atrocious on 'When My Blue Moon Turns to Gold Again.'"

Edna nodded. "Not particularly good on 'When I Lost You,' either. Do you know 'When I Lost You?'"

"Why, hell, yes—*every*body knows 'When I Lost You.'"

Edna said, "Sing 'When I Lost You.'"

Lockington sang "When I Lost You."

The cab driver hauled his vehicle to a screeching halt, spinning in his seat. He was a big man with a handlebar mustache. There was a skull and crossbones embroidered on his black T-shirt. He said, "Hey, I know that one! Sing it again!"

Lockington sang it again and the cab driver chimed in. He had an excellent tenor, Lockington thought.

Edna Garson was dabbing at her eyes with her handkerchief. She said, "Such a beautiful song."

34

CHICAGO-LANGLEY/ ATTN MASSEY/ 0900 CDT/ 5/27/88
BEGIN TEXT: **BIRD DOG ARRESTED**/ END TEXT/
CARRUTHERS

LANGLEY-CHICAGO / ATTN CARRUTHERS/ 1000 EDT/ 5/27/88
BEGIN TEXT: **WHY?**/ END TEXT/ MASSEY

CHICAGO-LANGLEY/ ATTN MASSEY/ 0901 CDT/ 5/27/88
BEGIN TEXT: **DISTURBING PEACE**/ END TEXT/
CARRUTHERS

LANGLEY-CHICAGO / ATTN CARRUTHERS/ 1001 EDT/ 5/27/88
BEGIN TEXT: **HOW?**/ END TEXT/ MASSEY

CHICAGO-LANGLEY/ ATTN MASSEY/ 0902 CDT/ 5/27/88
BEGIN TEXT: **SINGING MIKE'S TAVERN**/ END TEXT/
CARRUTHERS

LANGLEY-CHICAGO / ATTN CARRUTHERS/ 1003 EDT/ 5/27/88
BEGIN TEXT: **WHEN ARRESTED?**/ END TEXT/ MASSEY

CHICAGO-LANGLEY/ ATTN MASSEY/ 0903 CDT/ 5/27/88
BEGIN TEXT: **DURING SECOND CHORUS I GET BLUES
WHEN IT RAINS**/ END TEXT/ CARRUTHERS

LANGLEY-CHICAGO / ATTN CARRUTHERS/ 1004 EDT/ 5/27/88
BEGIN TEXT: **WILL REPHRASE/ AT WHAT TIME
ARRESTED?**/ END TEXT/ MASSEY

CHICAGO-LANGLEY/ ATTN MASSEY/ 0905 CDT/ 5/27/88
BEGIN TEXT: **APPROX 1730 YESTERDAY**/ END TEXT/
CARRUTHERS

LANGLEY-CHICAGO / ATTN CARRUTHERS/ 1005 EDT/ 5/27/88
BEGIN TEXT: **SPRING BIRD DOG**/ END TEXT/ MASSEY

CHICAGO-LANGLEY/ ATTN MASSEY/ 0906 CDT/ 5/27/88
BEGIN TEXT: **BIRD DOG SPRUNG LAST NIGHT BY EDNA
GARSON**/ END TEXT/ CARRUTHERS

LANGLEY-CHICAGO / ATTN CARRUTHERS/ 1007 EDT/ 5/27/88
BEGIN TEXT: **WHO EDNA GARSON?**/ END TEXT/ MASSEY

CHICAGO-LANGLEY/ ATTN MASSEY/ 0907 CDT/ 5/27/88
BEGIN TEXT: **PROBABLE ROLL IN HAY**/ END TEXT/
CARRUTHERS

LANGLEY-CHICAGO / ATTN CARRUTHERS/ 1008 EDT/ 5/27/88
BEGIN TEXT: **SINGING IN TAVERN MASKED BIRD DOG'S
PURPOSE?**/ END TEXT/ MASSEY

CHICAGO-LANGLEY/ ATTN MASSEY/ 0908 CDT/ 5/27/88
BEGIN TEXT: **LIKELY/ BIRD DOG SHREWD OPERATOR**/
END TEXT/ CARRUTHERS

LANGLEY-CHICAGO / ATTN CARRUTHERS/ 1009 EDT/ 5/27/88
BEGIN TEXT: **ANY IDEA WHAT BIRD DOG LEARN MIKE'S
TAVERN?**/ END TEXT/ MASSEY

CHICAGO-LANGLEY/ ATTN MASSEY/ 0910 CDT/ 5/27/88
BEGIN TEXT: **AFFIRMATIVE/ DO NOT SING**/ END TEXT/
CARRUTHERS

LANGLEY-CHICAGO / ATTN CARRUTHERS/ 1011 EDT/ 5/27/88
BEGIN TEXT: **WILL REPHRASE/ WHAT INFORMATION
PERTINENT TURKEY BIRD DOG GAIN AT MIKE'S
TAVERN?**/ END TEXT/ MASSEY

CHICAGO-LANGLEY/ ATTN MASSEY/ 0912 CDT/ 5/27/88
BEGIN TEXT: **NO KNOWLEDGE THIS TIME**/ END TEXT/
CARRUTHERS

LANGLEY-CHICAGO / ATTN CARRUTHERS/ 1012 CDT/ 5/27/88
BEGIN TEXT: **BUG BIRD DOG OFFICE**/ END TEXT/ MASSEY

CHICAGO-LANGLEY/ ATTN MASSEY/ 0913 CDT/ 5/27/88
BEGIN TEXT: **WILL NEED COURT ORDER**/ END TEXT/
CARRUTHERS

LANGLEY-CHICAGO / ATTN CARRUTHERS/ 1013 CDT/ 5/27/88
BEGIN TEXT: **FUCK COURT ORDER/ NATIONAL
SECURITY**/ END TEXT/ MASSEY

CHICAGO-LANGLEY/ ATTN MASSEY/ 0914 CDT/ 5/27/88
BEGIN TEXT: **DURING COMING HOLIDAY WEEKEND
BEST OPPORTUNITY**/ END TEXT/ CARRUTHERS

LANGLEY-CHICAGO / ATTN CARRUTHERS/ 1015 EDT/ 5/27/88
BEGIN TEXT: **UNDERSTOOD**/ END TEXT/ MASSEY

LINE CLEARED LANGLEY 1015 EDT 5/27/88

35

At 9:26 on the steamy morning of Friday, May 27, Lacey Lockington came slowly down the vestibule stairs to make his faltering way into the Classic Investigations office, nearly one-half hour late, badly hungover, physically exhausted. It'd been a hectic evening, winding down after midnight, and Lockington could have handled that, but there were times when Edna Garson's morning-after desires exceeded those of her night before, and this had been one of those.

Moose Katzenbach was leaning against the front edge of the desk, basking in the breeze of the new fan, observing Lockington's approach with educated eyes, pivoting to watch him drop heavily into the swivel chair. Lockington looked up with haunted eyes. He said, "Any calls?"

Moose shook his head. "Not one jingle."

Lockington grunted, "Good."

Moose said, "Uhh-h-h, Lacey, if it's any of my business, just where the hell did you disappear to yesterday afternoon? I called the Shamrock and I called your apartment."

138

Lockington caught the burrs of annoyance in the big man's voice. Wearily he said, "Look, Moose, I have been through a trying period. I have been drunk, arrested, thrown into jail and bailed out. I have been mounted and ridden like a Texas cow pony, I have been pawed, clawed, and gnawed, I have met sexual demands that would have chased the average satyr into a fucking monastery, I am but a battered shell of the man you once knew, and bearing these facts in mind, is it really important just where the hell I disappeared to yesterday afternoon?"

Moose said, "Normally, no, but this time was different. I tried calling you all the way up to midnight—apparently you didn't make it home last night."

"Apparently—Moose, what are you trying to tell me?"

"Well, when I got to the Club Howdy yesterday, the joint was closed up tight, so I went down the street to that crummy Nashville Corners."

"All right. So?"

"So Bobbie Jo Pickens got herself murdered sometime Wednesday evening."

Lockington sucked in an audible deep breath, sagging deeper into the swivel chair. After a while he said, "I don't think I'm all that surprised. How was she killed?"

"Pistol-whipped, the barkeep at Nashville Corners told me. Nobody heard a ruckus, he said."

"How would anybody hear a ruckus? In that rotten neighborhood nobody would hear the world come to an end."

Moose nodded glumly, not contesting the point.

Lockington said, "Who found her?"

"She lives upstairs above the Club Howdy, and she didn't come down for the Wednesday night show—she's usually there by eight o'clock. Her phone didn't answer, so they hammered on the door. Then they called the cops."

"What time do they figure it happened?"

"Seven o'clock or so—that was the opinion of the coroner's office."

"Who handled it?"

"Bill Starbuck."

Lockington nodded. "Starbuck's good—he doesn't miss by much."

"She put up a fight—they say the place was a mess."

"Anything to go on?"

"No stick-outs, far as I know."

"Forcible entry?"

"Yes and no—the night chain was snipped, but the door wasn't jimmied."

"It'd take a key to get to the night chain."

"Nothing to it—pick the lock or have a key cut from a wax impression."

"Unless the chain was cut on the way *out*."

"There's a thought."

"Yeah, but hardly original."

"The Nashville Corners bartender said that the bathtub was full and she was wearing a robe. With bath water running, she wouldn't have heard somebody messing with the door."

"Theft a likely motive?"

"Naw—they found a few hundred in her bureau drawer."

Lockington was awake now, wide awake, his mind plunging through a jungle of possibilities in quest of probabilities, colliding with a certainty—the Devereaux matter was getting worse instead of better, and it wasn't about to go away. When they act up like that, they have to be dealt with.

36

Moose hollered, "Boo!" jolting Lockington from his thoughts, reminding him of an incident when he'd been a youngster in the fourth grade. There'd been a big kid on the block, Howard Mayberry, four or five years Lockington's senior. When you're in the fourth grade, four or five years is a whole bunch. Lockington had always spoken respectfully to Howard Mayberry, but Howard had never responded. One morning Lockington had met Howard's mother at the corner grocery store and he'd said, "Mrs. Mayberry, how come Howard never says boo to me?" Mrs. Mayberry had patted Lockington on the head. She'd said, "Howard never says boo to you? Well, don't you worry, Lacey, I'll take care of *that!*" The next evening Lockington had been coming home at dusk and his route had taken him past the Mayberry residence and the big lilac bush in its front yard. As Lockington had gone by, Howard Mayberry had jumped from behind the lilac bush, roaring, "Boo!" and he'd frightened Lockington out of seven years' growth. The

Mayberrys had been a strange family.

Moose was saying, "Jesus Christ, Lacey, I been talking to you for ten *minutes!*"

Lockington stretched in the swivel chair, wishing he were in bed. Alone, of course. He said, "Yeah? What have you been talking about?"

"I been trying to find out who goes to lunch first—it's eleven forty-five."

"You go first."

Moose said, "You coulda told me that ten minutes ago."

Lockington yawned. "On your way back, see if Information Brown's at the newsstand."

Moose nodded and went out in a bit of a huff. Lockington hadn't responded because his thoughts had been elsewhere. So had Howard Mayberry's, obviously. At the age of twenty-four, Howard Mayberry had invented a timed lubricator for conveyor lines and he'd become a millionaire. Lacey Lockington had spent *his* twenty-fourth birthday drunk in a Saigon whorehouse.

It'd been a matter of priorities.

37

The Judson Cafeteria's Friday special had been fried perch, but Moose Katzenbach had gone with the salisbury steak and mushroom gravy, which had been excellent, he said, adding that Information Brown hadn't been at his newsstand.

If Information Brown wasn't at his newsstand, then it followed as must the night the day that he'd be at the Squirrel's Cage. Lockington put on his hat and walked over there. Information Brown was nowhere in sight. Lockington took a seat at the bar, ordered a double Martell's cognac, and asked about Information Brown. He'd just returned to the newsstand, Avalanche MacPherson said, but he'd be back within the hour, because Information Brown had never been known to go longer than an hour without a drink.

Lockington nodded, watching a woman slip onto the barstool next to his. She was one helluva woman—she was pert-breasted, slender-waisted, slim-hipped, she had glossy auburn hair done in a neat pixie style, she had large pale-blue eyes, a perfect, slightly uptilted nose, a full-lipped gentle mouth, and a firm jawline. Her complexion was without blemish and Lockington detected no signs of makeup. Her short, simple dark brown dress was form-fitting, her beige suede pumps and matching handbag were quality merchandise, her perfume was bewitchingly vague, her smile was sudden and appealingly off-center. Her gaze was unflinching but not brazen. She was beyond doubt the most beautiful female Lacey Lockington had ever laid eyes on. She said, "Good afternoon." Her voice was soft, throaty.

Lockington gave her a perplexed smile, watching her put a tiny Colibri lighter to a cigarette. She ordered a shot of Smirnoff's vodka, drinking it without benefit of a wash, raising her hand for another before returning her attention to Lockington. She said, "I know who you are."

Lockington said, "So do I."

"You're Mr. Lockington."

"By golly, you're right."

"My pleasure, Mr. Lockington—I'm Natasha Gorky, and we're going to get along just fine."

"I'm glad to hear that."

Natasha Gorky said, "You're a private investigator."

Lockington nodded. "Now and then."

"I'm a linguist at Chicago's Polish consulate—seven languages. Eight, if you count American, which bears no resemblance to the British tongue."

"*Gorky* isn't Polish."

"I didn't say it was Polish."

"That's right, you didn't."

"It's Russian, of course."

"And there's a gun in your handbag."

"Well, yes, now that you mention it—a Mikoyan

snubnosed thirty-two—ten-round clip, German-designed, Soviet manufactured, deadly accurate."

"And with your Mikoyan snub-nosed thirty-two, you can shoot the eyes out of a potato at seventy-five yards."

"No, but I'll take a bet on fifty." A chillingly matter-of-fact response, Lockington thought. She sucked on her cigarette, smoke drifting from slightly flared nostrils, appraising him for a few moments. Then she said, "Correct me if I'm in error, but I believe that you are interested in a matter that concerns me greatly—namely the death of Rufus Devereaux."

She wasn't in error so Lockington didn't correct her. He said, "You're KGB?"

"Yes, Mr. Lockington, I'm KGB. Can we talk?"

"About what?"

"Devereaux—what else?"

"There's nobody stopping us."

"Privately, and at length, please."

"It's important?"

"Terribly—to your country and to mine. For a change, our respective governments are trying to skin the same cat."

"You'll have to explain that."

"I will, and in detail, if you'll grant me the opportunity."

Lockington thought it over, but not for long. He said, "All right, Ms. Gorky, my office is across the street, three-quarters of a block west."

"I know the location of your office. My apartment is less than ten minutes from here."

Lockington shrugged assent. There was a genuine urgency about her—she was letting it all hang out. They finished their drinks, leaving the Squirrel's Cage to dodge traffic crossing West Randolph Street. She opened the door of a black Mercedes sedan, popping lightly into the car, her short brown skirt flashing briefly to her upper thighs. She smoothed it demurely into place. She had wonderful legs, Lockington just happened to notice. He went around the back of the Mercedes to pile in beside her. She pulled away from the curb, flicking a glance into her rearview mirror, her face expressionless. She said, "You're being followed—I assume that you're aware of that."

Lockington said, "I rarely pay attention unless I'm running heroin." He wondered what the hell he was doing riding around in a Mercedes-Benz automobile with a woman from Russia, instead of waiting at the Squirrel's Cage for Information Brown. Actually, he shouldn't have been doing either—he'd pulled out of the Devereaux business, hadn't he? Sure, he had—the way old ball players pull out of baseball. It was worth a shot—she might light a candle.

Natasha Gorky was wheeling through Loop traffic with calm self-assurance and Lockington appreciated that. Most female drivers spooked him. She was saying, "There'll be three automobiles behind us now—a black Ford Escort driven by a CIA operative, a green Pontiac Trans Am driven by a Mafia employee, and a white Cadillac driven by an elderly overweight man with crazy eyes and silver hair."

Lockington didn't respond and she continued. "The CIA fellow's name is Hargan—Hargan is competent enough. The Mafia man's name is Mercurio—he's a heavy-handed dolt, slow-witted. The man with silver hair frightens me."

Lockington said, "Billy Mac Davis?" It was a shot in the dark, but Davis was in Chicago, Lockington had seen him behind the wheel of a white Cadillac, and a man answering

Davis's description had barged into Mike's Tavern to ask questions—a man driving a white Cadillac.

Natasha Gorky was nodding. "Then you *do* know. This Davis man—he's been an evangelist, then a politician, and he's *always* been a zealot. That's a toxic mixture—Davis is frustrated, treacherous, utterly ruthless."

Lockington turned slowly on the seat of the Mercedes, peering at Natasha Gorky. He said, "Now, look, isn't this just a bit out of the ordinary—a KGB agent walking out of the closet, identifying herself, laying it on the line to a man she doesn't know from Genghis Khan? It would seem to be carrying detente to an extreme—or does this come under the heading of *glasnost?*"

She shook her heard impatiently. "It's neither—put it down as common sense. Incidentally, KGB doesn't necessarily translate to an unshaven Bolshevik brandishing a lighted stick of dynamite—that's a nineteen twenties' stereotype and you Americans dredge it up every time you become alarmed. Also, I know you from Genghis Khan—I know a great deal about you. For example, I know that you don't believe there's a LAON."

"Do *you?*"

"Most assuredly—it's a red-baiting underground version of your infamous Ku Klux Klan. More about you, Mr. Lockington. You're clever, you manipulate with remarkable expertise."

Lockington frowned. "*Manipulate?* I don't know that I like the word."

"Manipulate...arrange—whatever. I refer to events of late last summer—the Denny-Elwood affair in which justice was served without trial, without error, and without mercy.

What was *your* term for it?"

"I didn't have one. I *still* don't. Any other observations?"

"Yes. Your tenor isn't bad, but you should brush up on 'I Get the Blues When It Rains.'"

38

She lived on the east side of North Lake Shore Drive. The building was of recent vintage and well-kept—eight stories of white brick and smoked glass with parking at basement level, revolving doors, a uniformed armed guard in the snappy little foyer, a brace of silently swift elevators, and reproductions of Picasso paintings all over the place. Lockington didn't understand Picasso and he didn't trust people who claimed that they did. Lockington's appreciation of art dimmed perceptibly when he was unable to determine whether the fucking picture was right side up or upside down.

Natasha Gorky's apartment was on the seventh floor, its sliding glass doors and wrought-iron balcony facing Lake Michigan. It was a small place, cool, dim, tidy, modestly furnished—white sofa and overstuffed chair, dark blue Naugahyde recliner, smallish maple coffee and end tables, spindly white-shaded lamps, and a half-barrel magazine container circled by bright brass hoops and stuffed with copies of *Newsweek*. There was a stereo receiver with tape deck on an end table. When Lockington saw no television set he advanced Natasha's intellectual stock several points in his ledger. He took off his hat, placing it on the back of the overstuffed chair before turning to seat himself at an end of the sofa, noting that a bottle of Smirnoff's vodka, a bottle of Martell's cognac, and a pair of double shot glasses had appeared on the coffee table as if by sleight of hand. Natasha poured Martell's into Lockington's glass, pushing it toward him, winking. "You've been thoroughly researched, Mr. Lockington."

Lockington said, "Obviously." He looked around the room. "Where's Vladimir?"

Natasha squinted, "Vladimir?"

"Vladimir Lenin. Shouldn't you have a picture of Vladimir Lenin?"

"Do you have a picture of George Washington?"

"No."

"Well, I don't have a picture of Vladimir Lenin." She offered him a cigarette. He didn't like filters but he took it. She said, "Vladimir had wonderful ideas—the problem is they haven't worked worth a damn."

Lockington said, "Have you noticed that wonderful ideas *never* work worth a dam?"

She sat at the other end of the sofa, pouring vodka, raising her glass to him. She said, "To the memory of your good friend Rufus Devereaux."

Lockington nodded approval of the toast and they drank. He said, "All right, Ms. Gorky, let's have it."

She leaned back on the sofa, blowing a smoke ring to the ceiling, watching it disintegrate like a wonderful idea. She said, "Devereaux—how well did you know him?"

"Not too well—we were baseball fans. That can do a lot for an association."

She smiled, tongue in cheek. "You'd do nicely in Dzerzhinsky Square."

"Is that where the nightingale sang?"

"No, the nightingale sang in *Berkeley* Square—KGB headquarters is in Dzerzhinsky Square. You know nothing of Rufus Devereaux's mission, or his obsession, or whatever it may have been?"

"Yes, he wanted to lay every woman in America." Lockington shrugged. "That didn't make him a bad guy."

She bowed her head into the palm of her left hand, laughing softly. It was a musical laugh, Lockington thought—like distant chimes. She said, "Oh, but aren't we evasive? Mr. Lockington, your friend is dead, we can't hurt him. He never spoke of the Copperhead?"

"The Copperhead—yes, on one occasion."

"No more than that?"

"It was a casual reference—he gave no indication of involvement. The Copperhead's a paid killer, they tell me."

"The best—in *your* country, that is. In certain circles it's believed that Devereaux was stalking the Copperhead. Beyond that, the Copperhead may have been stalking Devereaux. You knew Devereaux—was he good enough to mix in that sort of company?"

"I'd say yes."

"Based on what?"

"On a gut feeling, on impressions I received—he'd have been a bad man to go up against."

Natasha shrugged. "There's no iron-clad guarantee that he was killed by the Copperhead, but it was a chess match that'd been going on for nearly four years."

"Tell me about the Copperhead. Who is he—who does he work for?"

"His identity's unknown, he's used several names. He's killed in Miami—a two-hundred-yard rifle shot from an apartment rented by a Samuel Sheckard. He's killed in San Antonio—a point-blank pistol shot from an automobile rented by an Orval Overall. In Birmingham a man was knifed to death in a restaurant booth reserved by a Carl Lundgren—the Copperhead has no established pattern and he doesn't use the same alias twice."

"All right, if there's no clear-cut M.O., why does it have to be the Copperhead?"

"In Miami the victim was Wallace Vernon, an ultraliberal publisher. In San Antonio it was Grady James, a leftist columnist. In Birmingham it was Gordon Sheetz, a union organizer with known Communist ties, a radical by American standards. All had been threatened by LAON and each killing carried the Copperhead's trademark."

"What's his trademark?"

"Perfection—no loose ends. He leaves a trail of thin air. Our assumption is that he kills liberals for LAON and that he's eliminated at least one Mafia man."

"*Our* assumption?"

"The KGB's."

"How do you link him to the Mafia murder?"

"Wallace Vernon was killed in Miami on the night of June ninth, 'eighty-seven. A major cocaine transporter died there two hours later—a man by the name of Juarez. Juarez was Mafioso, a link between Colombia, Panama, and the United States. Wallace Vernon and Juarez were killed by the same weapon—Miami law enforcement recovered both slugs—the riflings were identical."

Lockington whistled. "You're well informed."

Natasha Gorky's smile was of the type usually reserved for the very young. "Mr. Lockington, the Komitet Gosudarstvennoi Bezopasnosti employs some five hundred thousand people. More than half of these are in the United States. I *should* be well informed."

Lockington said, "I see." He really didn't. The implied logistics were mind-boggling. He said, "And the Copperhead learned that Rufe was on his trail, so he doubled back on him?"

"A plausible theory." She was refilling their glasses. "On the other hand, Rufus Devereaux knew too much—*much* too much."

"About whom—what?"

"About the CIA, about the Mafia, about LAON."

"And about the KGB?"

There was that pale-blue unflinching stare. "Yes, and about the KGB."

"Which explains your interest."

"Indeed it does. You see, Rufus Devereaux had considerable knowledge of collusion between opposing ideologies, about bargains made and better left unmentioned."

"You've lost me—I fell off on the first turn."

"Well, by way of example—you remember the so-called Cuban missile crisis of nineteen sixty-two, I'm sure."

"Vaguely."

"*Vaguely?* You were twenty-two years of age in 1962!"

"Yes, but I was in the Marines—those were foggy years."

"Why foggy?"

"Because I was drunk."

"Was that all the Marines did—drink?"

"No, there were whorehouses. Back to the Cuban missile crisis, if you will."

"All right, what do you know of it?"

"Khrushchev installed nuclear missiles in Cuba. Kennedy made him take 'em out."

Natasha was shaking her head. "A half-truth at best. There were United States missiles in Turkey—they'd been there for *years*. Khrushchev countered by placing Soviet missiles in Cuba, agreeing to remove them if Kennedy would pull U.S. missiles out of Turkey. Kennedy jumped at it, using the alibi that the missiles in Turkey were obsolete. If I'm not mistaken, an obsolete nuclear missile will kill as many people as a state-of-the-art nuclear missile."

Lockington said, "Hell, I didn't know that we *had* missiles in Turkey."

"At that time, how many Americans *did*? Rufus Devereaux was privy to such information. For instance, he knew that the United States Government had sponsored a half-dozen attempts on the life of Fidel Castro, and that every one of them was made by the Mafia at the request of the CIA."

"That's substantiated?"

"No, but Devereaux could have substantiated it. He'd occupied any number of key CIA posts—he could have supplied dates, times, places, *names*."

"So could a lot of other people, undoubtedly."

"Undoubtedly, but a lot of other people haven't been willing to bring the facts to light."

"And Rufe was willing?"

Natasha frowned. Lockington liked her frown, realizing

that when a man likes a woman's frown he may be getting into deep water. She was saying, "It's possible—he may have become embittered."

Lockington was studying her—studying Natasha Gorky was a pleasure. He said, "He was in the same game as you. Have *you* become embittered?"

After what seemed a very long time she put a hand to her throat. "Yes, Mr. Lockington, and I'm *choking* on it."

Lockington joined in a silence that could have been chopped with an axe. In a while he said, "There are other cases too sensitive for public scrutiny?"

Her smile was frigidly tight. "Too numerous to mention. There've been no big winners, but all participants stand an excellent chance of losing."

"Losing *what?*"

"Leadership, backing, prestige, secrecy, the ability to function effectively. I refer to the KGB, the CIA, the Mafia, LAON—we're all in the same leaky canoe."

"All deal in assassination?"

"All, but of the four, LAON is on the thinnest ice—by comparison it's a fledgling organization."

"But gaining strength?"

"Oh, yes—it's established beachheads in government, it has highly influential supporters. At this stage in the game full exposure would prove catastrophic."

"The KGB believes that LAON hired the Copperhead to kill Devereaux?"

"It sees that as a definite possibility."

"Then who hired Devereaux to kill the Copperhead?"

"Perhaps no one—it could have been an ego trip for Devereaux. Had he spoken of retirement?"

"Several times."

Natasha's slow nod was a thoughtful thing. She said, "An excellent way to close an illustrious career, wouldn't you think—the frosting on the cake?"

Lockington downed his Martell's, grinding the stub of his cigarette into the ashtray on the coffee table. He gritted, "I'm out of my element—I don't think I should know about such things."

She'd gotten to her feet, stretching like a cat. She said, "Perhaps not, but if you stay on the Devereaux trail, you'll *learn*."

Lockington's discouraged sigh was audible. He said, "Would you believe that I was making an honest effort to stay out of this mess?"

"I believe that you *think* you were."

"But not that I—" He was staring in dismay. Natasha Gorky's short dark-brown dress had been pulled up over her pixie hairdo, her beige half-slip had slithered to the floor. She stepped clear of it, walking toward him, turning her back to him, peering at him over a tawny shoulder. She said, "My brassiere clasp, if you will, please."

Lockington unhooked the clasp, feeling her breasts spill out, watching her shrug free of the brassiere to catch it and toss it onto her overstuffed chair. She pivoted to face him, smiling her off-center smile, her pale-blue eyes sparkling with challenge, her nipples jutting like pink flint. She said, "You'll excuse my lack of panties?"

Lockington nodded, saying nothing.

She took his hand, tugging him from the sofa. "I'm from Odessa, Mr. Lockington. In Odessa the girls never bother."

She was unbuttoning his shirt when he said, "I hardly ever get to Odessa."

39

Granted the identical opportunity with the identical lady, deducting the shock of her direct approach and adding a few hours of continence, Lockington might have performed considerably better, or a great deal less poorly, depending on how Natasha Gorky saw it. A recuperation period of less than half a day had been inadequate for a man of Lockington's years. Still, he'd managed to get it done, the spirit willing, the flesh faltering, and she'd appeared to enjoy their hour. Appearances meant nothing, of course—Lockington knew that a clever woman will convince a man that he's done very well when he hasn't done very well at all. He figured that she'd registered him between a zero and a five, which was fair because he'd never been a ten, and eight was beyond him now—thirty years beyond him.

Her auburn pixie-cut was snuggled into his shoulder and she was murmuring, "Thank you—I was in need."

Lockington said, "So was I." It was a lie, but a noble lie.

She said, "May I call you Lacey?"

"I've been called worse."

"After—well, after *this,* Lacey would seem in order, don't you agree?"

Lockington agreed and he said so.

"I felt so foolish saying, 'Oh, my God, Mr. Lockington, I'm coming!' when 'Oh, my God, Lacey, I'm coming!' would have been more apropos. Did I *sound* foolish?"

"Not at all, but Communists shouldn't say, 'Oh, my God,' should they?"

"That would depend on the Communist, I suppose." She wiggled closer to him. "Uhh-h-h, Lacey, not to be talking shop after so pleasant a dalliance, but—well, about Devereaux—just what are you looking for?"

"I didn't know that I was looking for *any*thing, I'd tried to throw it out of my mind, but the *why* of it seems most important. Whys usually lead to whos."

"The why appears obvious."

"To shut him up?"

"Can you think of a better reason?"

Lockington pushed it around in his mind, trying to sight it from another angle. He said, "Rufe was with a woman when he got into Chicago—he'd had a relationship with another. One has disappeared, the other is dead."

"I know. What do you see in that?"

"Not a great deal. I suppose that one of them could have shot him."

"Farfetched. We've heard that he was killed with a heavy-caliber, high-velocity weapon—possibly a Magnum three fifty-seven with a silencer. How many women carry three fifty-seven Magnums with silencers?"

"Probably less than fifty percent. Could Devereaux have

been killed with his own gun?"

"Definitely not. Devereaux carried a bone-handled Smith & Wesson thirty-eight."

"How would you know that?"

"Firearms identification is a KGB requisite."

"Who identified Rufe's gun as a Smith & Wesson thirty-eight?"

"A KGB woman—one of our best."

"When and where?"

"June third of last year—here in Chicago."

"Rufe wasn't in Chicago in June of last year—if he'd been here I'd have heard from him."

"He was here briefly, staying at the home of an out-of-town friend in the unincorporated area of Leyden Township."

"The address?"

"Three thousand North Onines Avenue."

"Why was he here?"

"She doesn't know. He was leaving for Miami the next day. Now it would appear that he was attempting to catch up with the Copperhead and head off the assassination of Wallace Vernon."

"How would Rufe have known that Vernon was to be assassinated?"

"It was CIA information, apparently."

"How did your operative wangle a contact with Devereaux?"

"Easily—she let him pick her up at a country music honky-tonk. The KGB maintains dossiers on known CIA people—Devereaux's dossier was being updated."

"She took him to bed, of course."

"Of course."

"Who was your operative?"

"Natasha Gorky, if you must know."

"Doggone, woman, you *do* get around!"

"Lacey, that's my job."

"Your job—like taking *me* to bed?"

Natasha lifted her head from Lockington's shoulder, turning to peer at him. "All right, let's call a spade a spade—the KGB can use you in this matter, that's the way this *started* and I have no idea how it'll end, but in the last couple of hours I—you—let it pass, please. Where were we?"

"I was right here—you were in bed with Rufe Devereaux."

"And that disturbs you?"

"You're goddamned right that disturbs me!"

"Why?"

"I don't know, but it does."

"I'm glad."

"Why?"

"I don't know, but I am."

Lockington sat up in bed, groping for his cigarettes on the nightstand, lighting two, passing one to her. She accepted it, thanking him, her smile contented, the smile of the cat that's just polished off the canary. He said, "Let's swap corners. What does the KGB want from this?"

"The same thing the others want—silence and lots of it. At one time or another we've all gotten egg on our faces, we've all stepped in manure, we've been compromised, bought, sold, and bartered. Even God can't change the past, but silence can preserve the future."

"Silence won't flush LAON and the Copperhead into the open."

"LAON and the Copperhead are America's problem—so is the Mafia, so is the CIA. But Rufus Devereaux has become a problem for the Soviet Union."

"Rufe's gone—dead men tell no tales."

"What if he'd told tales prior to his death? What was in his missing attaché case—where is it?"

"Are you acquainted with the theory that he delivered its contents to *me?*"

"I've heard it, considered it, and dismissed it. If you knew the answers why would you be asking questions?" Natasha rose to a cross-legged sitting position, a sight to behold, her breasts full, firm, her belly flat and tight, her pixie hairdo tousled, her face lovely despite its perplexed expression. "Look, Lacey—why can't we work together on this? You know Devereaux personally, you know things that you don't *know* you know, and I have virtually immediate access to a wealth of information. We could get to the bottom of this, you and I!"

Lockington shrugged. He'd have joined this one in a wild turkey chase. She was straightforward, there was a blunt trustworthiness about her, he *liked* her—it was a chemical thing, a matter of instinct. She was as beautiful, as keen-witted, as glib-tongued, as poised and polished as they came, but he sensed a vulnerability. She had a faint aura of insecurity—she could have been the girl next door instead of a highly trained KGB agent. He said, "I call the shots?"

"You call the shots."

Lockington said, "All right."

She kissed him. He'd expected that, but it wasn't a brusque, businesslike kiss—it was soft, clinging, and it spun his senses. They looked at each other in the ensuing silence, probing with their eyes, a Martian and a Venusian stranded on Jupiter. After a while she said, "What—what if Rufe Devereaux wrote a book?"

Lockington said, "There'd be blood on the moon."

The silence returned.

Lockington put out his hand.

Natasha Gorky gripped it.

Lockington said, "Odessa?"

"That's right—Odessa."

He pulled her to him.

He kissed the hell out of her.

She bit his lower lip.

Hard.

She said, "Sorry!"

Lockington said, "It's all right—some do and some don't."

40

CHICAGO-LANGLEY/ ATTN MASSEY/ 1431 CDT/ 5/27/88
BEGIN TEXT: **BIRD DOG CONTACTED BY NATASHA GORKY**/ END TEXT/ CARRUTHERS

LANGLEY-CHICAGO / ATTN CARRUTHERS/ 1532 EDT/ 5/27/88
BEGIN TEXT: **WHEN APPROACH?**/ END TEXT/ MASSEY

CHICAGO-LANGLEY/ ATTN MASSEY/ 1432 CDT/ 5/27/88
BEGIN TEXT: **LUNCH HOUR/ SQUIRREL'S CAGE TAVERN WEST RANDOLPH ST**/ END TEXT/ CARRUTHERS

LANGLEY-CHICAGO / ATTN CARRUTHERS/ 1533 EDT/ 5/27/88
BEGIN TEXT: **PREARRANGED?**/ END TEXT/ MASSEY

CHICAGO-LANGLEY/ ATTN MASSEY/ 1433 CDT/ 5/27/88
BEGIN TEXT: **DOUBTFUL**/ END TEXT/ CARRUTHERS

LANGLEY-CHICAGO / ATTN CARRUTHERS/ 1534 EDT/ 5/27/88
BEGIN TEXT: **PREVIOUS CONTACTS?**/ END TEXT/ MASSEY

CHICAGO-LANGLEY/ ATTN MASSEY/ 1434 CDT/ 5/27/88

BEGIN TEXT: **UNKNOWN**/ END TEXT/ CARRUTHERS

LANGLEY-CHICAGO / ATTN CARRUTHERS/ 1535 EDT/ 5/27/88
BEGIN TEXT: **REASON THIS MEETING?**/ END TEXT/
MASSEY

CHICAGO-LANGLEY/ ATTN MASSEY/ 1435 CDT/ 5/27/88
BEGIN TEXT: **NO KNOWLEDGE**/ END TEXT/ CARRUTHERS

LANGLEY-CHICAGO / ATTN CARRUTHERS/ 1536 EDT/ 5/27/88
BEGIN TEXT: **VISIBLE RESULTS?**/ END TEXT/ MASSEY

CHICAGO-LANGLEY/ ATTN MASSEY/ 1436 CDT/ 5/27/88
BEGIN TEXT: **AFFIRMATIVE/ BIRD DOG IN NATASHA
GORKY APARTMENT**/ END TEXT/ CARRUTHERS

LANGLEY-CHICAGO / ATTN CARRUTHERS/ 1537 EDT/ 5/27/88
BEGIN TEXT: **HOW LONG?**/ END TEXT/ MASSEY

CHICAGO-LANGLEY/ ATTN MASSEY/ 1437 CDT/ 5/27/88
BEGIN TEXT: **LONG ENOUGH**/ END TEXT/ CARRUTHERS

LANGLEY-CHICAGO / ATTN CARRUTHERS/ 1538 EDT/ 5/27/88
BEGIN TEXT: **OPINION ONLY/ HOW LONG?**/ END TEXT/
MASSEY

CHICAGO-LANGLEY/ ATTN MASSEY/ 1439 CDT/ 5/27/88
BEGIN TEXT: **TWO HOURS SO FAR**/ END TEXT/
CARRUTHERS

LANGLEY-CHICAGO / ATTN CARRUTHERS/ 1539 EDT/ 5/27/88
BEGIN TEXT: **ALLIANCE?**/ END TEXT/ MASSEY

CHICAGO-LANGLEY/ ATTN MASSEY/ 1440 CDT/ 5/27/88
BEGIN TEXT: **REMOTELY POSSIBLE**/ END TEXT/
CARRUTHERS

LANGLEY-CHICAGO / ATTN CARRUTHERS/ 1540 EDT/ 5/27/88
BEGIN TEXT: **CODE GORKY PIGEON/ ASSIGN TAIL PIGEON**/ END TEXT/ MASSEY

CHICAGO-LANGLEY/ ATTN MASSEY/ 1441 CDT/ 5/27/88
BEGIN TEXT: **UNNECESSARY/ PIGEON TAGGING BIRD DOG/ ONE COVERS BOTH**/ END TEXT/ CARRUTHERS

LANGLEY-CHICAGO / ATTN CARRUTHERS/ 1542 EDT/ 5/27/88
BEGIN TEXT: **REPEAT/ ASSIGN TAIL PIGEON IMMEDIATELY**/ END TEXT/ MASSEY

CHICAGO-LANGLEY/ ATTN MASSEY/ 1443 CDT/ 5/27/88
BEGIN TEXT: **WILCO**/ END TEXT/ CARRUTHERS

LANGLEY-CHICAGO / ATTN CARRUTHERS/ 1543 EDT/ 5/27/88
BEGIN TEXT: **MERCURIO & BROWN STILL IN ACT?**/ END TEXT/ MASSEY

CHICAGO-LANGLEY/ ATTN MASSEY/ 1444 CDT/ 5/27/88
BEGIN TEXT: **AFFIRMATIVE/ BOTH PARKED PIGEON APARTMENT BUILDING**/ END TEXT/ CARRUTHERS

LANGLEY-CHICAGO / ATTN CARRUTHERS/ 1545 EDT/ 5/27/88
BEGIN TEXT: **GLUE TO BIRD DOG/ MOVE CERTAIN**/ END TEXT/ MASSEY

CHICAGO-LANGLEY/ ATTN MASSEY/ 1446 CDT/ 5/27/88
BEGIN TEXT: **WILCO**/ END TEXT/ CARRUTHERS

LINE CLEARED LANGLEY 1546 EDT 5/27/88

41

They'd sat at her kitchen table, conversing over coffee and cigarettes, Lockington realizing that for better or for worse, he'd been sucked back into the middle of something he'd just gotten out of. She'd whetted his appetite for the campaign, not with a pep talk that the battle-scarred Chicago police veteran would have scorned, but by permitting him to show the way, listening to his story of the empty matchbook and the thousand dollars, bowing to his experience and knowledge. She'd given him his head, a subordinate maneuver obvious to Lockington, one that he'd seen no reason to question. In essence, their goals were the same—if Natasha reached hers, he reached his. Lockington had sketched the opening phase of a plan, going no further, because there was no further to go. She'd listened attentively, nodding occasionally, making no comment until he'd said, "I don't know what we're looking for, but it's in the Youngstown, Ohio area."

Her gaze had been quizzical. "And from there, where?"

Lockington had shrugged. "Damned if I know, but we

have to get off of this treadmill, don't we?"

She'd spread her hands. "All right, then *go*—you'll be needing me in Ohio?"

"Yes, but not immediately."

"How soon?"

"Very, probably."

"And often?"

"Uhh-h-h—are we on the same railroad?"

She said, "Choo-choo-choo!"

At four o'clock he called Edna Garson's apartment. No answer. He called the Shamrock Pub and Edna was there—she'd just come in. Lockington talked to her for a couple of minutes and she said, "Well, okay, I'll do it, but I'm gonna miss you!" She growled deep in her throat. "There'd better not be a woman involved!"

Lockington chuckled an insincere chuckle. He said, "Strictly business."

"How long will you be gone?"

"Just a few days."

"Hurry back—we'll make up for lost time."

Lockington broke the connection and called Moose Katzenbach at the Classic Investigations office. He said, "There's a thousand bucks under the baseball encyclopedia in the bottom left-hand desk drawer. Put a couple hundred in your pocket and get the rest busted into twenties for me."

Moose said, "Holy Christ, Lacey, we must be in the *black!*"

"You'll find my spare keys in the top drawer. Lock up the office, get over to the Randolph Street lot, and pick up my car. Fill the tank and drive to my apartment—Edna Garson will be there, packing my suitcase."

"You on the lam, Lacey?"

"Just a little bit."

"For what—singing tenor?"

"Nothing quite that serious—there's a matter that requires looking into." Lockington gave him further instructions and a tight schedule. He said, "Got that, Moose?"

"Got it. You'll be in touch?"

"You still drinking at the Roundhouse Café?"

"Every night but Sundays."

"Why not Sundays?"

"It's closed on Sundays."

"Okay, if I need you I'll call the Roundhouse—eight o'clock or so."

"Which way you headed?"

"East."

"Devereaux?"

"Right."

"I knew it, goddammit!"

Lockington hung up, glancing at his watch, then at Natasha. "We'll leave here in an hour."

She nodded. She'd been perched on the arm of the sofa, watching, listening. She said, "You're highly efficient. When will you contact me?"

"Tomorrow afternoon. Where can I reach you?"

"Why not here?"

"Not a chance—your phone will be tapped by then."

"And yours?"

"You can bet on it—our little get-together will rattle some cages."

"All right—I know a nice old lady on the fifth floor. I'll give you her number. I'll spend the afternoon in her apartment."

"Can you get the name of the owner of the house in unincorporated Leyden Township—the place where Rufe Devereaux was staying before he went to Miami?"

"Three thousand North Onines—I'll have it in the morning."

"By the way, what if your lady friend isn't home?"

"She won't be—she's in San Bernardino, visiting her daughter."

"Then how will you get in?"

Natasha Gorky smiled at Lockington.

Put to a top-echelon KGB operative, it'd been a stupid question.

42

At 5:34 Natasha Gorky's black Mercedes-Benz sedan purred through the late afternoon heat, pulling to a halt on the south side of Belmont Avenue, directly in front of Mike's Tavern. Natasha squeezed Lockington's arm. "Take care!"

Lockington nodded, getting out of the car, pausing briefly at Mike's doorway to look westward. Four automobiles had stopped less than a quarter-block behind the Mercedes—a pair of black Ford Escorts, a white Cadillac, a green Pontiac Trans Am. The big parade, Lockington thought—strike up the band.

He entered Mike's Tavern, glancing around, spotting Mike at the far end of the bar, pouring a glass of wine for an elderly man wearing a straw hat. At 5:35 Lockington took a stool near the door, availing himself of an unobstructed view of Belmont Avenue traffic. Mike Kazman sauntered over in Lockington's direction, yawning. He said, "The cops told me that we was having one helluva fine time the other night."

Lockington said, "It must be true—I heard the same thing."

Kazman lowered his voice. "The TV weather guy said it was gonna hit ninety-five today, so first thing this morning I went down in the basement and turned on Nellie Carson's heat. Let the old crocodile call the fucking police about *that!*"

Lockington nodded approvingly. He said, "Is your alley door unlocked?"

"Sure—hell, some of my best customers come from the alley, you know that. Why?"

"On account of I'm operating on a theory which says nobody will be expecting lightning to strike twice in the same place."

At 5:39 a rattling old blue Pontiac Catalina approached, passing the window of Mike's Tavern, headed east. Right on time. The Pontiac swung south on Kimball Avenue and Natasha Gorky's Mercedes whipped away from the curb to follow it. One of the black Ford Escorts shot into view, closing fast to trail the Mercedes by no more than twenty feet. Lockington waved so-long to Mike Kazman, hustling through the rear door. Moose Katzenbach was waiting, the Pontiac parked in the beer-car-cluttered single-lane alley, its motor running. Moose bailed out, leaving the door open. He said, "She's full of ninety-two octane and your suitcase is on the backseat." He stuffed a roll of currency into Lockington's shirt pocket. He said, "Forty twenties."

Lockington said, "Thanks."

Natasha Gorky's Mercedes had stopped in the alley close behind the Pontiac, the black Ford Escort had screeched to a tire-smoking halt behind the Mercedes, blocked. Lockington grinned at Natasha. Natasha blew Lockington a kiss. Lockington got into the Pontiac. A big man in a dark blue suit was clambering out of the Ford Escort, waving his arms frantically, shouting something at the top of his lungs. Lockington didn't catch all of it, just the dirty-rotten-motherfucking-cunt-lapping-no-good-asshole-cocksucking-sonofabitch-bastard part. Moose said, "Luck, Lacey!"

Lockington nodded and pulled away, throwing gravel.

It'd been relatively easy.

43

CHICAGO-LANGLEY/ ATTN MASSEY/ 1755 CDT/ 5/27/88
BEGIN TEXT: **HARGAN REPORTS BIRD DOG LOOSE**/ END
TEXT/ CARRUTHERS

LANGLEY-CHICAGO / ATTN CARRUTHERS/ 1856 EDT/ 5/27/88
BEGIN TEXT: **HOW?**/ END TEXT/ MASSEY

CHICAGO-LANGLEY/ ATTN MASSEY/ 1756 CDT/ 5/27/88
BEGIN TEXT: **USED TURKEY WRINKLE/ IN FRONT
DOOR TAVERN OUT BACK DOOR TAVERN INTO CAR/
GONE**/ END TEXT/ CARRUTHERS

LANGLEY-CHICAGO / ATTN CARRUTHERS/ 1857 EDT/ 5/27/88
BEGIN TEXT: **WHOSE CAR?**/ END TEXT/ MASSEY

CHICAGO-LANGLEY/ ATTN MASSEY/ 1757 CDT/ 5/27/88
BEGIN TEXT: **HIS/ 78 BLUE PONTIAC CATALINA ILLINOIS
PLATES ZN940**/ END TEXT/ CARRUTHERS

LANGLEY-CHICAGO / ATTN CARRUTHERS/ 1858 EDT/ 5/27/88
BEGIN TEXT: **YOUR STATION WARNED BIRD DOG MOVE**

ROSS H. SPENCER

IMMINENT/ NOBODY LISTENING?/ END TEXT/ MASSEY

CHICAGO-LANGLEY/ ATTN MASSEY/ 1759 CDT/ 5/27/88
BEGIN TEXT: **BIRD DOG ASSISTED**/ END TEXT/ CARRUTHERS

LANGLEY-CHICAGO / ATTN CARRUTHERS/ 1859 EDT/ 5/27/88
BEGIN TEXT: **BY WHOM?**/ END TEXT/ MASSEY

CHICAGO-LANGLEY/ ATTN MASSEY/ 1800 CDT/ 5/27/88
BEGIN TEXT: **PIGEON**/ END TEXT/ CARRUTHERS

LANGLEY-CHICAGO / ATTN CARRUTHERS/ 1901 EDT/ 5/27/88
BEGIN TEXT: **SON OF A BITCH**/ END TEXT/ MASSEY

CHICAGO-LANGLEY/ ATTN MASSEY/ 1801 CDT/ 5/27/88
BEGIN TEXT: **RECOMMEND IMMEDIATE ILLINOIS APB BIRD DOG**/ END TEXT/ CARRUTHERS

LANGLEY-CHICAGO / ATTN CARRUTHERS/ 1902 EDT/ 5/27/88
BEGIN TEXT: **NEGATIVE/ NO COPS**/ END TEXT/ MASSEY

CHICAGO-LANGLEY/ ATTN MASSEY/ 1803 CDT/ 5/27/88
BEGIN TEXT: **UNDERSTOOD/ INSTRUCT NEXT MOVE THIS STATION**/ END TEXT/ CARRUTHERS

LANGLEY-CHICAGO / ATTN CARRUTHERS/ 1904 EDT/ 5/27/88
BEGIN TEXT: **TAP PIGEON PHONE ASAP/ CONTACT LANGLEY 0900 EDT 5/28/88**/ END TEXT/ MASSEY

CHICAGO-LANGLEY/ ATTN MASSEY/ 1805 CDT/ 5/27/88
BEGIN TEXT: **WILCO**/ END TEXT/ CARRUTHERS

LINE CLEARED LANGLEY 1905 EDT 5/27/88

44

Leaving the alley, Lockington had cut south, away from Belmont Avenue, then west to Pulaski Road, south again some half-dozen miles to the Eisenhower Expressway, and west on the final leg of his run to Route 294. Chicago's rush hour had reached its saturation point and the Eisenhower Expressway hadn't been dubbed the world's longest parking lot for nothing. The sun was lowering in the west, blindingly bright, the traffic was bumper to bumper, moving at tortoise speed, and before Lockington reached Route 294, his decrepit Pontiac was running in the red.

He slid into 294's southbound torrent and with the return of circulating air the engine heat dropped back to normal. Within forty-five minutes he was plucking his ticket from the slot of the gadget at the Indiana Tollway gates and at that point he reckoned that he was slightly under four hundred miles from Youngstown, Ohio. He herded the Pontiac into the righthand lane, wound it to sixty, held it there, and leaned back to watch dusk begin to stain the western Indiana countryside purple.

A nondescript eastbound dump truck rumbled ahead of him from an entrance to his right, its tailgate sporting two bumper stickers. The sticker to the left was white on blue—YES, JESUS LOVES ME! The sticker to the right was red on white—GOD'S WILL BE DONE. Lockington pondered the right-hand sticker. As a wide-eyed, highly impressionable youngster, he'd been given to understand that God's will is *always* done, that the sun wouldn't come up if God didn't will it to come up, that the family car wouldn't start if God didn't will it to do so. Every hurricane, every earthquake, every flood was willed by God, as was the budding of every rose, the daybreak song of every bird, the twilight rustle of every leaf. Which brought Lockington to the core of one of his countless doubts. If God indeed willed *all*, then it followed that a man's ascent to the glories of Paradise, his descent to the horrors of Hell, had been ordained long prior to his first stirrings in his mother's womb. The blind acceptance of the theory that God's will is always done led invariably to God having willed the Hitlers and Stalins to slaughter millions of innocents, and if God had willed these crimes, why should he punish their perpetrators? If we are God-controlled, God-destined to be what we are, to do what we do, a truly just God wouldn't be sitting in judgment on *anybody*.

Such thoughts had blurred the Indiana miles and Lockington found himself paying his toll, crossing the line to the Ohio Turnpike entrance, getting Youngstown directions from a woman in a booth at the gates. Ohio Exit 15, she told him, then pick up Route 11 South. He was down to less than a quarter-tank of fuel, probably enough to get him into the vicinity of Toledo, he figured. He'd stop there, fill 'er up, grab a sandwich and a cup of black coffee, and he'd be rolling into Youngstown about three o'clock on Saturday morning, having lost an hour to Eastern Time.

Darkness had set in and in his rearview mirror Lockington could see headlights closing rapidly. He was holding at a steady sixty and he estimated the speed of the vehicle at upwards of eighty. The headlights pulled close behind the Pontiac, then dropped back, turning onto the shoulder to stop and fade from view. Probably an unmarked state police car, he thought—Ohio was noted for its unmarked state police cars. Then, five minutes later, here came fast headlights again, nothing behind them, nothing between them and Lockington's car. Fifty yards behind the Pontiac they swung into passing position, pulled alongside, then slowed, keeping pace. The car was a Cadillac, it was white, and Lockington felt a cool spray sting his cheeks—*glass*, and he knew its meaning. He jammed the accelerator to the floorboard, spinning the Catalina in the direction of the Cadillac, watching it give ground, swerving onto the north shoulder, gaining speed to draw clear of the threat, its JESUS SAVES bumper sticker bright in the glare of Lockington's headlights.

He'd righted the Pontiac, the crisis was behind him, the Cadillac's taillights were twin red pinpoints in the distance, and bullet holes, three of them, were clustered in the window glass inches to the rear of Lockington's head. Not bad marksmanship considering that it'd hailed from a moving vehicle—if it'd been any better, he'd never had known what hit him. He'd heard no shots—a silencer. Major league equipment for the killing of a minor league private detective.

Lockington backhanded sudden cold sweat from his forehead, drawing a raspy deep breath. He was alive, wondering why Billy Mac Davis had opened fire on him, concluding that it'd been God's will.

45

Leaving the first rest stop east of the Toledo exits, a sub-average hamburger under his belt, his tank full of gasoline, Lockington checked his rearview mirror for fast-closing headlights, seeing none. He drove toward Youngstown under a glittering canopy of stars. Stars had become a rarity in the Chicago area—there was a grayish moon on occasion, but honest-to-Christ stars, the kind that actually *twinkle*, were hard to come by. The situation was due to too many people, too many factories, millions of automobiles, thousands of trucks, hundreds of diesel locomotives, and more jet airplanes than a man could shake his fist at—during its busiest hours, O'Hare Field handled a flight every twenty seconds. The racket was awesome, you could have carved the pollution with a butcher knife, and Lockington was glad to get away from it, however temporarily.

He wondered what'd clued Billy Mac Davis to his route. Moose Katzenbach had been told what direction he'd be taking, but Moose didn't slip on matters of that nature. Natasha Gorky had known his destination, but if she'd wanted him eliminated, she'd have had him shot in Chicago where his death wouldn't have caused a ripple. Billy Mac Davis had been playing for keeps—there were half a dozen wind-whistling holes in his windows to prove it, three coming in, three going out. Davis had figured Lockington for Ohio following his departure from Mike's Tavern, and it hadn't been a random shot like a raffle ticket pulled from a hat. Davis's guess had been educated, it'd been based on knowledge. Somewhere in the Youngstown area there was someone or something that Lockington wasn't supposed to come into contact with. There are no Chicago-to-Youngstown shortcuts—Interstate 80 is the most direct route and Davis had been flying low on that course, overtaking everything ahead of him, knowing that he'd catch a tired blue Pontiac within three or four hours.

The Pontiac clattered past the Cleveland and Akron exits and Lockington was less than an hour's drive from Youngstown when he turned onto the ramp of the next rest stop, rattling by the truck park where dozens of over-the-road cowboys slept in their cabs, awaiting daybreak and the haul to the east coast. Lockington wasn't a chronic hunch-player, but he was a firm believer in taking precautions and this stop amounted to a precaution.

The passenger-car parking area was empty. It was 2:03 A.M., and at 2:03 A.M. most decent people were in bed—doing any number of indecent things, perhaps, but in bed nevertheless. He parked well clear of the building, leaving the Catalina where it'd be clearly visible from the glassed-in foyer. He climbed out, stretching, moving at an unhurried pace, ostensibly the bored traveler, which was hardly the case—Lockington was covering his ass, as they say in the infantry. Once inside, he took stock of the place. The lobby was deserted, so was the dining hall. He heard the clanking of pans in the kitchen. These places didn't come to life much before daybreak, when they became beehives of activity. He leaned against a wall, lighting a cigarette, staring into the morning darkness, waiting. It was a short wait. A white Cadillac was slipping into the parking lot, lights out, stopping alongside Lockington's car. Billy Mac Davis had ducked into a rest stop, letting Lockington pass, or he'd left the turnpike and looped back onto it—however it'd gone, he'd been tracking his quarry for a hundred miles and Lockington gave him an A for determination.

So, what to do? There was a crackpot out there with a gun. Lockington considered barging through the kitchen to leave the building through a service door and turn his opponent's flank, thus leveling the odds, boiling it down to a one-on-one shootout. Or he could call the Ohio state police and wait for their arrival—a thankless proposition at best. By the time Lockington could get the situation explained, Billy Mac Davis would be in the next county, establishing another ambush, and Lockington would be in the nearest mental facility, sharing a room with a guy who'd just returned to planet Earth after having been kidnapped by extraterrestrials. Or…or *nothing!*—a green Pontiac Trans Am had wheeled into the rest stop parking lot. The passenger's door opened, a man got out, walking to Billy Mac Davis's white Cadillac, revolver in hand, pumping half a dozen rounds into the Cadillac's interior. Talk about coldblooded efficiency—within twenty seconds of its arrival, the Trans Am was gone. Lockington had recognized the executioner—

Vince Calabrese.

He left the building at a long-legged stride. There were no signs of life in any direction save for a Peterbilt snorting from the west end of the truck park, trailing a long filthy plume of diesel smoke. Early start. Lockington got into his Pontiac, kicking it to life, pulling away to roll down the outbound ramp, blending with I-80's sparse dead-of-the-night traffic. Billy Mac Davis would be back there in his white Cadillac, deader than a fucking mackerel, looking a great deal like a volleyball net. Lockington shrugged. What the hell—Jesus saves.

46

CHICAGO-LANGLEY/ ATTN MASSEY/ 0800 CDT/ 5/28/88
BEGIN TEXT: **STILL NOTHING BIRD DOG**/END TEXT/
CARRUTHERS

LANGLEY-CHICAGO / ATTN CARRUTHERS/ 0901 EDT/ 5/28/88
BEGIN TEXT: **POSSIBILITY BIRD DOG EDNA GARSON
APT?**/ END TEXT/ MASEY

CHICAGO-LANGLEY/ ATTN MASSEY/ 0802 CDT/ 5/28/88
BEGIN TEXT: **CHECKED/ NEGATIVE**/ END TEXT/
CARRUTHERS

LANGLEY-CHICAGO / ATTN CARRUTHERS/ 0902 EDT/ 5/28/88
BEGIN TEXT: **PIGEON APT?**/ END TEXT/ MASSEY

CHICAGO-LANGLEY/ ATTN MASSEY/ 0803 CDT/ 5/28/88
BEGIN TEXT: **CHECKED/ NEGATIVE/ HOLD/ HOLD/
HOLD**/ END TEXT/ CARRUTHERS

CHICAGO-LANGLEY/ ATTN MASSEY/ 0807 CDT/ 5/28/88
BEGIN TEXT: **PRIORITY CLEVELAND DISPATCH/ OHIO**

STATE POLICE REPORT BILLY MAC DAVIS DEAD/ END TEXT/ CARRUTHERS

LANGLEY-CHICAGO / ATTN CARRUTHERS/ 0909 EDT/ 5/28/88
BEGIN TEXT: **HOW?**/ END TEXT/ MASSEY

CHICAGO-LANGLEY/ ATTN MASSEY/ 0809 CDT/ 5/28/88
BEGIN TEXT: **QUITE**/ END TEXT/ CARRUTHERS

LANGLEY-CHICAGO / ATTN CARRUTHERS/ 0909 EDT/ 5/28/88
BEGIN TEXT: **WILL REPHRASE/ HOW BILLY MAC DAVIS DIE?**/ END TEXT/ MASSEY

CHICAGO-LANGLEY/ ATTN MASSEY/ 0810 CDT/ 5/28/88
BEGIN TEXT: **INSTANTLY**/ END TEXT/ CARRUTHERS

LANGLEY-CHICAGO / ATTN CARRUTHERS/ 0910 EDT/ 5/28/88
BEGIN TEXT: **WILL REPHRASE/ WHY DAVIS DIE?/ BUBONIC PLAGUE?/ STRUCK BY METEORITE?/ INGROWN TOENAIL?**/ END TEXT/ MASSEY

CHICAGO-LANGLEY/ ATTN MASSEY/ 0811 CDT/ 5/28/88
BEGIN TEXT: **NONE OF ABOVE/ SHOT 6 TIMES 38 FIREARM I–80 REST STOP EAST OF AKRON OHIO/** END TEXT/ CARRUTHERS

LANGLEY-CHICAGO / ATTN CARRUTHERS/ 0912 EDT/ 5/28/88
BEGIN TEXT: **WHEN?**/ END TEXT/ MASSEY

CHICAGO-LANGLEY/ ATTN MASSEY/ 0812 CDT/ 5/28/88
BEGIN TEXT: **APPROX 0215 EDT**/ END TEXT/ CARRUTHERS

LANGLEY-CHICAGO / ATTN CARRUTHERS/ 0913 EDT/ 5/28/88
BEGIN TEXT: **REASON DAVIS DEATH?**/ END TEXT/ MASSEY

CHICAGO-LANGLEY/ ATTN MASSEY/ 0813 CDT 5/287/88

BEGIN TEXT: **BULLET WOUNDS HEAD NECK CHEST**/ END TEXT/ CARRUTHERS

LANGLEY-CHICAGO / ATTN CARRUTHERS/ 0914 EDT/ 5/28/88 BEGIN TEXT: **WILL REPHRASE/ WAS REASON POLITICAL?**/ END TEXT/ MASSEY

CHICAGO-LANGLEY/ ATTN MASSEY/ 0815 CDT/ 5/28/88 BEGIN TEXT: **UNKNOWN THIS TIME**/ END TEXT/ CARRUTHERS

LANGLEY-CHICAGO / ATTN CARRUTHERS/ 0915 EDT/ 5/28/88 BEGIN TEXT: **ADVISE PROMPTLY FURTHER DEVELOPMENTS**/ END TEXT/ MASSEY

CHICAGO-LANGLEY/ ATTN MASSEY/ 0816 CDT/ 5/28/88 BEGIN TEXT: **WILCO**/ END TEXT/ CARRUTHERS

LINE CLEARED LANGLEY 0916 EDT 5/28/88

47

He verified his directions when he paid his Ohio Turnpike fare at Exit 15. He picked up Route 11 South, departing it at the Mahoning Avenue turnoff, finding that he was in Austintown, three miles west of the Youngstown city limits. It was five minutes after three o'clock in the morning, there wasn't a lighted beer sign in sight, so he checked into a dilapidated motel operated by a sly-eyed, silent Indian who'd probably bought the place with profits from practicing thuggee, Lockington figured. The man appeared clad in a nightgown, he took Lockington's money, handed him a key, and vanished like a wraith. Lockington entered his damp, dingy room, opened his suitcase, found a bottle of Martell's cognac wrapped in socks and shorts, toasted Edna Garson's thoughtfulness with a hefty belt of the stuff, and rolled into bed.

He'd slept dreamlessly until 11:30, awakening to cloudless blue skies and silence. Excluding his military time, Lockington had spent every day of his life in the Chicago area. Silence was strange to him, and he sat on the edge of his bed, listening, fearful that he'd gone deaf during the night. He showered, shaved, and left his room to behold the green splendor of the Mahoning Valley. The New Delhi Motel was a twelve-room, L-shaped affair, eight units running parallel to Mahoning Avenue, four branching to the north, all lopsided and badly in need of paint, but the place was half-ringed by dense forest to its south—a compensating factor, in Lockington's opinion. In Chicago trees were scarce, most likely to be found in Grant Park where a man could get mugged at high noon during a police convention, probably by a policeman.

He paid another day's room rent, tangled with an order of sausage, eggs and hash browns at a next-door restaurant, and drove east into Youngstown, Ohio. It was time to get the lay of the land, a relatively simple task, he knew—it'd amount to no more than locating the right bartender. He wouldn't be found in a first-class drinking establishment— the right bartender would be working the bar of a crummy blue-collar joint, the kind with a sagging beer sign, a cracked plate-glass window, a filthy men's room with an empty towel dispenser. There'd be a busted electronic dart game in a corner, an out-of-order jukebox, a 1977 naked-cutie calendar on a wall, an ancient cash register that sounded like a head-on steam locomotive collision, a drunk sleeping in a booth, and a red-nosed, half-crocked woman at the bar.

Lockington tooled the Pontiac slowly along Mahoning Avenue, passing taverns, sorting them out. When he came to the Flamingo Lounge, he hit the brakes. *Both* plate-glass windows were cracked and that was good enough for Lockington. He drove to the rear of the ramshackle building, parking in a graveled lot strewn with bricks and shards of glass. He went in through the rear door to find himself in a bistro that met all of his requirements save one—there was no drunk sleeping in a booth. There were, however, two red-nosed women at the bar, sloshing down spigot beer. Lockington pulled up short, seating himself as far as possible from the pair, but one of them, a toothless redhead, said, "Hi, dearie!"

Lockington nodded to her, an ill-advised move, because her sidekick, a menacing-looking creature whose upper lip sported more hair than Lockington's chest, took matters a step further. She said, "Say, honey—you buying or being?"

Lockington said, "I'll need time to consider the question."

The redhead turned to the hairy one. "He ain't gonna buy, he's gonna *be!*"

The bartender walked in Lockington's direction, winking, grinning. Under his breath he said, "The Sugar sisters—just ignore 'em."

Lockington mumbled, "Is that possible?"

The bartender shrugged. "Probably not." He put out his hand and they shook. He said, "I'm John Sebulsky." Lockington looked him over. This was the right bartender, no doubt about it—mid-thirties, alert dark eyes, obviously intelligent. He'd know exactly where the possum pooped in the petunia patch. Lockington said, "Howdy, John, I'm Lacey Lockington—can you scare me up a double Martell's?"

Sebulsky grabbed a bottle and poured. He said, "That'll be two dollars, Lacey."

Lockington paid him. He said, "Bargain day—it'd be four in Chicago."

Sebulsky said, "Hey, for four you can take an eight-year lease on the joint."

Lockington said, "Uhh-h-h—do the Sugar sisters go with it?"

Sebulsky said, "Sure thing—we aim to *please!*"

The redheaded Sugar sister had lost her balance on her barstool, listing precariously to starboard, then to port, then teetering backwards, clutching desperately at the hairy one for support. They went over together in a wildly flailing flurry of arms and legs. The crash was awesome. John Sebulsky was yawning. He said, "You from Chicago, Lacey?"

Lockington nodded. "Yeah. Would you believe I used to brag about that?"

Sebulsky said, "No good anymore?"

Lockington said, "Shot in the ass, but it used to be the greatest."

Sebulsky said, "The whole damned country's going to hell."

The Sugar sisters were thrashing about, trying to get up. The redhead was saying, "For Christ's sake get *offa* me, I gotta *pee!*"

The hairy one said, "How can I get offa you? *You're* on *top!*"

Sebulsky sighed a weary sigh. He said, "Y'know, I blew a golden opportunity to take this job. I coulda been number-one towel boy in a Pittsburgh whorehouse." He spread his hands resignedly. "Too late now."

Lockington said, "Sure is—one of the Sugar sisters just pissed on the floor."

Sebulsky didn't turn his head. He stared fixedly at nothing. He said, "Which one?"

Lockington said, "Hard to tell. Does it make

a difference?"

Sebulsky was squinting, thinking about it. After quite a long time he didn't say anything at all.

There was a touch of the philosopher about John Sebulsky, Lockington thought.

48

The Sugar sisters had stormed from the premises in a righteous huff, vowing to return with a battery of attorneys, and but for John Sebulsky and Lacey Lockington, the Flamingo Lounge was devoid of human presence. They talked. Sebulsky had been Youngstown-born-and-raised, he knew the territory and its history. What he didn't know, he could damn sure find out, he said. It hadn't been a smart-aleck statement— he had a brother in the real estate business, a cousin who was with the Mahoning County police, an uncle who was a surgeon, serving on the staff of St. Elizabeth's Hospital, and, as a bartender, Sebulsky had become acquainted with hoodlums, bookies, drug pushers, prostitutes and pimps— what did Lockington want to know about the Youngstown area? Well, nothing that came readily to mind, Lockington told him, but he might have a couple of questions later—he figured to be in town for a few days. Sebulsky nodded, giving him a long penetrating look. Lockington knew that look— it said that John Sebulsky was trying to figure him. What was a man from Chicago doing in Youngstown, Ohio? The reaction was natural—a stranger rides into Gopher Gulch, mentions Dodge City, and the natives get inquisitive.

Youngstown was hurting, Sebulsky said. It was called the Rust Belt now—wags had gone so far as to put up white crosses here and there—Rust in Peace. He told Lockington of the steel industry collapse some ten years earlier when fifteen thousand good-paying Youngstown jobs had gone down the drain virtually overnight. He tried to put that into perspective for Lockington—what if the Chicago area lost a *million* jobs in the same span of time? There'd be hell to pay, wouldn't there? Lockington said, well, there'd be concern, of course, but the effects probably wouldn't be quite so pronounced because there was always hell to pay in Chicago over one damned thing or another, and if there *wasn't* hell to pay over *something*, people became alarmed.

The conversation drifted to the young baseball season, leading to agreement that the Cleveland Indians were going nowhere, and so were the Chicago Cubs. Then Lockington inquired about the Club Crossroads. He'd heard mention of it, he said—what sort of place was it?

Sebulsky said, "I know the bookkeeper at the Crossroads. It's a country music dive—big frame building, south side of Mahoning Avenue, something like four miles west in Austintown. Used to be a cattle barn—some out-of-town guy bought it a little over a year ago. He put it back on the tracks. It's a good place to get your teeth kicked out."

Lockington said, "Rough?"

Sebulsky nodded. "The thing is, they get the country music types out there—none of 'em ever been south of Columbus, but they wear the Stetson hats and the neckerchiefs and the fancy western shirts and the tight jeans and the cowboy boots, and when they get a few beers in 'em, they think they're in fucking El Paso and they kick the shit out of each other."

"Why?"

"Hell, they don't need a reason at the Crossroads—it's just the thing to do."

"Who owns the joint?"

"Guy named Jack Taylor—nobody knows much about him, Ace says."

"Ace?"

"Ace Loftus—the bookkeeper at the Crossroads. He comes in now and then. You figure on going out there?"

Lockington shrugged. "Depends on the entertainment. How is it?"

"Pretty good, if you're into country. They don't do that new crossover crap that's floating around—the music is kosher." Sebulsky rolled his dark eyes. "They got a canary that'll blow your drawers off!"

"Worth a listen?"

"Yeah—Pecos Peggy. She got her own band, the Barnburners—piano, dobro, lead guitar, rhythm guitar, drums."

"Where they from?"

"I dunno—deep South somewhere, I'd say, after hearing 'em talk. Peggy's straight—sings country like it should be sung. She's been at the Crossroads ever since Jack Taylor took over—she draws a crowd."

"Good-looker?"

"Hey, you *know* it! Every stud who comes in wants to get her on her back, but she dazzles 'em with footwork—far as

I know, she ain't been scored on."

"Ought to be a good night tonight."

"Sure—Saturday night of a holiday weekend, I figure twenty, maybe thirty fights!"

Lockington frowned. "Jesus, I wonder if it's worth the risk."

"Take a table—most of the trouble's at the bar."

"Tell me more about Pecos Peggy."

Sebulsky said, "She's a full eclipse—a real class item! She got the bluest eyes in this whole fucking solar system!"

Lockington nodded, motioning for a refill. Here he was in a major league stud poker game, the blue chips were down, and he'd just caught a deuce in the hole. Not bad. Deuces were wild, dealer's choice, and Lockington was dealing, he kept telling himself.

49

He drove a mile or so south on Raccoon Road before locating a cozy little restaurant—Giamotti's, typically Italian. Red lamps, red tablecloths, red carpeting, travel posters on the walls—Venice, Rome, Naples, Genoa. He ordered a bottle of beer and a small antipasto. The beer was the way Lockington liked it, bitter cold, and the antipasto was excellent. He lit a cigarette, found a pay telephone, and rang the number of Natasha Gorky's fifth-floor lady friend. Natasha answered on the first ring. "Lacey?"

"Yep."

"You're in Youngstown?"

"Yep."

"Are you all right?"

"By the skin of my teeth."

"What do you mean?" There was concern in her voice.

"I'll explain later. How about you?"

"So far, so good. I haven't seen the Mafia man in the green Trans Am since yesterday afternoon, but the CIA fellow is tagging along. I can lose him when I want to."

"The green Trans Am is in Ohio—the Mafia eliminated Billy Mac Davis early this morning."

"He's *dead?*"

"Just a bit."

"But *why?*"

"I don't know. We'll talk about it when you get here."

"When should I come?"

"Tomorrow, if possible."

"All right, I'll get clearance at the embassy in the morning. Where are you staying?"

"Room Twelve, New Delhi Motel, Mahoning Avenue, Austintown—Austintown's the first suburb west of Youngstown." He gave her directions. "What about the house on Onines Avenue?"

"It's owned by a James Slagle. Apparently he's a traveling man—he's never at home and the neighbors know nothing about him."

"How did you get this?"

"I sent a man out there this morning—an insurance salesman, ostensibly. Have you been to the place you mentioned—the Club Crossroads?"

"I'll make it later this evening. Who's the honcho at the Chicago CIA office?"

"Do you want to contact him?"

"Not yet—he's just a kicker."

"His name's Carruthers—Stanley Carruthers. He's a graduate of Cornell University, he played basketball there—he's six-three, he weighs one-eighty, he lives in Wilmette, he's thirty-six, brown-eyed, balding, he has a habit of tugging at his left ear, he wears tinted spectacles, he's Missouri Synod

Lutheran, he has two children, twelve and ten, Harry and Estelle, Estelle wears braces. Carruthers is a good family man, he doesn't smoke, drink, or gamble—he drives an 'eighty-eight white Toyota Camry, Illinois license plates TK two-nine-seven-eight."

"And you've been in bed with him."

"Just once."

Lockington said, "Oh, my *God*."

"Lacey, it's my *job*—can't you understand that?"

"Well, I gotta say *one* thing—you're certainly a *frank* bitch!"

"Why are you shouting—where are you?"

"In a restaurant—who's shouting?"

"*You're* shouting. Are you angry?"

"No, I'm in a state of fucking euphoria!"

Natasha Gorky's silvery laugh tumbled over the line. She said, "You're *slahduhk!*"

Lockington snarled, "If that means stupid, I *know* it!" He slammed the telephone onto its hook, turning to go back to his table. He stopped, reversed course, and called again, dropping several quarters in the process.

Natasha answered immediately. Lockington roared, "And what's more, you be mighty goddamned careful coming through Indiana—they got a whole bunch of road repair work going on there!"

He hung up. From a corner table an elderly white-haired lady was staring apprehensively at him. This baffled Lockington. At her age she must have seen *hundreds* of broken-down private detectives who'd just fallen ass-over-tea-kettles in love with beautiful young KGB agents.

50

Fearful that his welcome might have worn a bit thin, Lockington paid his tab at the little Italian restaurant and looked for a place with a telephone. He wanted to call Moose Katzenbach in Chicago. He found a tavern further south on Raccoon Road—Moo-Moo's Place. There wasn't a customer in sight but the woman behind the bar smiled hospitably. She had a huge pink ribbon in her mouse-colored hair and she weighed somewhere in excess of three hundred pounds. She said, "Hi, I'm Moo-Moo."

Lockington said, "Hi, I'm thirsty—let me have a bottle of beer, please."

Moo-Moo popped a glass onto the bar, jerked a bottle of Rolling Rock out of the cooler, opened it, and spilled half of it into Lockington's lap. She said, "Oooops!"

Lockington shrugged. He said, "Think nothing of it. Hardly a day goes by but what I get a bottle of beer poured in my lap."

Moo-Moo said, "Sorry about that."

Lockington said, "You see, on those days when I *don't* get a bottle of beer poured in my lap I become disconsolate and ill at ease."

Moo-Moo said, "Hey, looky, I told you I was sorry, didn't I?"

Lockington said, "Why, just yesterday I didn't get a bottle of beer poured in my lap, and I developed a severe case of indigestion and constipation set in."

Moo-Moo's hands went to her hips. She said, "Now listen, buster, I already apologized! Whaddaya want, a fucking seven-piece fucking string ensemble playing fucking 'Moonlight and Roses?'"

Lockington shook his head. "I never liked that one—could they maybe do 'When My Fucking Blue Moon Turns to Gold Again?'"

Moo-Moo said, "Take your pants off."

Lockington stared at her. He said, "Well, I'm a sonofabitch!"

Moo-Moo said, "Get outta those pants and I'll dry 'em over the stove in the back room."

Lockington said, "All I want is a telephone—I gotta call Chicago."

"There's a phone in the basement. Throw your pants up to the landing and I'll get 'em dried out while you're calling Chicago. The call's on the house. That's fair, ain't it?"

Lockington shrugged. She showed him the stairs, Lockington went down, took off his pants, threw them up to her, found the telephone and called the Roundhouse Café in Chicago. Sadie Berlitz answered. Lockington recognized Sadie's voice instantly. Sadie sounded just like Betty Boop. She said, "Lacey, I recognized your voice instantly! You sound just like Popeye!"

Lockington said, "Is Moose Katzenbach there?"

"Sure is."

"Can I speak to him?"

"You can if I can pry him loose from that blonde in his booth."

Lockington waited, listening to a polka on the Roundhouse Café's jukebox. Polkas had always been popular at the Roundhouse Café. Eventually Moose took the phone and Lockington said, "Sadie just told me that you're hooked up with a real hot item."

There was a guarded silence before Moose said, "Right about now the hot part ain't all that important. What's important is this is a woman I can *talk* to. Y'know, Lacey, there's some things that men just can't discuss with men. You get where I'm coming from?"

"Yeah, Moose, I get where you're coming from. What's happening in Chicago?"

"Hotter than Kelsey's nuts here—might rain tomorrow. Cubs lose to Houston seven–one, Nolan Ryan beat the Moyer kid. Something on your mind?" Moose seemed vague, preoccupied. A blonde in the booth can really mess up a man's thinking.

Lockington said, "There's a house out in unincorporated Leyden Township—Three Thousand North Onines Avenue. Know where Onines is?"

"No, where is it?"

"A few blocks east of Wolf Road, north of Grand Avenue, as I figure it."

"What about it?"

"Bust into it."

"Jesus, Christ, Lacey, you *serious?*"

"Damn right, I'm serious—it could be important."

"*When?*"

"Pronto—tonight."

"What if I get nailed?"

"You won't get nailed—they got county police protection in unincorporated Leyden. The county cops spend their time holed up in Mannheim Road greasy spoons, gargling coffee and goosing waitresses—takes 'em two hours to answer a call."

"What am I looking for?"

"Hell, I don't know—anything of interest. The owner doesn't spend much time there, apparently."

"*Apparently? Apparently* ain't so fucking encouraging!"

"Just do the best you can with it, Moose—play it by ear."

"Okay—where can I reach you?"

"Room Twelve, New Delhi Motel, Austintown, Ohio. I may be out late tonight—if you run into something, keep ringing until you get me."

Moose hung up. Lockington went to the foot of the stairs. He hollered, "My pants dry yet?"

Moo-Moo threw the pants down. They landed at Lockington's feet, a smoking hole in their crotch. Moo-Moo said, "You wanna call Winnipeg?"

51

In his old blue Pontiac Catalina and his new blue K-mart pants, Lacey Lockington closed in on the Club Crossroads. It was set back some seventy-five yards south of Mahoning Avenue, the several acres surrounding it covered by neatly yellow-lined blacktop. A half-dozen uniformed men patroled the expanse, waving flashlights, shouting instructions, guiding automobiles into parking slots. It was shortly before ten o'clock on the last Saturday evening in May, the Ohio night air was balmy. There was a fragrant light breeze out of the west, there were more stars than Lockington had seen in one sky since he'd been in Vietnam, there was a huge yellow crescent moon nuzzling the flank of a wispy stray cloud. A carnival atmosphere drenched the parking area, men laughed, women tittered, and Lockington slammed the Pontiac's rusty door, joining the holiday weekend throng in the long hike across the macadam to the big red building with the bright green neon CLUB CROSSROADS sprawled across its roof peak.

He passed a belligerent-looking security man at

the entrance and he paused momentarily, taking in his surroundings before seating himself at a small rough-hewn table, the splintered surface of which supported a black tin ashtray and a guttering candle in a red glass chimney. There were more than a hundred such tables, Lockington figured. They poked mushroomlike from the sawdust floor, encircling the gaunt wooden stage in the center of the place, and better than half of them were occupied at that comparatively early nightclubbing hour. The Club Crossroads bar took up the entire east wall of the building. It was crowded, its five blue-jacketed bartenders hustling to handle the demand. A dozen or so young ladies wearing floppy western hats, sequined shirts, imitation cowhide vests, brown corduroy shorts, and highheeled cowboy boots ranged the compound, smiling, chatting, jotting orders on pads. One of them pulled up at Lockington's elbow and he asked for a bottle of Rolling Rock beer. She nodded and moved on, pausing at other tables on her way to the service bar. Lockington leaned back on a wobbly wooden chair, lighting a cigarette, frowning an appreciative frown. In a financially depressed area the Club Crossroads amounted to a major league operation.

The beer arrived—one dollar fifty, a fair nightclub price. In Chicago it was averaging two and a half in the sleaziest of joints. Lockington handed his waitress three singles, accepting fifty cents in change. He said, "When does Pecos Peggy come on?"

The girl tilted the brim of her Stetson, glancing at an old-fashioned Sessions clock high on the wall. "Right away—about ten minutes. She works half hour on, half hour off."

He'd just started on his second bottle of Rolling Rock when the turnout began to murmur. Then the Club Crossroads erupted in a jungle roar and Lockington turned to the stage. Pecos Peggy was coming up the steps, waving, smiling, some five feet eight inches of dark-haired lissome female clad in a skin-tight short black satin dress, black-seamed fishnet stockings, and four-inch-heeled red pumps. There was a tight double strand of pearls at her throat and a slim bold bracelet on her right wrist. John Sebulsky had been dead right—she was beautiful, nearly as beautiful as Natasha Gorky, and her eyes were as blue as an October sky. She paused on the lip of the stage, a veteran show-woman, sizing up her audience before lifting a hand microphone from its stand and stepping to centerstage, laughing now, waiting for the commotion to die down. She was queen of the Club Crossroads, mistress of all she surveyed, the darling of that multitude, and she knew it. The overhead lights dimmed and there was something undeniably regal about Pecos Peggy when she turned to her lead guitar player, a slim, bearded, hatchet-faced fellow in gray denim jacket and jeans. She said, "Marty, let's kick it off with 'Down to My Last Broken Heart.'" The crowd roared affirmation of her choice and Marty twanged out an introduction, repeating it several times before the torrent of sound subsided.

Then Pecos Peggy was clutching the mike with both hands, holding it as she might have held the face of a midnight lover, singing *to* it, not *at* it. Her left foot was planted forward, her right leg was slightly cocked at the knee, she was leaning into her song, *feeling* it, caressing it, giving of herself. This was no gravel-throated hog-caller from southeastern Georgia. Her voice was gentle, crystal clear, her tremolo controlled; she had range, dropping to low notes effortlessly, floating to upper registers with unconcerned ease. Her stage mannerisms reminded Lockington of Bobbie Jo Pickens, but they were less pronounced. Bobbie Jo's bawdy gaudiness wasn't there, and he didn't miss it. She was a singer, not a belter, a portrait in oils, not a cartoon, and when she'd finished "Down to My Last Broken Heart," Lockington found himself on his feet, joining in the tumult. He was no critic, country music had never topped his list of preferences, but if Bobbie Jo Pickens had been good, Pecos Peggy was excellent.

She sang "I Wish That I Could Fall in Love Today" and the roof nearly came off the Club Crossroads. She took a short breather, stepping to one side, snapping her fingers, doing a nifty little dance step to an instrumental of "Roadside Rag." When it was over, she thanked her musicians, introducing them individually, then collectively as "the best darned country band in the business," leading the applause for them. Then she took a deep breath, lifted the mike close to her lips, and slid into "Does Fort Worth Ever Cross Your Mind?" That threw the switch. Lockington counted half a dozen simultaneous but unrelated fistfights at the bar, three more at the tables. Bouncers materialized, moving in with barracuda speed, tossing the brawlers about like cordwood, sifting them, ejecting the chaff from the building. Pecos Peggy sang on, covering the ruckus with "Break It to Me Gently," and "Old Flames Can't Hold a Candle to You." The big red barn on Mahoning Avenue was filling with people, swelling with sound, Pecos Peggy was an *event*—with one more like her, the wrong promoter could have started World War III. When she left the stage at ten-thirty, tripping light-footedly down the bouncer-lined sawdust aisle leading to her dressing room, the crowd went limp, like a fighter on his ring-stool, conserving energy for the next round.

Lockington's waitress returned and he ordered another

bottle of Rolling Rock before taking the flyer he'd come prepared to take. He tossed a five-dollar bill onto her tray. He said, "Tell Pecos Peggy that a friend of Rufe Devereaux is in the audience—tell her that he'd like to meet her."

The girl's face was blank, the name meant nothing to her, but she tucked the money into a pocket of her imitation cowhide vest. She said, "Rufe Dev-er-oo?"

Lockington nodded. "You got it—'Dev-er-oo.'"

The waitress frowned. "Okay, I'll tell her, but you're wasting your time—Peggy doesn't date customers."

"Honey, I'm not trying to date her—Peggy and I had a mutual acquaintance, there's nothing more to it than that."

"*Had*, did you say?"

"That's right, *had*—he's dead."

"Oh—well, I'm—I'm sorry. Does Peggy know?"

"Probably."

She turned toward the service bar, picking up an order at a table of four on her way. In a couple of minutes she was back with Lockington's Rolling Rock. She said, "I'm going on break now—I'll talk to Peggy."

Lockington nodded, sipping at his beer. A wild goose chase, possibly, but an empty matchbook had brought him 425 miles to the Club Crossroads, and a beautiful dark-haired, blue-eyed woman had accompanied Rufe Devereaux to Chicago, or so the story had gone. The matchbook was real, so was the thousand dollars that'd come with it, and Pecos Peggy was a beautiful dark-haired, blue-eyed woman.

In a few minutes the waitress was back, plunking a fresh bottle of Rolling Rock on Lockington's table. She said, "That's on Peggy."

Lockington said, "My thanks."

She took a small lavender-colored card from her vest pocket, handed it to him, and left without another word. Lockington cupped the card in his hand, peering at it in surreptitious fashion like a spy in a B-movie, he thought. The ink was blue, the handwriting dead-vertical, the handwriting of a woman who stood squarely on her own two feet. *Clancy's— Market St.—Boardman—1:45.* Lockington finished his beer.

In the parking lot he approached an attendant, a big bushy-haired man. He said, "Where the hell is Boardman?"

The attendant said, "Any particular place in Boardman?"

"Yeah—Clancy's on Market Street."

"You're new in the area, right?"

"Right."

The attendant scratched his head. "Well, let's see—I'm gonna try to make this simple, understand?"

"I understand."

"Okay, a stranger's best bet would be to drive east on Mahoning Avenue and pick up six-eighty just this side of the bridge. Check?"

"Check."

"All right, stay on six-eighty like maybe ten minutes to the Canfield exit. The Canfield exit will put you on two-twenty-four headed west—got that?"

"Got it."

"You'll go a couple miles and there'll be a big hairy-assed shopping center on your left—that'll be Southern Park Mall and the next traffic light will be at the Market Street intersection. Okay?"

"Okay."

"Turn left on Market—you'll be in Boardman, heading south, and Clancy's will be out there a little better than a mile, right-hand side—small joint, big red neon sign."

Lockington said, "Nice place?"

"Matter of opinion—they got women and a late license, but if you're looking for a high you don't have to drive clear to Clancy's."

"No?"

"There's a couple joints out on Meridian Road, couple more down on Steel Street."

Lockington said, "I'll pass."

The attendant shrugged, turning away to handle an incoming car.

Lockington said, "Thanks, chief."

"Any time."

Lockington got into his Pontiac and the attendant threw him a highball with his flashlight. Lockington waved, easing out of the parking lot, liking the brusque friendliness of Youngstown people, wondering about the out-of-the-blue reference to cocaine, then shrugging. Cocaine had become a way of life in Emlenton, Pennsylvania and Anderson, Indiana. New York was up to its ears in the stuff, so was Chicago, so was Los Angeles, and there was no reason for Youngstown, Ohio, to be an exception. You could purchase it in municipal buildings, in schools, on playgrounds, in churches, and messing with it was like raising a king cobra. If it didn't kill you today, it'd get you tomorrow—it wasn't a matter of *if*, it was a matter of *when*. Lockington was a pragmatist—if a man was determined to commit suicide, a .38 slug through the temple was quicker and less expensive.

He'd swung right on Mahoning Avenue and he found the 680 entrance right where the parking lot attendant had said it'd be—at the west end of the bridge.

52

He drove, following directions to the letter. The once bustling Youngstown downtown district loomed briefly to his left, a dreary, unlighted mile of skeletal buildings, sad sentinels awaiting a better day. It'd come, John Sebulsky had told him—fully one-third of the fifteen thousand jobs lost had been regained over the years following the crash, small industries were slipping unheralded into the green Mahoning Valley, tool-and-die shops, small plastics concerns, food distribution outfits, an automotive corporation, taking up the slack a little at a time, fifty jobs here, one hundred fifty there. Lockington was glad for this. Youngstown was a good city with good people, and it had *trees*. Lockington had a thing for trees.

He thought again of relocating—he'd thought of it often, so often that his mind turned to the subject unbidden, like an old horse that knows its way home. The Chicago he'd known and loved was gone and it'd never come back. There wasn't much in Youngstown, but there was hope, a light at the end of the tunnel. In Chicago, the fucking tunnel had collapsed.

Clancy's was a small white stucco building approximately four times the size of Lockington's room at the New Delhi Motel, shabby on the outside, dim and smoky on the inside, a silent jukebox on its south wall, a dusty cigarette machine on its east wall, a sleek-black-haired Valentino-type behind its circular bar. There were a dozen barstools, four occupied by women, hard-faced, middle-aging things. Professionals look pretty much the same in Youngstown, Chicago, or Saigon—they have dollar signs stamped all over them. And the Valentino-type working the bar probably had a tongue like a whitewash brush, Lockington thought—Valentino-types usually do. There were half a dozen booths clustered along the west wall of Clancy's and Lockington carried his double Martell's in that direction. The young couple in the left-hand corner booth might have abided by the dictates of propriety when they'd first come in, but that was no longer the case. Their conduct failed to disturb Lacey Lockington to any great degree, but the likelihood of getting splashed did, causing him to veer sharply into the booth in the righthand corner.

It was 9:55 according to Lockington's Japanese wristwatch which hadn't been set since Central Daylight Time had arrived in Chicago better than a month earlier. It was a twenty-dollar Yamahachi and it'd always been a free soul, ticking to the beat of a different drummer, so it could have been 10:55 Youngstown time, or 10:45, or 11:05. Rarely had time been of the essence in Lockington's life—if he was late he apologized, if he was early he waited, and he let it go at that, Greenwich be damned.

He had time to kill and he spent the vigil drinking Martell's cognac and considering the matter of the now late Billy Mac Davis. Davis had been a fanatic, his own doctrine had branded him as such, but, Jesus H. Christ in the morning, how fanatic can one man *get?* He'd blazed away at Lockington in the early evening on Interstate 80, and he'd been set to stage an encore at an Ohio Turnpike rest stop scant hours later. He'd had a following—more than fifteen thousand people had poured into Chicago Stadium to hear him rant and rave, and he'd had money—religious and political lunatics can raise millions with the twitch of an eyebrow. So why hadn't one of his disciples handled the dirty work? Among Davis's followers there must have been dozens of crackpots who'd have taken the assignment out of sheer dedication to the white supremacy cause. Or why hadn't the job been handed to the Copperhead, an expert with skills readily available to LAON, according to Natasha Gorky. Yes, Virginia, there *was* a LAON, and Billy Mac Davis had been connected with it—his views had paralleled those attributed to LAON too closely for coincidence. They'd been essentially of the same fabric, the red-baiting and the black-hating, beliefs short of reason and devoid of intelligence. LAON as a body harped on the Communist threat and the individual Billy Mac Davis had gone after the blacks—it'd been six of one, half a dozen of the other. Lockington was a staunch conservative, but conservatism without brakes proves every bit as dangerous as unbridled liberalism—give either its head and you wind up with guys in long black overcoats hammering on your door at two-thirty in the morning.

Lockington sat in the booth at Clancy's, shaking his

head. There was a troublesome point here—Billy Mac Davis had been tagging him around the city of Chicago for days, he'd had innumerable opportunities to take a whack at Lockington, and he'd never made a move. But when Lockington had set sail for Youngstown, Ohio, Davis had jerked out all the stops. The Mafia—it could have killed Davis at its leisure, but it hadn't. Yet, when Davis had lit out in pursuit of Lockington, the manure had hit the windmill. Lockington's eyes narrowed—Davis had tried to keep him out of Youngstown, and the Mafia had thwarted Davis, obviously wanting Lockington to get there. Why? What the hell was in Youngstown?

He sensed movement to his left and he shook himself free of his thoughts, glancing up to see Pecos Peggy coming his way. She stopped at his booth, peering down at him, her blue eyes dark with intensity. She said, "Lacey Lockington, what took you so goddamned *long?*"

53

Their eyes met briefly. When she averted hers, he said, "Maybe I ain't Lockington."

She slid into the opposite side of the booth, smiling. She said, "There are three men in the place—a pimply-faced kid, a greaseball gigolo bartender, and you. There's a Pontiac with Illinois plates in the parking lot."

"And my waitress pointed me out at the Club Crossroads."

"Uh-huh."

"Okay, I'm Lockington."

"How did your car come by the bullet holes?"

"Ventilation—my windows don't work."

"You don't want to talk about them?"

"Not really. Drink?"

"Just one—bourbon and water."

Lockington went to the bar, ordering her drink and another double Martell's for himself. The Valentino-type's eyes were glued to Pecos Peggy in the booth. He said, "Daughter?"

Lockington said, "Naw—great-grandmother—well-preserved."

"Remarkable! *National Chatter* would be interested."

Lockington shook his head. "*National Chatter* prints gross exaggerations."

Lockington returned to the booth, carrying the drinks. She *could* have been his daughter with a dozen years to spare—she wasn't much beyond twenty, her skin was alabastrine, her dark hair fell to her shoulders in loose waves, the depths of her eyes seemed bottomless, blue, bluer, bluest, her chipper chin was slightly cleft, her hands were steady, long-fingered, the thumbs upturned. Upturned thumbs indicate self-confidence. She'd swapped her Club Crossroads attire for a gauzy gray crepe dress with a high frothy collar, she reminded Lockington of a nineteenth-century cameo—there was a simple purity about her, and he was unable to associate her with the Pecos Peggy who'd just stood the Club Crossroads on its ear. She was raising her glass to him. "Here's to you, Lacey Lockington—I've heard nothing but good about you."

Lockington shrugged and they drank. He said, "You expected me earlier?"

She was lighting a cigarette. Through the smoke she said, "Yes, no later than Thursday. I mailed the envelope late Monday night."

"When Rufe realized he was being followed."

"No, after that—I mailed it from the International Arms. Rufe knew that we were being followed before we reached Cleveland. At Hopkins Airport he told me that they'd be waiting for us at O'Hare. From then on, it was cats and mice." She was remembering that night, her blue-eyed gaze was a faraway thing. She said, "Rufe was clever."

"You'd figured to get into Chicago clean, evidently."

"Rufe saw it as a possibility—we'd been there before without incident. When he realized that we'd failed, he planned to double back to Youngstown and lie low. He wanted you to come here—he said that you were a good man in the clutch. Rufe needed help."

"Why—what was he involved in?"

"Later on that, please—later on the whole story."

"Why not now?"

"Because this is neither the time or place." There was unswerving finality in the reply. Pecos Peggy was quietly in command, she knew it, so did Lockington. He said, "Where were you when he was killed?"

"At the mailchute—it was on the far side of the building. When I came back..." Her voice trailed off.

Lockington nodded. "When can we talk about it? I'm not here to intrude, I'm here to be helpful."

"I know—I didn't mean to be abrupt. You'll learn all there is to learn tomorrow night, when I'm through working."

Lockington said, "There's a discrepancy here— according to one source of information, Rufe was killed somewhere around nine-thirty in the morning. You say that it happened nine or ten hours earlier."

"Look, let's drop it for now. You'll see it through a different window tomorrow night. Can you take me home?"

"You aren't driving?"

"No, Marty Davis dropped me off."

"Marty—your lead guitarist?"

"Uh-huh—you're observant. It was on Marty's way—he lives out in Columbiana."

Lockington was studying her. After a silence, she smiled. "You're undressing me—I hope."

He let it go by. "You're one helluva singer."

She didn't say yes, she didn't say no, but she thanked him. "I have roots in the field—that helps a bit, I suppose."

Lockington said, "Pecos Peggy—Pecos Peggy *who?* I don't know your last name."

"Nor my first, for that matter. Let's try Smith—I'll be one of the Smith girls."

Lockington frowned. He said, "If all the Smiths got laid end to end, there just ain't no telling what might happen."

She grinned an engaging white-toothed grin. "If all the Smiths got laid, there'd be a lot more Smiths, don't you think?"

He offered her another drink. She said, "Not tonight, but we'll tie one on one of these evenings—I'll do backflips and you can make droll remarks."

Lockington said, "What part of the country do you hail from, Smitty?"

She was extinguishing her cigarette, her eyes focused on the ashtray. She said, "Mississippi—originally, that is. I just happened to wind up in Youngstown."

Originally, that is hadn't told him much. Adolf Hitler had been from Austria. Originally, that was. He'd just happened to wind up in Berlin.

54

When they were leaving Clancy's parking lot, pulling onto Market Street, Peggy said, "How did you come out here—Route Six-eighty?"

"Yeah—I got directions from a guy in the parking lot."

"We'll go back another way. Take Market straight through to Indianola Avenue, then turn left. Where are you staying?"

"Room Twelve, New Delhi Motel on Mahoning. How will I know Indianola Avenue?"

"I'll tell you—Good Lord, why don't you trade this car in? It's going to disintegrate before we *get* to Indianola!"

Lockington nodded, saying nothing, and when they'd turned left on Indianola, she said, "Take a right at the bottom of the hill—that'll be Glenwood Avenue. Be careful on Glenwood, it's a tough street—one little fender-bender and we could get lynched. I've never heard an engine howl like this!"

"That isn't the engine, it's the transmission."

They rumbled north on Glenwood Avenue, passing

seedy taverns with soul music cascading through open doors. Peggy said, "Left at the next traffic signal—Falls Avenue." Following the turn they swung into a tight left-hand curve to plunge down a long, twisting hill. She said, "You're in Mill Creek Park now. Biggest city-limits park in the United States—Youngstown's Chamber of Commerce stresses that."

On either side, tall pines were silhouetted against a starlit sky, towering over the Pontiac, dwarfing the worn-out vehicle. The area was probably in constant shade, Lockington thought. He said, "This'd make one helluva bobsled run."

They careened down the hill and she was gesturing for him to slow down. "Right at the bottom, cross the bridge, then right again."

Lockington said, "Why the circuitous route?"

"It saves time, really. Also, we'll learn if we're being followed." She spun on the seat, peering through the rear window. "My God, we're trailing smoke—I think we're on *fire!*"

"Naw, she burns a little oil. Why should we be followed?"

She shrugged noncommitally. They were skirting a narrow body of placid water. She said, "This is Lake Glacier—it's beautiful." She'd continued to look back, squinting into the darkness. "Still no sign of a tail."

"If we're being followed, they could be driving with their lights out."

"Uh-huh, well, they'll turn 'em on when they're enveloped by smoke."

"Who?"

"Maybe nobody, maybe the CIA, maybe the Mafia—in Chicago, Rufe said that if we got one, we'd get both."

"Did he say why?"

"No. Take the left-hand fork to the top of the hill. That'll be Belle Vista Avenue. Go right on Belle Vista to the traffic light, turn left, and you'll be on Mahoning Avenue, headed back to the New Delhi Motel."

"Where do you get out?"

"Should I?"

"Should you *what?*"

"Should I get out?"

"Shouldn't you?"

"I don't think so, but it's a matter of opinion."

"You're joking."

"*Try* me."

"It wouldn't work."

"You're Mr. Clean?"

"No, but I'm forty-eight—you'd eat me alive."

"Only in little bites." They were on Mahoning Avenue, heading west. "For your information, I prefer older men."

"Apparently you do—I'm a dinosaur, and Rufe was older than I am."

"Don't get off on the wrong foot—I never spent one moment in bed with Rufe! We were close friends, no more than that!"

"Uh-huh. Wanna buy a unicorn?"

"All right, have it your way. At any rate, the older man is gentler, more considerate."

"Depends on the older man, I'd say."

"I speak only from my own experience. Oh, well, it's off to the nearest convent—Novitiate Peggy Smith who doesn't even know 'Ave Maria.'" She sounded pensive. They were passing the Flamingo Lounge, lair of the Sugar sisters. Its lights were out. She said, "Turn right at the next corner."

Lockington said, "All these turns—I feel like a cross-eyed corkscrew."

"This is the last of them—North Dunlap Avenue. Take it to the end of the line—I live on the cul-de-sac."

"Alone?"

"Why—does it matter?"

"It might."

"Alone since Rufe, yes."

"He lived with you?"

"I did his laundry."

"For how long?"

"Not long enough."

It was a neat white ranch-style house with dark brown trim and silver gray hip roof. There was a trellised white fence along the south side of its front yard and there were pink roses. She motioned him into the driveway. He stopped behind a red Porsche. A fifty-thousand-dollar house and a sixty-thousand-dollar automobile. Odd. He said, "Your car?"

She nodded and got out. "One more try—nightcap?"

Lockington shook his head. "It's been a long day."

Pecos Peggy said, "Tomorrow night, then. Just a bit after twelve-thirty—I'll blow my last set. I'll pick you up at your room. Can you find your way back to the motel?"

"I'll get there."

"Wait just a moment." She slammed her door, coming around the front of the Pontiac into the critical glare of the headlights, taking her time. Lockington could see through her gray crepe dress like it was that much thin air and she knew it. Her lines were exquisite and she knew that too. She opened the door on the driver's side. She said, "Rufe talked about you incessantly, but he omitted one highly pertinent fact."

Lockington didn't say anything.

She leaned into the car to kiss him, hanging on like a pit bull until Lockington was seeing orange and purple pyrotechnics. Her tongue tasted of cloves and her perfume was fragrant mist at the open gates of Paradise. She drew back, catching her breath, stroking his cheek. She said, "He never mentioned that you're a gentleman."

55

It was nearly three o'clock on Sunday morning, the shabby motel room was warm and stuffy, its air-conditioner setting up a frightful din but accomplishing nothing else. Lockington sat on the edge of the lumpy bed, chain-smoking, nipping at the fifth of Martell's cognac so thoughtfully tucked into his suitcase by Edna Garson. He'd been out of Chicago for less than thirty-six hours, and the glowering gray city on the polluted lake seemed so long ago and far away. He'd been shot at and nearly ambushed, he'd witnessed a murder, he'd had a hole burned in his trousers, he'd established his contact at the Club Crossroads and he was probably hot on the trail of whatever he was supposed to be hot on the trail of, he'd received a straightforward proposition from a very young, very beautiful woman, and he'd chickened out. So far, not a dull moment.

There'd been more to Pecos Peggy's offer than had met the eye. If a man's riding the fence, undecided as to which way to throw his weight, getting hauled into bed by a creature of Pecos Peggy's class is likely to tip the balance. Lockington knew this from experience—he'd gone down that road a couple of times, once during the previous summer, again on the afternoon before yesterday. He wasn't damned fool enough to believe that his physical and intellectual appeal had driven Natasha Gorky to frenzied desire for his sexual favors—it just didn't work that way. Natasha Gorky was a professional seeking professional assistance, and she'd taken the shortest route to market, swinging him from uncertain withdrawal to enthusiastic participation with the finest implement yet devised for the purpose of altering a man's thinking. Natasha had brought an axe to be ground, and so had Pecos Peggy. The difference was that Natasha's purpose had been perfectly obvious, and Peggy's hadn't. She'd been trying to win him over, but to *what?*

She'd promised explanation of the affair and Lockington found himself dwelling on that between jolts of Martell's cognac. What if there was a *fifth* factor? Good God, he hoped not—there were too many cooks in the kitchen as matters stood. The CIA, the KGB, the Mafia, LAON, strange bedfellows indeed—*unimaginable*—but hardly further-fetched than an aging, down-at-the-heels private detective and a lithe and lovely country singer. There was more to be learned—otherwise, why all this bother? Peggy could have told him that the matchbook had been mailed when Rufe Devereaux was alive, but Rufe Devereaux was dead now, so run along back to Chicago and peddle your papers. She hadn't done that. She was attempting to hold him in Youngstown, Ohio and she was willing to use her body to do it.

Lockington wasn't a connoisseur of talent, but he

knew it when he saw it. Pecos Peggy was top-drawer and top-drawer performers don't bed down in a city of 150,000 people. The good ones go where big bucks can be turned, and if they stop in smaller towns it's for one-night stands in high-school football stadiums that've been sold out for months. A few of the better-known country thrushes had slept their ways onto the charts, and had Pecos Peggy Smith been a woman of staunch moral convictions, her absence from the upper brackets might have been understandable, but at the tender age of one score years she'd been around the block a few dozen times, so morals accounted for nothing. She lived in a modest house, she drove a very expensive car, and *that* didn't figure. People who drive Porsches park them in triple garages on country estates, not in the side-street driveways of middle-class neighborhoods.

Well, maybe time would tell and maybe it wouldn't, but it'd already told on Lacey J. Lockington—he was bushed. He capped the bottle of Martell's—it was almost half-gone, he noted with regret, recalling a couple of lines from an old country ballad:

> The trouble with new love is that old love must
> die, And the trouble with whiskey is the bottle
> runs dry—

There was something to be said for those barnyard philosophers, Lockington thought—they had the knack of expressing themselves.

He slept. For five minutes or less. The phone was ringing. Lockington pawed for it, dragged it into bed and said, "This is a recording. Fuck you."

Moose Katzenbach said, "I been trying to get you for

three hours!"

Lockington said, "Okay, here I am."

Moose said, "I got into that house—jimmied a window."

"And?"

"I found a couple things of interest. One was a postcard, mailed from Miami to a James Slagle at that address. It was postmarked June eighth of last year."

"What did it say?"

"It thanked Slagle for his hospitality. It was signed *Rufe*—that'd be Rufe Devereaux, right?"

"Yeah, I guess Slagle let Rufe use the house once in a while—Slagle spends a lot of time out of town, as I understand it."

"That gotta be straight information—I doubt if he's *ever* home! The refrigerator's empty, and there's dust half an inch thick in there!"

"Anything else?"

"There was a bottle of peppermint schnapps and a bottle of Smirnoff's vodka on a table by the bed—both almost empty."

Lockington wished he hadn't asked. He gritted, "Okay, Moose—that was it?"

"Not quite."

"Then let's wrap it up—I can use some sleep."

"Slagel got three kilos of cocaine stashed in his living room closet."

Lockington whistled. "Good stuff?"

"Top grade. I found a jug of laundry bleach in the basement—I poured some into a water glass, threw in a pinch of coke, and, man, you shoulda seen the *streams!* I'd say it's damned near *pure!*"

"Three kilos—you're talking a couple *million!*"

"Cut it, and you got *twice* that much, street prices!"

Lockington said, "I wonder if Rufe knew that Slagle's a wholesaler."

"Maybe he found out—maybe that's why he's dead."

"Yeah, could be—Jesus, Rufe sure picked up with some strange types."

"Uh-huh—drug dealers, ex-cops—"

"Good night, Moose—say hello to your new girlfriend."

"That won't take long, she's right here."

Lockington hung up, glancing at his watch. Damned near four A.M.—nearly three in Chicago. They wouldn't be at the Roadhouse Café, it closed at two. Lockington grinned—they were in the hay! Way to go, Moose, he thought—she couldn't have happened to a nicer guy!

56

Lockington's telephone blew its top at eight-fifteen in the morning. Ohio sunlight was rollicking into the little gray room, staining its walls bright yellow. He corralled the offending instrument, grunting something unintelligible into its mouthpiece. Natasha Gorky said, "A happy Sunday morning to *you!*"

Lockington said, "There ain't never *been* a happy Sunday morning."

Natasha said, "I should get out of Chicago sometime late this afternoon—in the meantime, you must be very, *very* careful."

"Where are you calling from?"

"A restaurant on North Michigan Avenue."

"Are you still drawing a crowd?"

"The CIA's with me, yes—parked right out front. Did you hear what I said? *Be careful.*"

"I'm always careful."

"Then be *doubly* so. You're in trouble with LAON—there's a price on your head. LAON believes that you killed Billy Mac Davis."

Lockington thought that one over. He said, "Yeah, judging from appearances, it *could* have been me. LAON knows where I am?"

"It knows that you're in Youngstown—it may not know *where* in Youngstown."

"How did you get this?"

"We have people in Memphis—LAON's headquarters is there."

"The KGB has penetrated LAON?"

"Just its fringes, but deeply enough. It'll be the Copperhead, you can depend on that—you're worth fifty thousand dollars."

Lockington made a swishing sound between his lips. "Two hundred fifty a pound."

"This isn't funny!"

"So who's laughing?"

"I should make it to Youngstown by midnight, Eastern Time—after that you'll have an extra pair of eyes. What have you learned?"

"I made the contact indicated by the matchbook—the girl who was with Rufe in Chicago. She told me that I'll be getting the whole picture tonight."

"From whom?"

"She didn't say—I assume that it'll be from her. She lived with Rufe. She's to pick me up at the New Delhi, twelve-thirty or so."

"Listen, damn you—stay out of bed until I get there!"

"Okay."

"You're *slahduhk!*" She hung up.

That'd been her second *slahduhk*. Lockington didn't understand Russian. It was probably just as well. Great oaks from little *slahduhks* grow.

57

Sunday's early afternoon sky was sapphire, cloudless but for a few tiny white puffs scudding high along a soft breeze out of the west. John Sebulsky sat on a teetery wooden stool behind the battered bar of the Flamingo Lounge, his jaded vacant stare returning to focus with Lockington's arrival. Sebulsky said, "Hello, Lacey—you just missed it."

Lockington said, "I'm glad. What did I just miss?"

"The Sugar sisters kicked the living shit out of Burt Soltis."

"Why?"

"He wouldn't buy them a drink."

"Who's Burt Soltis?"

"Burt used to be middle linebacker for the Steelers."

"Soltis—he was all-league few years ago?"

"Yep."

"Where are the Sugar sisters now?"

"Down at Bailey's Bar, I think. I heard sirens in that area half an hour ago."

"Where's Soltis now?"

"Southside Hospital—that redhead got a lethal left hook."

Lockington squeezed onto a barstool and Sebulsky said, "Martell's?"

Lockington nodded. He appreciated bartenders who remembered. He said, "Have one with me."

Sebulsky nodded, pouring the Martell's and popping the top on a bottle of Michelob Dry. He said, "Thanks."

Lockington said, "I went out to the Club Crossroads last night. Interesting joint."

"See Pecos Peggy?"

"Sure did."

"Whaddaya think?"

Lockington whistled.

Sebulsky said, "Damned wonder she ain't been discovered."

Lockington said, "Getting discovered is one-quarter luck, three-quarters fuck. What's her last name?"

Sebulsky frowned. "Don't believe I've ever heard it. Why?"

Lockington shrugged. "In case she makes it big, I'll be able to say I saw her before she got there. Like I saw Belinda Darkhorse back in 'eighty-two at some carnival."

"Belinda Darkhorse?"

"Yeah—she juggled half a dozen grapefruits and took off her clothes at the same time. Belinda ain't got there yet."

Sebulsky didn't say anything for a while. He sat on the edge of the wooden stool, hunched forward, peering through the open door, watching Mahoning Avenue traffic and the afternoon roll by. Then he said, "Y'know, I've been thinking about you. You're some kind of Chicago cop, ain't you?"

Lockington shook his head. "Nothing official—just another private investigator. I'm looking into an insurance matter."

"Uh-huh. How come the interest in Pecos Peggy?"

"Inheritance thing, maybe—no point in getting people all shook up until identities are established."

"She's in line for money?"

"Possibly, if her name's Gagliano."

"Gagliano doesn't ring a bell. A bundle?"

"If eighty grand's a bundle."

"In Youngstown, eighty grand's a bundle."

"Didn't you say something about knowing a bookkeeper at the Crossroads?"

"Ace Loftus—I went to high school with Ace."

"Could you ask him how Pecos Peggy signs her paychecks? It'd help."

"I already know the answer to that one. There ain't no checks—it's cash only. He got no idea how much she gets—guess that's been worked out with the owner."

"Out-of-town man, you said—Jack Taylor?"

"Yeah—you got a good memory."

Lockington said, "The IRS takes a dim view of those cash-only transactions."

Sebulsky grinned. "What the IRS doesn't know about cash-only deals would make one helluva big book."

"Okay, the check angle's out. Pecos Peggy drives an 'eighty-eight red Porsche—Ohio plates nine-eight-oh PRK. Her name'll be on the title registration. You said that you have a cousin with the county cops."

Sebulsky snapped his fingers. "Damn right—he could

run it through as a check on an abandoned vehicle!"

"It's worth fifty."

"I think I could have that in an hour or so. Anything else?"

"How do I find out who owns the property at Five fifty-one North Dunlap Avenue?"

"Is it worth fifty?"

"Right."

"Well, like I told you, my brother's into real estate—it's a holiday, but he's a *beaver*, he knows all the wrinkles. I'll give him a jingle. You talking cash on the barrelhead?"

"Yep. There's one other thing—you know anybody who speaks Russian?"

"Hell, yes—my grandfather. He was born in Russia—Sebulsky's a Russian name. What's the problem?"

"There's a word I want to get translated."

"That might be tough—Russian got a bunch of languages and dialects. What's the word?"

"*Slahduhk*—I can't spell it, but that's the way it sounds —*slahduhk*."

Sebulsky chuckled. "*Slahduhk?* I've heard it all my life! *Slahduhk* means sweet."

Lockington said, "I'll be back in an hour." He left a twenty on the bar. Cooperation in a strange town is hard to come by. There was bounce in his step when he headed for the door. The Sugar sisters were coming in. The redhead said, "Hello, there, you living *doll!*"

Lockington said, "Hi, gorgeous!" He returned to the bar with a five-dollar bill. He said, "John, give these lovely young things a drink, please." Then he said, "Helen, thy beauty is to me like those Nicean barks of yore!"

The hairy one said, "Helen my *ass*—I'm *Alice*,

she's *Leona!*"

Lockington's voice was mellifluous. His hands were clasped to his chest. He said, "They walk in beauty like the night of cloudless climes and starry skies!"

The redhead groaned, "Oh, my *God*, whaddaya *want? Take* me, TAKE me!"

The hairy one said, "Jeez, ain't it a pleasure to meet a real, genuine, honest-to-God *gentleman?*"

The redhead said, "You're fucking A!"

58

He drove toward the New Delhi Motel. He needed time for thought. He was probably missing something, and he didn't have the remotest notion of what it might be. He parked the Pontiac in front of Room 12. The door was wide open. Lockington went in. Room 12 looked like the site of a rodeo *after* the rodeo. His suitcase had been turned upside down and inside out, the mattress and box spring were on the floor, his pillow had been stripped of its casing, the little overstuffed chair was on its side, its cushion against a wall, the dresser drawers were scattered about the room, the top of the toilet's flush box was off, sitting on the sink. Lockington righted the chair, replaced the cushion and sat there, contemplating the Christ-awful mess. Then he smiled. His half-bottle of Martell's cognac was intact. Thank God for small favors.

He had a jolt of the stuff and hiked over to the office to discuss the matter with the manager. He said, "Who tore up my room?"

The manager said, "Speak little English."

"You see anything suspicious in the last couple hours?"

"Speak little English."

"What's more, my air-conditioner ain't working worth a damn!"

"Speak little English."

Lockington said, "How would you respond if I were to inform you that I am a State of Ohio hotel inspector, operating on behalf of Governor Richard Celeste, may his name be praised?"

The manager repeated, "Speak little English," but he blinked and Lockington regarded this as an encouraging sign. He jerked out his wallet, flashing his old City of Chicago Police badge.

The manager said, "Mr. Lockington, Your Excellency, it is the policy of this establishment to make its guests as comfortable as possible! The management attempts to extend every service, every courtesy! Rest assured, Your Excellency, that your room will be restored to order immediately, and your air-conditioner will be replaced within the hour! May your stay at the New Delhi Motel be a long and enjoyable one, Your Excellency!"

Lockington said, "Allah Akbar!" He went out, feeling slightly drunk with power, wondering what the hell *Allah Akbar* meant.

59

CHICAGO-LANGLEY/ ATTN MASSEY/ 1517 CDT/ 5/29/88
BEGIN TEXT: **BIRD DOG PIGEON PHONE TAPS COMPLETE/ NO ACCESS PIGEON APT/ PIGEON TAPPED AT POLE**/ END TEXT/ CARRUTHERS

LANGLEY-CHICAGO/ ATTN CARRUTHERS/ 1618 EDT/ 5/29/88
BEGIN TEXT: **RESULTS?**/ END TEXT/ MASSEY

CHICAGO-LANGLEY/ ATTN MASSEY/ 1518 CDT/ 5/29/88
BEGIN TEXT: **NONE BIRD DOG/ PIGEON ARRANGED BEAUTY APPT END NEXT WEEK**/ END TEXT/ CARRUTHERS

LANGLEY-CHICAGO/ ATTN CARRUTHERS/ 1619 EDT/ 5/29/88
BEGIN TEXT: **BIRD DOG WHEREABOUTS?**/ END TEXT/ MASSEY

CHICAGO-LANGLEY/ ATTN MASSEY/ 1520 CDT/ 5/29/88
BEGIN TEXT: **UNKNOWN**/ END TEXT/ CARRUTHERS

LANGLEY-CHICAGO/ ATTN CARRUTHERS/ 1620 EDT/ 5/29/88

BEGIN TEXT: **GODIVA?**/ END TEXT/ MASSEY

CHICAGO-LANGLEY/ ATTN MASSEY/ 1521 CDT/ 5/29/88
BEGIN TEXT: **UNKNOWN**/ END TEXT/ CARRUTHERS

LANGLEY-CHICAGO/ ATTN CARRUTHERS/ 1621 EDT/ 5/29/88
BEGIN TEXT: **PIGEON?**/ END TEXT/ MASSEY

CHICAGO-LANGLEY/ ATTN MASSEY/ 1522 CDT/ 5/29/88
BEGIN TEXT: **ENTERED POLISH CONSULTATE 1955 CDT
YESTERDAY/ STILL THERE**/ END TEXT/ CARRUTHERS

LANGLEY-CHICAGO/ ATTN CARRUTHERS/ 1623 EDT/ 5/29/88
BEGIN TEXT: **CERTAIN STILL THERE?**/ END TEXT/
MASSEY

CHICAGO-LANGLEY/ ATTN MASSEY/ 1523 CDT/ 5/29/88
BEGIN TEXT: **BLACK MERCEDES STILL PARKED
CONSULATE**/ END TEXT/ CARRUTHERS

LANGLEY-CHICAGO/ ATTN CARRUTHERS/ 1624 EDT/ 5/29/88
BEGIN TEXT: **ADVISE CLEVELAND CONCENTRATE
YOUNGSTOWN BIRD DOG**/ END TEXT/ MASSEY

CHICAGO-LANGLEY/ ATTN MASSEY/ 1525 CDT/ 5/29/88
BEGIN TEXT: **WHY YOUNGSTOWN?**/ END TEXT/
CARRUTHERS

LANGLEY-CHICAGO/ ATTN CARRUTHERS/ 1625 EDT/ 5/29/88
BEGIN TEXT: **LOGICAL/ TURKEY LIVED YOUNGSTOWN/
BIRD DOG WOULD START AT BEGINNING**/ END TEXT/
MASSEY

CHICAGO-LANGLEY/ ATTN MASSEY/ 1527 CDT/ 5/29/88
BEGIN TEXT: **CONTINUE PIGEON SURVEILLANCE?**/ END
TEXT/ CARRUTHERS

LANGLEY-CHICAGO/ ATTN CARRUTHERS/ 1628 EDT/ 5/29/88
BEGIN TEXT: **AFFIRMATIVE/ POSSIBILITY MAY JOIN BIRD DOG**/ END TEXT/ MASSEY

CHICAGO-LANGLEY/ ATTN MASSEY/ 1529 CDT/ 5/29/88
BEGIN TEXT: **WILCO**/ END TEXT/ CARRUTHERS

LINE CLEARED LANGLEY 1629 EDT 5/29/88

60

The Sugar sisters were sprawled unconscious in the corner booth of the Flamingo Lounge, the hairy one snoring, the redhead drooling in her sleep. John Sebulsky shook his head. He said, "Y'know, I've been working here for going on five years—they come in two, three times every day, and they've been soused to the scuppers every goddamned time I've seen 'em. I think they were plastered when Washington crossed the fucking Delaware!"

Lockington threw a wary glance into the booth. He said, "Yeah, and they probably pissed in it."

"They sleep for an hour and they get up and start all over again—it's some kind of perpetual motion!"

Lockington said, "You dig up anything?"

Sebulsky shrugged, dipping into a shirt pocket to produce a folded white slip of paper. He said, "Well, yes and no—probably mostly no."

Lockington tossed five twenties onto the bar. "Whadda we got?"

Sebulsky studied the paper, frowning. "That Porsche don't belong to Pecos Peggy—it was bought a couple weeks ago at European Motors out in Trumbull County by a guy named Patrick Moran. The property at Five fifty-one North Dunlap was purchased March before last through Cosmos Realty in Boardman. A man by the name of Harry Steinfeldt took it. Moran lives in Hubbard, Ohio—Steinfeldt's from Warren. Both deals were cash—no credit checks, no red tape."

"You get their addresses?"

Sebulsky said, "Yeah, they're on here." He pushed the paper to Lockington. Lockington folded it and stuffed it into his wallet. Sebulsky said, "Does that tell you anything?"

Lockington said, "Not yet, and I still don't have Pecos Peggy's last name."

"I gave you a little extra effort—I called Ace Loftus at the Crossroads half an hour ago. He doesn't know her last name. He says that she uses Smith with customers but he thinks that's a throwaway. He's not even sure of her *first* name, but he came up with one thing. He thinks that she's from some place called Petal—during rehearsals he's heard the guys in her band rib her about it. You know how that goes—if you're from Houston, you needle the guy from South Bend, and if you're from South Bend you pour it to the guy from Murphysburg."

Lockington nodded. Sebulsky poured a double hooker of Martell's, opened a bottle of Michelob Dry, picked up Lockington's five twenties, and said, "Call it square. Maybe next time."

Lockington shrugged. He said, "Maybe *this* time. Where can I get hold of a road atlas?"

Sebulsky said, "I got one in my car, but it's a couple years old."

"Mississippi's in it?"

"I dunno—I'll get it and you can find out." He ducked through the rear door, returning in a matter of moments with the atlas. He placed it on the bar. "It's a mess—it was in the trunk."

Lockington picked it up. It'd been issued by the All State Motor Club, its cover was torn, a streak of rust had nearly obliterated Michigan, but Mississippi was in tolerable condition and Pecos Peggy Smith was originally from Mississippi, or so she'd told him.

He lit a cigarette and ran a forefinger down the list of Mississippi towns that had names beginning with the letter P—Pachuto, Panther Bum, Parchman, Pascagoula, Pass Christian, Pearl, Pelahatchie, Percy, Petal—*Petal,* by God! Petal, Mississippi, population 8,476, was on Route 42 and it was located some three or four miles east of Hattiesburg— southern part of the state, down toward the Gulf of Mexico. All right, so there was a town named Petal in southern Mississippi—what about it? Lockington wasn't sure what about it—it'd been a flicker, flare, and fizzle thing.

John Sebulsky was staring into the corner booth, gripping the edge of the bar with white-knuckled hands. Lockington followed his gaze.

The Sugar sisters were stirring.

61

Lockington drove east, finding a small pizza parlor near Steel Street, ordering a small cheese pizza, browsing through the Youngstown area telephone book while waiting to be served. He found no listing for a Patrick Moran and none for a Harry Steinfeldt. Two and a half hours later he pulled into the New Delhi Motel parking lot, weary to the bone. Moran's address had turned out to be a vacant lot on the north side of Hubbard, Steinfeldt's had been a whorehouse near the railroad tracks in one of Warren's seamier districts.

In light of the fact that a night of activity lay ahead of him, he felt that a nap was in order, and he'd have taken one had not an oversexed young couple checked into Room 11. Following a prolonged period of oohings and ahhings there'd come a merciless barrage of thumpings and bumpings, crashings and smashings, highlighted by assorted moanings and groanings and ecstatic gnashings of teeth, and Lockington, sensibilities numbed, stumbled into the twilight to seek refuge in the backseat of his Pontiac where he caught forty winks, but no more than that. Now, at 12:30 A.M., he sat on a rusty fender, feet dangling, smoking a cigarette, studying an Ohio moon twice the size of a manhole cover, waiting for Pecos Peggy Smith or Natasha Gorky, whichever showed first.

It was Pecos Peggy Smith, if that was her name. She drove up in the tomato-red Porsche that belonged to somebody else, pushing its door open, waving him in, and they left the New Delhi parking lot to turn west on Mahoning Avenue. Lockington said, "How did tonight's show go?"

She shrugged. "As well as most, I guess—I hit a clinker on 'I Dreamed of an Old Love Affair' but it was during the midnight set and I think they were too drunk to notice. We had a nice turnout—you should have dropped in."

"I meant to do that, but I dozed off. Where are we going?"

"Southwest of Canfield, not far—fifteen minutes, usually."

"*Usually*—you've been there before?"

"Many times." She'd wheeled the Porsche from Mahoning Avenue north on Route 46.

Lockington said, "Would you believe that some sonofabitch busted into my hotel room and ransacked it?"

"Sure, I'd believe it. There's been a wave of that—kids looking for something to sell so they can buy crack. What'd they steal?"

"There was nothing *worth* stealing—I travel light."

The Porsche's dashlights were casting an ethereal glow on her face. She was smiling. She said, "Then they didn't get your red tuxedo."

"Nor my blue suede combat boots."

"There's nothing frilly about Lacey Lockington—that was obvious from scratch." The radio was tuned to a country music station and she reached to cut the volume to a murmer before she said, "Uhh-h-h, look—about last night—I was feeling horny—you know how it goes, I guess—sometimes we get urges."

Lockington nodded. "I've had a few."

"You see, Rufe spoke of you so often—you've become a legend, sort of. I've never gone to bed with a legend."

"Legends are usually disappointing—in or *out* of bed."

"So far, you've lived up to your advance billing—you're exactly as he said you were. Taciturn, unassuming—I get the feeling that you're dangerous. Danger excites me."

Lockington said, "It excites me, too—you're driving eighty-five miles an hour."

She eased off on the accelerator. "Sorry! Anyway, I'd be grateful if you'd forget about last night—not that the offer doesn't stand, but I'd rather you didn't mention it tonight."

"To whom?"

"To whomever."

"Guaranteed."

She slapped him on the knee, one of those affectionate, younger-woman-older-man, attaboy-Pops slaps. She said, "Thanks, Lacey."

They drove in silence for a couple of minutes. Then Lockington said, "Incidentally, what part of Mississippi do you hail from?"

"Do you know Mississippi—ever been there?"

"No, but I had an uncle who did some time at Camp Shelby just before the war. He liked the area." She didn't respond and Lockington went on. "He said that Camp Shelby was near Hattiesburg—he talked a lot about Hattiesburg. Is it a big town?"

"Hattiesburg? Oh, forty thousand, give or take." She turned right, leaving the subject on Route 46. The sign at the junction had said Western Reserve Road. Peggy said, "We're nearly there. I'll drop you off and pick you up in a couple of hours—let's make it two-thirty sharp."

Lockington said, "Hold it! What the hell am I getting into?"

Her smile was back. "Lacey, you've wanted an explanation and you've deserved one. After tonight you can go back to Chicago and live happily until the cows come home."

"No hurry. I like Youngstown."

"So do I—it's served its purpose."

"There's a cryptic remark if I've ever heard one."

"No, not cryptic—just slightly veiled."

Western Reserve Road was heavily wooded on both sides. They'd passed residences set back in clearings, but they'd been few and Lockington was beginning to experience an unfamiliar isolated feeling—he'd nearly forgotten that there were places where a man could watch cloud formations, smell clover, hear songbirds. Peggy turned left, pulling into a long blacktopped driveway, rolling to within a few feet of a long, low ranch house.

Lockington said, "What happens now—does a sorcerer appear?"

Peggy said, "Damned right! Just ring the bell!"

Lockington got out and she dropped the Porsche into reverse to back from the drive and head east on Western Reserve Road with a short beep of the horn. He stood for a moment, staring upward, awed by a limitless star-spangled sky, stunned by Mahoning Valley silence. He shook free of the spell, stepping onto the carpeted stoop of the dwelling, locating the doorbell button, pressing it, listening to muffled chimes from within the house. The door swung open immediately. A man stood in the doorway, silhouetted against the dim glow of a table lamp, waving him in. Lockington opened the storm door, entering, extending his hand.

He said, "Hello, Rufe."

62

They stood in the half-light of the living room, shaking hands, grinning, Devereaux squinting at Lockington. He said, "Lacey, are you gonna stand there and tell me that you ain't *surprised?*"

Lockington shook his head. "Not like I would have been five days ago."

"Why *not?*"

Lockington shrugged. "It's been dawning on me that there's one helluva lotta attention being paid to a dead man. By the way, thanks for the thousand dollars."

"Expense account money—don't mention it." Devereaux was locking the door, taking Lockington by the elbow to guide him into the kitchen. It was a pleasant room with a huge braided rug and an old-fashioned ceiling fan and a wood-framed clock on the wall. It had a small maple table and captain's chairs. The table held a red-shaded brass lamp, an oblong ceramic ashtray, a pair of martini glasses, a bottle of Shady Valley peppermint schnapps, and a fifth of Martell's cognac. Devereaux said, "There just ain't no place like a cozy kitchen for down-to-earth drinking."

They sat at the table, staring at each other, trying to bridge the dusty gap between their old days and their moment at hand. Rufe had lost weight—some fifteen pounds, Lockington figured—and his hairline had receded a trifle but he was pretty much the same old Devereaux, a twinkle in his hard eyes, his hand steady as Gibraltar when he poured schnapps and cognac. Lockington said, "You on some kind of diet?"

Devereaux grinned. "Yeah, all the pussy I can eat."

Lockington said, "All right, Rufe, what the hell's happening? What am I doing here—what's the problem?"

Devereaux was smiling. He said, "Lacey, the Agency pulled a swifty—it buried an empty box. Nothing original about that, you understand, it's an old gimmick, it's been worked a half-dozen times with people the Agency was trying to protect. In my case it was different—I was being isolated from other elements that wanted me."

"Why?"

"Because the Agency wanted me for itself."

"Again, *why?*"

"We'll get to that shortly."

"Shortly, shmortly! When I headed for Youngstown, a guy named Billy Mac Davis tried to blow me away on Interstate Eighty! You'll remember Billy Mac Davis."

"Yeah, the loony who wanted to be president. He's the founder of an outfit called LAON—Law and Order Now—a spooky bunch of fanatics!"

"Uh-huh—well, Davis knew my destination, and he didn't want me to reach it. He knew that you're in Youngstown and he figured that I was coming here to help you. You're probably on LAON's list. You'd better watch out for a guy named the Copperhead—he works for LAON."

"I know that. The Copperhead better see me before I see *him*—I've been trailing that bastard for over a year."

"On CIA assignment or on your own?"

"On my own. That's the way I close it out, Lacey—by killing the Copperhead. The final feather in my cap!"

"What do you know about him—what's he look like?"

"No idea what he looks like, but I know the approximate location of his lair—I'm closing on him and he knows it!"

"Where does he work from?"

"I have him narrowed down to being somewhere in Mercer County, Pennsylvania, just over the Ohio line—I'll get the bastard!"

"It was intimated that the Copperhead nailed you at the International Arms."

Rufe nodded. "Oh, sure, that's CIA style. Throw up a smoke screen—bumfoozle the opposition."

"Well, Rufe, do me a favor and get him in a hurry—he may be on my track."

"On *your* track—what the hell for?"

"It's simple enough—Davis is dead, LAON thinks that I killed him, and the Copperhead works for LAON."

Rufe's mouth had dropped open. "Davis is *dead?*"

"As a doornail. He missed me the first time around and he was going to take another whack at it. The Mafia killed his ass while he was waiting to kill mine—it happened early Friday morning at an I-80 rest stop about fifty miles from here."

"LAON and the Mafia are in different leagues—there's no competition there. Why would the Mafia kill Davis?"

"Because Davis was trying to kill *me*."

"All right, why should the Mafia protect *you?*"

"Probably because it thinks that I'll show the way to Rufe Devereaux."

Rufe buried his head in his hands. He groaned, "Sonofa*bitch!* Have you been followed?"

"Not to the best of my knowledge, but somebody went through my motel room with a fine-tooth comb. I doubt that we were tailed tonight—your lady friend has a sharp eye and a heavy foot. Rufe, why would the Mafia want you?"

Rufe sighed a disconsolate sigh. "For the same goddam reason the CIA wants me. How many guesses you want?"

"Just one. You've written a book—you've blown the whistle."

Rufe was grinning. "Lacey, you're *good!*"

Lockington shook his head slowly. "Jesus Christ, Rufe, you're messing with people that shouldn't be messed with. It could get you *killed*—I mean for *real.*"

Devereaux banged the table with the flat of his hand. "Not a chance! They won't hurt me, Lacey, they wouldn't *dare!* I've taken precautions, there's a dozen copies of that manuscript stashed all over this area—they're insurance policies! They won't lay a hand on me until they've squelched the book—when it's been published, it'll be too damned late to hit me. The possum will be out of the pot! I got 'em by the short hair—they're fucked if they *do* and they're fucked if they *don't!*"

Lockington said, "Tell me about your book."

"Lacey, it's a *scorcher,* and there ain't one word of it that I can't back up! When it hits the market, there's gonna be royal hell to pay, the press is gonna have a field day, there'll be congressional investigations, heads will roll—you're gonna see a three-ring *circus!*"

"How do these people know that you've written a book?"

"I've contacted a few publishers—word gets around in the publishing industry."

"Any nibbles?"

"*Nibbles?* There were three companies kissing my ass! I signed with Center Court Press in Chicago—two hundred grand advance, twelve percent royalties! That's why *you're* here, Lacey—to deliver the manuscript to Center Court. It's on West Monroe near the Chicago River bridge."

"And that's why you were in Chicago last Monday?"

"Yeah, and they cut us off at the pass—we had to backtrack! Y'see, Lacey, it ain't only the money—this book just *has* to be published. It reveals stuff that should be known by the average working stiff! It's high fucking time that people become aware of what goes on behind closed doors!"

Lockington winked at Devereaux. "Well, Rufe, I can see where the money would be of secondary importance to you—what the hell, you got a girlfriend who drives a sixty thousand dollar automobile."

Rufe chuckled. "It isn't hers yet, but it will be—I'll sign it over to her on her birthday, next week, June tenth! She's earned every nut and bolt of it—I couldn't have turned a wheel without her. She's cooked for me, she's run my errands, she's been a wonder."

Lockington said, "Her talents are many—she's also the best damned female country vocalist I've ever heard."

Rufe nodded. "She's turned down a stack of Nashville recording offers."

"Nashville's the Promised Land. Why would she nix Nashville?"

"Because she loves me."

Lockington didn't take it further—there was a sentimental tear in Rufe's eye. After a while he said, "If they're watching you, how did you get your manuscript to Center Court Press in the first place?"

"I didn't—Center Court flew a guy in here. I met him out at Youngstown Municipal, we had lunch, he read the first seventy-five pages, wrote me a check for one hundred thousand on the spot—the rest comes on date of publication."

"Why didn't you just *mail* the damned thing?"

"I just *finished* it ten days ago, and there's no way I'd risk the U.S. Postal Service. The CIA has access to the mails—national security, y'know."

"Yeah, that was how they shut the Chicago police out of your 'murder'—national security."

Rufe said, "What do you think of the Club Crossroads?"

"Obviously a money-maker."

"I own it, lock, stock and barrel, a steal at fifty grand!"

Lockington blinked an involuntary blink. "How—how come?"

"The price was right. I've always been partial to country music and when I first got here I took to hanging around the Crossroads—what the hell, it's the only country joint in town. Peggy's outfit auditioned and they should have signed 'em but they didn't, so I bought the place. Now she can stay as long as she damn well pleases!"

Lockington shrugged his way free of the subject. Pecos Peggy Smith had a sugar daddy and that was none of Lacey Lockington's business. He said, "Did you know that Bobbie Jo Pickens was killed?"

Devereaux froze. "Aw, *no!*"

"I thought you might know why."

"Damn, I liked that woman! Yeah, I know why—because she told me all about LAON. LAON's very big in my book. I got to know Bobbie Jo—she was a good person."

"She'd broken off from the Billy Mac Davis crusade, apparently."

"Sure, she broke off—she quit when she learned about LAON and what it was doing. Davis was the ultimate conservative, about fifteen degrees to the right of Attila the Hun—with Davis there were no grays, only black and white."

"And he hated black."

"It didn't stop there—he hated *liberals.* LAON burned the *Chicago Sentinel* Building last summer, and in December it torched the *Beacon Banner* Building in Duluth—both were liberal newspapers. It's arranged the assassinations of any number of pinkos—well, hell, never mind, you can read about that stuff in my book. Center Court believes it can publish before the first of the year."

"What's the name of the book?"

"*Blueprint for Chaos.* By 'Joseph B. Tinker.'"

"Joseph B. Tinker—your nom de plume?"

"Right—why take chances? *Blueprint for Chaos* is dedicated to you, by the way—'To Lacey J. Lockington, the only man I've ever trusted.'"

Lockington said, "Thanks, Rufe—I never thought I'd be immortalized in print."

Rufe said, "I may do another one when I've killed the Copperhead—I'd have to fictionalize it, of course, but the ingredients would be kosher."

"Why not? You could write it under a different pen

name—'John J. Evers,' maybe."

Rufe was staring at Lockington without a smile. "Helluva fine idea—'John J. Evers'—gotta remember that!"

Lockington said, "Look, Rufe, how did Bobbie Jo Pickens get involved with Billy Mac Davis anyway?"

"Davis was a holy-rolling preacher, she was an impressionable kid, barely out of high school, fifteen years younger than Davis. He put her to work, singing gospel songs at his revival meetings, then more popular stuff when he went political."

"Where was he preaching when they hooked up?"

"I don't know—he worked the Bible Belt from one end to the other. Davis was out of Memphis, Tennessee."

Lockington pushed his glass toward Rufe and Rufe filled it. He said, "Jesus, Lacey, it's good seeing you again!"

Lockington said, "Likewise. Your Chicago trip didn't work out worth a damn?"

Rufe exhaled loudly. "Hectic, Lacey, *hectic!* I had the manuscript in an attaché case. We took a cab from North Dunlap Avenue where I was living at the time. I'd seen no signs of surveillance earlier, but I spotted our tail before we got out of Mahoning County. At Hopkins I called Chicago to reserve a Jaguar V-Twelve—fast car. The Jag was waiting for us at O'Hare. So was the CIA. I outran 'em on the Kennedy."

"But you couldn't outrun the Mafia."

"No, the hoods had a souped-up Pan Am."

"The CIA was following you, but how did the Syndicate know you were coming in?"

Rufe shrugged. "An employee at Center Court Press, possibly—anyway, when I couldn't shake the Pan Am, I stopped at a tavern at Belmont and Kimball, not far from your place. I called a cab and instructed it to pick me up in the alley. I went to another ginmill and blew about twenty dollars trying to get hold of somebody from Center Court Press so I could get rid of the manuscript. I couldn't raise a soul, so I went back, picked up Peggy, returned the Jag, took another cab to the International Arms, and noticed CIA people in the lobby—hell, I knew one of 'em personally, guy named Steve Dellick. We went up to our room and when I saw that the hallway wasn't monitored, I called room service for a couple of sandwiches and I paid the delivery kid fifty bucks to take us down on a service elevator and smuggle us out of the building through the kitchen."

"You figured that the CIA would muscle you during the night?"

"I knew damned *well* it would. There are times when the Agency takes off the gloves. It'd have strong-armed us for the location of the duplicates! If Peggy hadn't been with me, I'd have taken my chances with the bastards, but, as matters stood, it was best that we take it on the duffy. We walked over to State Street, grabbed a cab to O'Hare, caught a red-eye to Pittsburgh, took a cab back to Youngstown. Peggy called a few realtors and I took this furnished house last Tuesday. It's ideal—it's isolated, and on Western Reserve Road she can tell if she's being followed. I've been here ever since, peeking out of the window, keeping an eye open for the Copperhead, hoping that you received that envelope, watching for a lop-eared gumshoe from Chicago." Devereaux got to his feet, grinning, stretching, yawning. He said, "Peggy will be picking you up in a few minutes. Let's take a walk out back—I'll show you the Big Dipper. We get a terrific Big Dipper in Youngstown."

63

They were walking across the half-acre expanse of Rufe Devereaux's backyard. Lockington's shoes were soaked with dew. He said, "Rufe, you didn't bring me out here to show me the fucking Big Dipper—you brought me out here to tell me something that you didn't want to tell me in the house. What's up—is there a chance that the placed is wired?"

Devereaux said, "Well, I gotta admit that the possibility has crossed my mind."

"How could that have been accomplished? You say that you haven't been out of the house since you moved in."

"That's right—damned unlikely, but one never knows, does one?"

"You're more hep than I am—I've never been involved in the cloak-and-dagger racket."

"Well, Lacey, anything's possible, and when you start assuming that it *isn't*, that's when you get your ass burned! Now, I have to get my book to Center Court Press pronto. When do you plan on going back to Chicago?"

"Any old time. When do you want me to make delivery?"

"If you get out of Youngstown tomorrow morning—Tuesday—pretty early, like six A.M., you could be in the Loop by one in the afternoon, Central Time. That way you'll have a little over twenty-four hours to get ready for the trip."

"That'll be about twenty-four more than I had when I left Chicago. Who gets the manuscript?"

"The same guy who flew in to look at it—his name's Romanoff, Sidney Romanoff. Looks like a barn owl that's just been confronted by a stegosaurus."

"Okay, give me the manuscript."

"Not yet—I'll spend this afternoon on it, doing some touch-up. You be in your car, waiting in front of your motel room, six o'clock in the morning—I'll have Peggy swing around and hand it to you. Make damned sure you get out of Youngstown clean, Lacey—it's too late in the game for a fumble. If you have to wait to see Romanoff you can read some of it. Only problem is, it has no pictures to color."

"No matter, I left my crayons in my apartment."

Rufe slapped him on the back. "Peggy's here—I see her headlights in the driveway."

They rounded the corner of the house, stepping into the white torrent of light. Lockington stopped short, snarling, "*Down*, Rufe, *now!*"

They hit the wet grass together, face down, rolling toward the building for cover as automatic weapon fire burned the night air, screaming into the darkness, chewing into a corner of the dwelling. Amid a hail of splinters Devereaux said, "I hope he doesn't move out where he can *see* us!"

Lockington's .38 police special was in his hand. He rasped, "If he does, he's one dead sonofabitch!"

There was a moment of silence before a door slammed and tires screeched on the asphalt drive. Lockington peered around the corner of the house. A low-slung dark coupe had hurtled onto Western Reserve Road and Lockington scrambled to his knees, two-handing the .38. He squeezed off three rounds as the car rocketed away to the east, burning rubber, its rear end fish-tailing. They got to their feet, brushing themselves off. Devereaux said, "*Shit!* How did you know it wasn't Peggy?"

"The headlights—the outline—it wasn't a Porsche." Another car went by, traveling east at high speed.

"Then what *was* it?"

"Damned if I know!"

"I'd have been suckered—I'd have thought it was somebody who'd pulled in to turn around."

Lockington snapped, "If they'd pulled in to turn around, they wouldn't have waited two minutes to *do* it."

"That gun had a chugging sound and I've heard it before—a TEC-9, sure as hell. Thirty-six-round magazine and it'll take a silencer."

Lockington said, "Yeah, you can buy one in Texas for three and a quarter."

Devereaux said, "Plus tax."

They sat on the front stoop, smoking, not saying much, waiting for Peggy. Lockington broke a long silence. He said, "Rufe, do you know 'I Get the Blues When it Rains?'"

Rufe grunted, "Me, too."

"It's a song, Rufe."

"Is it country?"

"No, it's an old barbershop number."

"If it ain't country, fuck it."

Lockington said, "Okay, just thought I'd ask."

After a while, Rufe said, "She's late—shoulda been here twenty minutes ago."

Lockington didn't reply. The silence was uncomfortable.

Then she came, her red Porsche gliding down Western Reserve Road and into the driveway. Lockington shook hands with Rufe. He said, "See you in Chicago sometime."

Rufe said, "Damn betcha!"

Lockington got in. Peggy blew Rufe a kiss, backing from the drive. She said, "We'll go straight through on Western Reserve—there's a terrible mess on Forty-six—ambulances, police cars—I had trouble getting through."

"Big wreck?"

"No, there were two men in a green Pontiac Trans Am. They were run off the road and shot—well, shot is hardly the word—they were *shredded!* Someone said that the police thought it was AK-47 fire. What's an AK-47?"

"It's a Soviet-designed, Chinese-manufactured infantry rifle. They sell 'em in Texas for four hundred bucks— four and a half if you want a seventy-five-round drum." Lockington frowned, suddenly remembering that neither he nor Rufe Devereaux had mentioned the KGB. Or the house at 3000 North Onines Avenue. Or any number of things.

64

Rufe Devereaux had summed it up accurately enough, Lockington thought—they'd have to get the manuscripts before they got Devereaux. If they got hold of the manuscripts they'd *have* to eliminate Rufe because there'd be no guarantee that he wouldn't sit down and write *Blueprint for Chaos* all over again. But if the book were to be published and in the stores, the cat would be out of the bag and Rufe's death would serve no purpose other than to multiply those pressures exerted by its revelations.

Of the four factions involved, which had attempted the Western Reserve Road massacre? Lockington crossed the KGB from the list of eligibles. Natasha Gorky was heading up KGB efforts, her alliance with Lockington had been of her own volition, she had the rail stall and no logical reason to kick over the traces. Lockington couldn't bring himself to associate the Central Intelligence Agency with the aborted effort—the CIA *arranged* murders, rarely did it *commit* them. And there was LAON, a squad of racist lunatics recruited by a demented Fascist zealot who'd shot at Lockington on Interstate 80. LAON's multitudinous transgressions were listed in Devereaux's book. One player remained—the Mafia, also eligible for dishonorable mention in *Blueprint for Chaos*. Every one of the four would be delighted to see the book vanish without a ripple. The most likely to throw caution out the window and go for broke would be LAON— LAON lacked the organizational self-discipline possessed by the other three. But none of them had Rufe's manuscripts, and the manuscripts were the main ingredient of the entire stew. The outfit that would be least concerned about being lambasted in the book would be the Mafia. It was known for what it was, it had little to lose in an expose, bad press didn't mean diddly to the Mafia. But the car that'd left Rufe Devereaux's driveway could have been a Pontiac Trans Am, and a Pontiac Trans Am had been shot up on Route 46, its occupants undoubtedly Vince Calabrese and Slats Mercurio, stitched by a hail of rifle fire. Why? Certainly not because of Rufe's book—certainly not for *any* reason that Lockington could drum up.

"Lacey, you're almost home."

Lockington surfaced from his murky pool of thought, finding himself in Austintown rolling east on Mahoning Avenue. He said, "Yeah—guess I was dozing."

Peggy said, "You're going to take the manuscript to Chicago?"

"I'm going to try."

"Rufe's in danger, isn't he?"

Lockington shrugged. "Not just yet. Rufe Devereaux's lived with danger for a long time—he can handle it."

"He's such a sweet man."

"Yeah—helluva guy."

"And I'm such a slut."

"Are you?"

"Oh, my God, if you only *knew*." She was turning into the New Delhi Motel grounds, parking the Porsche next to Lockington's Pontiac. "If you'll invite me in for a drink, I'll give you a demonstration—Pecos Peggy Smith, the easiest fuck in the state of Ohio!" She smiled a sad smile. "But the *best*, beyond doubt!"

Lockington said, "Honey, it's damned near three in the morning and I'm a basket case—let's exchange rainchecks."

"How many can you spare?"

"How many can you use?"

"Lacey, you'd be *amazed!* Will you be at the Crossroads tonight?"

"We'll see."

"I'll sing one for you."

"Can you do 'Sleepwalkin' Mama?'"

"It's not my kind of song—it's horny. I'm never horny in public, only in bed. I'm world-class horny in bed. Got another?"

"I'll think about it."

Lockington started to get out. She caught his arm. She said, "What the hell, Lacey—the girl just can't help it."

She drove away and Lockington stopped to peer into his Pontiac. The back of the rear seat had been dislodged. It'd flopped forward onto the floor at an angle.

Lockington's nod was involuntary. Somehow, the development meshed with his recent thinking.

65

A long-haired brown-and-white dog came padding out of the early morning darkness, nose to the ground, passing within ten feet of Lockington. Lockington growled. The dog paid no attention. Somewhere in the distance a cat yowled. It was that time of year. A truck came out of Youngstown, pounding westward on Mahoning Avenue, its rumble dimming in the distance. That was all. Lockington unlocked his door, wondering about Natasha Gorky's whereabouts and learning quickly. He found her sitting on the edge of his bed, naked as a jaybird, smiling her wonderfully lopsided smile. She crooked an inviting forefinger. She said, "Come here, please."

Lockington said, "Breaking and entering really isn't nice."

Natasha's pale-blue eyes sparkled. She said, "Neither is sex out of wedlock." She dropped back on the bed, spreading her legs, running her hands across her flat, smooth belly. She said, "The *hell* it isn't!"

Lockington sat on the overstuffed chair, lighting a

cigarette. He said, "There are things we should talk about."

She said, "They won't keep until breakfast?"

Lockington's eyes were riveted to the succulent center of Natasha Gorky. He left the overstuffed chair, extinguishing his cigarette. He said, "Yeah, they'll keep until breakfast."

A few minutes later she pitched and yawed under him, moaning, "Oh, *dobry!*—ooh, *parfait!*—oooh, *meraviglioso!*—ooooh, *erstaunlich!*—ooooooh, *vunderlich!*—ooooooh, *storartad!*"

Lockington said, "What does that mean?"

Natasha gasped, "Later, dammit, *later!*"

They'd fallen asleep and she never did tell him, but he managed to figure it out for himself.

66

They'd gotten out of bed early, Natasha bouncy and bright-eyed, Lockington sluggish, looking like the parachute hadn't opened. Lockington asked about her Mercedes—he hadn't seen it, where was it? In Chicago, she told him—she'd driven it to the consulate and she'd left for Youngstown in the blue Thunderbird parked in front of Room 5. She'd rented Room 5, she said, her suitcase was there. Lockington wondered where Hargan was. In Chicago, Natasha opined, keeping an eye on the Mercedes. They had breakfast at the restaurant next door to the New Delhi, Natasha going through a Belgian waffle the size of a Chinese gong, Lockington settling for five cups of black coffee and several cigarettes. They'd talked, he'd brought her up to date, watching her facial expression when he'd told her that Devereaux was alive. There'd been none. He'd said, "Do you have his file?"

Natasha said, "Right here!" She tapped her forehead with a forefinger.

Lockington said, "I've been acquainted with Rufe for

four years, I know nothing of his past. Has he ever been in serious difficulty?"

"I suppose so, most secret service people are, at one time or another."

"But you have nothing definite on that?"

"Nothing of consequence. He's been a womanizer—that usually leads to complications." Her auburn hair was still damp from the shower they'd taken. The water had been cold, and she'd squealed at the beginning. "What sort of information do you want?"

Lockington shrugged. "An old enmity, maybe—something in his background that might have provoked last night's attack."

She shook her head. "Nothing like that. His CIA career was routine in its early stages—Alabama in the late fifties, Texas, Mississippi, Georgia in the sixties, but he had ability and it was recognized. He was dispatched to foreign duty in the seventies and early eighties—Europe, the Middle East, he's been in Russia. He persuaded two KGB operatives to defect—a devilishly clever man who's been highly respected in intelligence circles."

"The Mafia will do anything for money—it could have been hired to eliminate Rufe."

"I suppose so, but the Mafia deals in drugs—million-dollar sales. Who could have afforded Mafia services?"

"Possibly the CIA, possibly LAON, possibly the KGB—they're barking up the same tree."

"Then who'd kill Mercurio and Calabrese?"

"Maybe the same people who hired them.

Natasha's smile was less than a smile. "You don't trust me, do you?"

"For reasons as yet unknown to me, I trust you implicitly—I can't help that. But you aren't running the KGB—you're a tool, what you think is blue may be orange."

Natasha lit a cigarette. "All right, whatever—I'm here to help. You're calling the shots, that was our agreement. What can I do?"

"You can attempt to get a bit of information. It'll be difficult, perhaps impossible on Memorial Day."

"I have sources. Let me try."

"All right, I need a birth records check."

"From where?"

"Southern Mississippi."

"Be specific, please."

"You'd better have pencil and paper."

"Unnecessary—my memory is excellent." There'd been no braggadocio about it, she'd made the statement matter-of-factly.

"Okay, covering a five-year span, 'sixty-seven through 'seventy-one, I want particulars on female children born in Hattiesburg, Mississippi on June tenth—the mother probably lived in Petal, Mississippi."

"If she lived in Petal, why would she have her baby in Hattiesburg?"

"Petal's a small town, under ten thousand—it may not have a hospital. Hattiesburg has a population of over forty thousand and it's no more than ten minutes from Petal."

"Strange order. It's pertinent?"

"Probably."

She nodded. "I won't get this instantly, you understand. It'll take time—hours, more than likely."

"That'll be all right. There's a pay phone near the cashier.

You work on that, I'll work on something else, and I'll see you in Room 12 in an hour or so." He paid the breakfast check and walked back to the New Delhi Motel. He jammed the back of his rear seat into proper position and drove toward the Flamingo Lounge. There was a maybe in the back of his mind. It was an infinitesimal maybe, but considering its size, it was creating a terrible ruckus.

67

He found John Sebulsky seated on his wooden stool behind the bar, studying a Styrofoam cup of coffee. Sebulsky pointed to the coffee, making a sour face. He said, "Greek restaurant stuff."

Lockington said, "Oh, my God!"

Sebulsky said, "Greek restaurants were the real reason for the Japanese bombing Pearl Harbor."

Lockington said, "You'll have to explain that."

"Well, you see, generally speaking, the Japanese didn't have anything against the United States. What happened was, there was a Greek restaurant owners' convention in Hawaii and they were planning to open a chain of gyro joints in Tokyo."

Lockington nodded. "That explains it."

"Not a great many people are aware of that fact."

"I certainly wasn't."

Sebulsky said, "Did you know that all Greek restaurants are in the United States? All they got in Greece is

Burger Kings."

Lockington said, "I've never been to Greece."

Sebulsky said, "Me either. So far, I ain't lost a whole lot of sleep over that."

Lockington said, "Is there a private telephone here? I want to make a long distance call."

"There's a pay phone over by the dart game."

"Yeah, and what if the Sugar sisters come in?"

"I see your point—where you calling?"

"Chicago." Lockington plunked a twenty on the bar. "That'll more than cover it."

"Okay, there's one in the office."

The office was filled with beer cases. Four cases of Pabst Blue Ribbon served as a desk. Lockington sat on a case of Budweiser. He took out a pad and a ballpoint pen before dialing Mike's Tavern. Mike answered on the third ring. Lockington said, "You're under arrest."

Mike said, "Lacey! Where the hell are you?"

"I'm calling from Istanbul—there's a belly dancer I got the hots for."

"Them belly dancers ain't no good in bed—what you see ain't necessarily what you get. What's up, Lacey?"

"Mike, that old baseball encyclopedia of yours—can you get hold of it?"

"It's in the basement. They ain't got no baseball encyclopedias in Istanbul?"

"It's a holiday, the stores and libraries are closed, and I got a baseball bet with a harem eunuch. Would it be too much trouble to run downstairs and get it?"

"Yeah, it'd be too much trouble, but I'll do it anyway—hang on."

Lockington slouched on the case of Budweiser, waiting. From the bar area there came a muffled heavy thud, a sound that Lockington had learned to associate with a falling body. He got up to peer around the doorway frame. A portly man wearing a grayish-blue uniform was flat on his back in the middle of the barroom floor. The Sugar sisters were straddling him. The man was saying, "Jesus Christ, I don't have *time* to buy no drinks—I got *mail* to deliver!"

The redheaded Sugar sister said, "Hey, *you* got problems, *we* got problems—hell, all God's chillun got problems!"

The hairy Sugar sister said, "Yeah, looky all them people in fucking Beirut!"

The redhead Sugar sister said, "Besides, there *ain't* no mail on Memorial Day."

The uniformed man was gasping for air. He groaned, "For God's sake, John, give 'em a *drink!*"

Sebulsky said, "I poured it the very moment you came in."

Lockington pulled away from the doorway, shrinking back into the comparative safety of the office. Mike had returned to the telephone. He was puffing from the trip. He said, "Okay, Lacey, I finally found it. Whaddaya wanna know?"

Lockington said, "Give me the roster of the nineteen-oh-six Chicago Cubs."

Five minutes later he called 1–312–353–2980.

He'd just hung up when John Sebulsky appeared in the doorway. Lockington said, "I made *two* Chicago calls."

Sebulsky said, "Pecos Peggy gonna get her eighty grand?"

Lockington said, "Looks like she'll do better than that."

Sebulsky said, "You can come out now—the Sugar

sisters just left."

"Will they be back?"

"Is the Vatican in Rome?"

Lockington said, "There's a thought! How do I get to Rome?"

Sebulsky said, "I think you gotta start from Cleveland. Did you hear about two guys getting shot out on Forty-six last night?"

Lockington said, "Somebody mentioned it."

"They got chewed up pretty good—my cousin's on the Mahoning County police and he said that the coroner's office counted thirty-four holes in one guy and thirty-six in the other! You know what he thinks?"

"No, what does he think?"

"He thinks they ended up on the wrong end of an AK–47. What do *you* think?"

Lockington said, "I think those guys should be more careful in the future."

68

He parked the Pontiac in front of Room 12, getting out. The manager was standing in the office doorway, waving to him, smiling a white-toothed smile. He said, "Good morning, Mr. Lockington, Your Excellency!"

Lockington waved back. The door to Room 12 was partially ajar and Lockington went in, closing it behind him. Natasha Gorky had the telephone to her ear, waving him to silence, motioning for him to sit down, listening intently, nodding, saying, "All right, thank you—well done!" She hung up, turning her attention to Lockington. "How did you do?"

"Very well. You?"

She lit a cigarette before she said, "I put it into the network with instructions that I be contacted here. It came through just now."

"And?"

"And you've turned a corner—On June 10th, 1967, a girl was born in Hattiesburg, Mississippi—Margaret Beth Pickens. Seven pounds even, no birthmarks. The mother was a Bobbie Jo Pickens of Petal, Mississippi."

"The father?"

"Blank."

"Uh-huh."

Natasha said, "We can't leave him blank—let's color him Billy Mac Davis."

Lockington shrugged.

Natasha said, "She's the girl who was with Devereaux in Chicago?"

"Twice, possibly more—Pecos Peggy Smith, the singer at the Crossroads, the one who took me to Rufe's place last night."

Natasha said, "She's Devereaux's mistress?"

"So it would appear—he's spent a pile of money on her."

Natasha squinted, shaking her head. "Ironic—she sleeps with Devereaux and Billy Mac Davis hires the Copperhead to kill him. Talk about strong parental objections!"

Lockington was silent.

Natasha was having trouble getting it adjusted. She said, "A girl of twenty-one and a man in his late fifties—intellectual rhythms, possibly, but a physical mismatch, wouldn't you say?"

"I wouldn't say." Lockington corralled the bottle of Martell's, uncapping it, offering it to Natasha.

She shook her head. "I brought Martell's and Smirnoff's—it's over in Room Five. I'll bring it when I change clothes—I look like a train wreck."

Lockington took a slug of the Martell's before he produced his dime-store pad to riffle through it, find a page, and hand it to Natasha. He said, "Any of these names familiar to you?"

She studied the page, her facial expression locked at zero. Lockington would have hated to sit across a poker table from her. After a while she said, "Who are these people?"

Lockington said, "American baseball players from more than eighty years ago."

She closed the pad, returning it to Lockington. "Explain, if you will."

Lockington said, "Would you like to go for a walk in the woods?"

She smiled her off-center smile. She said, "Why—do you want to get my ass in the grass?"

Lockington said, "Well-l-l, yes, that's part of it."

69

CHICAGO-LANGLEY/ ATTN MASSEY/ 1027 CDT/ 5/30/88
BEGIN TEXT: **THIS STATION HAS CONTACT WITH BIRD DOG**/ END TEXT/ CARRUTHERS

LANGLEY-CHICAGO/ ATTN CARRUTHERS/ 1128 EDT/ 5/30/88
BEGIN TEXT: **EXCELLENT/ HOW ACCOMPLISHED?**/ END TEXT/ MASSEY

CHICAGO-LANGLEY/ ATTN MASSEY/ 1028 CDT/ 5/30/88
BEGIN TEXT: **BIRD DOG PHONED/ REQUESTS ASSISTANCE**/ END TEXT/ CARRUTHERS

LANGLEY-CHICAGO/ ATTN CARRUTHERS/1129 EDT/ 5/30/88
BEGIN TEXT: **PHONED FROM WHERE?**/ END TEXT/ MASSEY

CHICAGO-LANGLEY/ ATTN MASSEY/ 1029 CDT/ 5/30/88
BEGIN TEXT: **YOUNGSTOWN OHIO**/ END TEXT/ CARRUTHERS

LANGLEY-CHICAGO/ ATTN CARRUTHERS/ 1130 EDT/ 5/30/88
BEGIN TEXT: **WHY ASSISTANCE?**/ END TEXT/ MASSEY

CHICAGO-LANGLEY/ ATTN MASSEY/ 1030 CDT/ 5/30/88
BEGIN TEXT: **NOT EXPLICIT/ PRESUMABLY TURKEY INVOLVED**/ END TEXT/ CARRUTHERS

LANGLEY-CHICAGO/ ATTN CARRUTHERS/ 1131 EDT/ 5/30/88
BEGIN TEXT: **STATE LIGHT PLANE AVAILABILITY YOUR STATION**/ END TEXT/ MASSEY

CHICAGO-LANGLEY/ ATTN MASSEY/1031 CDT/ 5/30/88
BEGIN TEXT: **READY ACCESS CESSNA 182 SKYLANE**/ END TEXT/ CARRUTHERS

LANGLEY-CHICAGO/ ATTN CARRUTHERS/ 1132 EDT/ 5/30/88
BEGIN TEXT: **STATE APPROX FLY TIME THIS CRAFT CHICAGO TO YOUNGSTOWN MUNICIPAL**/ END TEXT/ MASSEY

CHICAGO-LANGLEY/ ATTN MASSEY/ 1033 CDT/ 5/30/88
BEGIN TEXT: **OFFHAND 3 HRS MAX**/ END TEXT/ CARRUTHERS

LANGLEY-CHICAGO/ ATTN CARRUTHERS/ 1133 EDT/ 5/30/88
BEGIN TEXT: **DISPATCH 2 OPERATIVES YOUNGSTOWN ASAP/ RESERVE RENTAL CAR YOUNGSTOWN MUNICIPAL**/ END TEXT/ MASSEY

CHICAGO-LANGLEY/ ATTN MASSEY/ 1034 CDT/ 5/30/88
BEGIN TEXT: **WILCO/ WILL SEND DELLICK & MAHONEY/ DELLICK IN CHARGE**/ END TEXT/ CARRUTHERS

LANGLEY-CHICAGO/ ATTN CARRUTHERS/ 1135 EDT/ 5/30/88
BEGIN TEXT: **NEGATIVE/ IN YOUNGSTOWN BIRD DOG IN CHARGE**/ END TEXT/ MASSEY

CHICAGO-LANGLEY/ ATTN MASSEY/ 1036 CDT/ 5/30/88
BEGIN TEXT: **COMPLETELY?**/ END TEXT/ CARRUTHERS

LANGLEY-CHICAGO/ ATTN CARRUTHERS/ 1136 EDT/ 5/30/88
BEGIN TEXT: **COMPLETELY/ CONTACT TO BE MADE BY BIRD DOG?**/ END TEXT/ MASSEY

CHICAGO-LANGLEY/ ATTN MASSEY/ 1037 CDT/ 5/30/88
BEGIN TEXT: **AFFIRMATIVE/ BIRD DOG ADVISES OPERATIVES TAKE ROOM NEW DELHI MOTEL MAHONING AVENUE AUSTINTOWN OHIO/ SAYS LEAVE BEER CAN FRONT WINDOW/ SAYS HIBERNATE AND WAIT**/ END TEXT/ CARRUTHERS

LANGLEY-CHICAGO/ ATTN CARRUTHERS/ 1138 EDT/ 5/30/88
BEGIN TEXT: **DO IT**/ END TEXT/ MASSEY

CHICAGO-LANGLEY/ ATTN MASSEY/ 1038 CDT/ 5/30/88
BEGIN TEXT: **WILCO**/ END TEXT/ CARRUTHERS

LINE CLEARED LANGLEY 1138 EDT 5/30/88

70

They'd rounded the small office enclosure, bearing south into the dense woods that half-encircled the New Delhi Motel. She'd looked up into the trees, taking Lockington's hand. "Virgin forest—I feel like a girl again."

"Because you were a virgin?"

"*Tawlsty gawluhvy!* Because of the *forest!*"

"There were forests near Odessa?"

"Miles of them—I played in them as a child. From the hilltops I could see Odessa's harbor—the whaling ships came to Odessa often." They walked on, Lockington stopping at short intervals, glancing toward the motel. Natasha said, "There was a young seaman—we met in the forest."

"And then you were no longer a child."

Natasha stooped to pick up a brown pin-oak leaf, caressing it with her fingertips. She said, "And then I was no longer a child."

They'd gone better than fifty yards into the woods and Lockington swung right, walking slowly to the west, his gaze fixed on the New Delhi. He stopped. They'd come to a tiny clearing, its floor matted with leaves. There were violets and a long hollow log. Lockington said, "This would appear to be a likely place."

They sat on the hollow log. Natasha said, "I can see the door of your room from here."

Lockington said, "That's why it would appear to be a likely place."

Natasha said, "Is this where you get my ass in the grass?"

Lockington shrugged.

Natasha said, "Ah, *nature!*" She slipped from the log into the leaves, peeling her skirt and half-slip upward to her navel. She wore no panties. The girls in Odessa didn't bother, she'd told him. She peered up at him with bright pale-blue eyes. She said, "Oh, I'd just *love* to get lost in the Everglades with you!"

"It's better here—dry ground."

"Come down here."

"Not so many mosquitoes."

"Come *down* here, *will* you?"

"Fewer alligators."

Natasha sat up, grabbing his knees. She said, "Are you coming down *here* or am I coming up *there?*"

Lockington said, "I'm coming down there."

Natasha smiled. She said, "How nice! Procrastination is the thief of time."

"That's a line from Edward Young."

"Who was Edward Young?"

"Damned if I know."

"Then why did you bring him up?"

"I didn't bring him up—*you* brought him up."

Natasha said, "I regret that. Are you coming down here?"

Lockington came down there. He said. "This time, let's try it in English."

71

Natasha's skirt was down, Lockington's pants were up, but they stayed there until they ran out of cigarettes. Then it was twilight and birds were returning to the trees around them. They listened to the flutter of descending wings and Natasha murmured, "It's been a long and risky flight—I should come down to earth and make a nest."

Lockington said, "Where?"

"Wherever." There was a wistfulness about her, the vulnerability that Lockington had detected in Chicago. He said, "When?"

"Soon—very soon. I'm tired."

"How soon is very soon?"

"I wish it could be tonight—or tomorrow—but there's this matter to be attended to."

Lockington blew the ash from his last cigarette. He said, "You don't quit the KGB easily, do you? I mean, you just don't walk in and say, 'See you later?'"

She was sprawled on her belly, her toes hooked over the

hollow log, plucking meditatively at stray blades of grass. "No, normally that isn't how it's done, but I just might get away with it."

"The KGB would make an exception in your case?"

"The KGB makes exceptions only for exceptional reasons."

"And you have an exceptional reason?"

"No, but perhaps I can convince the KGB that I *do*. Are you taking me to dinner?"

"I am."

They walked back to the motel and Natasha turned off in the direction of Room 5. "I'll be with you in half an hour."

Lockington nodded, noticing the silhouette of a beer can on the windowsill of Room 8. He knocked on the door and it opened instantly. Steve Dellick said, "Lockington, it's good to see you again—this is Kevin Mahoney."

Lockington waved to an angular, lantern-jawed young fellow, spotting a pair of flak jackets draped over the back of a chair. He said, "Boys, will you accompany me for just a few minutes?"

72

The feeling had come back to him—cold, creeping dread in the swirling mists before dawn in Vietnam.

They'd rolled out at four-thirty in pitch blackness and the first words out of Lockington's mouth had been, "No lights!"

They'd showered in the dark, dressed in the dark, sat on the edge of their badly rumpled bed in the dark, smoking, conversing subduedly, waiting—waiting. Natasha had said, "You're certain of this?"

Lockington had said, "As certain as I've been of anything." He'd considered the statement. "Which isn't saying much."

At five-thirty he said, "Okay, let's have some light—I'm out of bed now, getting ready to grab the manuscript and start the run to Chicago."

Natasha reached to switch on the nightstand lamp, squinting against its sudden glare. Lockington studied her—she was unruffled. With a few more like her, he could have ruled the world, he thought.

It was five-forty. Dawn was graying the Ohio sky, leaking

into the room through the tattered paper window blinds.

The silence was dense. Lockington stared at his twenty-dollar Japanese wristwatch. By that unpredictable timepiece it was five fifty-two when they heard it—a faraway rattle of gunfire sounding like a string of tiny firecrackers. Lockington slammed the mattress with his fist. "Sonofabitch, what are they *doing?* It sounds like the fucking Battle of the *Marne!*"

Natasha made no response—she was on her feet, heading for the door. Lockington grabbed her arm, spinning her heavily onto the bed. He said, "Not yet, for Christ's sake!" Natasha kissed him. Upwards of fifty shots, he figured. Too many. He rasped, "Something's wrong out there!"

Another thirty seconds and they went out, dog-trotting across the graveled expanse of the New Delhi Motel parking area. The manager was in his nightshirt, standing wide-eyed in his office doorway. He said, "Mr. Lockington, Your Excellency, what *is* it, sir?"

Lockington snapped, "Take cover—a Sikh regiment has penetrated our southwestern perimeter!"

The manager wailed, "Aaa—iii—eeeee!" He scooted into the office, slamming its door.

They plunged into the forest, Lockington leading the way, making for the little clearing they'd found. They reached it, scrambling through dewy thickets. Steve Dellick and Kevin Mahoney stood over the bullet-mangled body of a big man clad in blood-splotched black. He lay face down on the damp leafy floor of the clearing. There was a long brown leather case at his side. Lockington snarled, "This is *murder*—you were instructed to take him *alive!*"

Steve Dellick said, "Jesus Christ, Lockington, we didn't fire a *shot!* He came from the south through the woods—we were waiting for him to open his case before we accosted him! He'd just unsnapped it when the fusillade decked him—AK-47's, sure as hell!"

Lockington said, "From *where?*"

"Two locations!" Dellick pointed into the trees behind them. "We were there, completely out of sight! The shots came from there and there!" He was indicating positions considerably to the left and right of the area they'd occupied. "The first couple of rounds took him out, but they kept blazing away—he's gotta have five pounds of lead in him!"

Lockington said, "Did you see them?"

Dellick shook his head. "Not so much as a *shadow*—top-drawer talent!" He was peering at Natasha Gorky. "Lockington, who the hell is this woman?"

Lockington snapped, "Lieutenant Yulebell, Salvation Army—she's on *our* side." He turned to the dead man's leather case, raising its lid with the toe of his shoe, kneeling to study its contents. After a while he said, "Swiss—Mannerhorst Three-oh-three—telescopic sight—tripod—all the gingerbread."

Kevin Mahoney said, "He had an excellent field of fire—he'd have nailed you the moment you opened your motel room door!"

Natasha Gorky had dropped to her haunches beside Lockington. She said, "He was good—*very* good—but you were better. Devereaux ran second."

Lockington's stare would have withered fifty acres of ragweed. "No, Devereaux ran *third*—I ran *second*—a scheming little Russian minx won it going away!"

She spread her hands helplessly. In a small voice she said, "That was her job."

73

They'd returned to the New Delhi parking lot and Steve Dellick was standing at the side of an Austintown police car, talking to a man who wore a sharply pressed blue uniform. Dellick was saying, "Whistle up an ambulance—we have a casualty back in the woods. You can wrap it up when they've gotten the body out of here."

The uniformed man had a lot of gold braid on his cap, indicating that he was a general or an admiral or whatever they were in Austintown. He said, "I've been here since four this morning—no one has driven in."

Kevin Mahoney said, "Anybody go out?"

The field marshal said, "Yeah, two men in a blue T-bird, Illinois plates."

Steve Dellick said, *When?"*

"Ten, twelve minutes ago—you said to keep everybody *out,* not *in.*"

Lockington said, "It's all right—forget it."

Dellick said, "Now, wait just a minute!"

Lockington said, "Forget it, Dellick. Don't make waves—this is a national security matter, isn't it?"

Dellick said, "But who *were* they?"

Lockington said, "They were staying in Room 5—I saw 'em. Probably a couple fags on their way to New York—no connection."

Dellick said, "All right, so much for that, but where's Devereaux's manuscript?"

Lockington said, "*Damn*, I should have *mentioned* that—there *ain't* no manuscript."

Dellick said, "Aw, c'mon, Lockington!"

Lockington said, "There never *was* a manuscript—Rufe Devereaux couldn't have written a grocery list." He turned, walking away, Natasha Gorky following, catching up to grab his arm.

Dellick said, "That's all there *is?*"

Lockington paused. Over his shoulder he said, "That's all unless you're interested in three K's of coke in a closet at 3,000 North Onines in Leyden Township."

Natasha whispered. "Thank you."

Lockington said, "Now that your T-bird's gone, you may want a lift to Chicago."

"I'd be grateful for that! I'll throw my things into your car, then I'll help you with your packing."

When she came into Room 12, Lockington was sitting in the overstuffed chair. He took her by the hand, pulling her to him. He flipped her face-down over his knee. He hoisted her skirt, noting with approval that the lady from Odessa wore no panties. He tanned her tawny fanny, swatting it as rapidly and with as much force as he could muster. She didn't flinch, she didn't squirm, she didn't cry out, she took it like a soldier. When he was worn out, she slipped to the floor on her knees, facing him, smiling, tears streaming down her cheeks. She said, "Did you enjoy that?"

Lockington said, "Every goddamned *moment* of it!"

Natasha Gorky threw her arms around him, squeezing him hard. She said, "Oh, Lacey Lockington, so did I, so did *I!*"

There were times when Lockington realized that he had a lot to learn about women.

This was one of those times.

74

At 551 North Dunlap Avenue, the red Porsche was in the driveway and Lockington parked behind it, leaving Natasha Gorky in the Pontiac when he went to the front door. He rang the bell, waiting. He rang it another two times. Eventually she responded, brushing sleep from her eyes, wearing an extremely low-cut short blue nightie and an untied white chenille robe. She was barefoot. She said, "Needed you last night, here you come this morning." She stepped to one side, beckoning him in. Her breasts were two-thirds exposed and one was black and blue—the lady liked it rough.

Lockington parked himself at the end of a luxurious tufted gray sofa. He said, "Sit down, please."

She sat in a padded wooden rocker, taking a cigarette from a pocket of her robe, lighting it, staring at him. "What *is* it?"

"It's you father—he's dead."

Peggy didn't blink. "I—I knew it was coming—the chemotherapy wasn't taking—but, my God, not this *soon!*"

"He was shot—assailant unknown."

She lunged forward in the rocker, burying her face in her hands, silent for a time. Then she said, "Yes, one way or the other, he was on short time. It's probably better this way. He didn't suffer, did he?"

Lockington shook his head. "It was sudden."

"Do you know why?"

"Does it matter?"

"No."

Lockington said, "Listen, I'm here to give you sound advice. You're going to be very well off—you'll own your own home, you have a fancy car, you'll be the proprietress of a profitable night club, there has to be important money stashed somewhere. Get the hell out of this cocaine thing— you don't need it, and you could wind up doing big time in a federal lockup. You have a kilo of the stuff on the property right now, don't you?"

She raised her head. Blood trickled from a corner of her mouth. She'd bitten through her lower lip. She said, "Yes."

Lockington snapped, "Get rid of it—dump it into a ditch!"

Peggy said, "I did what he told me to do, said what he told me to say. He said that if there was trouble, he'd absolve me and accept full responsibility. I believe that he'd have done that."

Lockington said, "So do I."

"You see, he knew that he was dying—he wanted the money for my mother and me. He felt that he should square up with us for all the years he wasn't there—he meant well."

Lockington said, "You know about your mother?"

"Yes—he told me on the phone after I got home last

night. This is what they call a one-two punch, I guess. I'm an orphan."

"The syndicate killed your mother—it was trying to locate your father and its missing cocaine. You could be next. *Drop* it, do you hear me?"

She was nodding, trying to absorb the shock. "Where is my father's body?"

"I don't know—you'll have to check with the Austintown police."

Her hands were shaking, her poise dissolved. She said, "Look, I'm sorry—you've been used—my father did the planning—I just—oh, *shit!*" She broke into a series of hoarse, racking sobs.

Lockington was on his feet. He crossed the room to ruffle her hair. He said, "Pull your life together, kid—you're young, you have the world by the ass." He went out, closing the door quietly, not looking back.

• • •

He drove south to Mahoning Avenue, then east. Natasha broke the silence. "How did she take it?"

Lockington said, "She'll get over it—she's tough."

They stopped at a restaurant but they didn't eat. They spent an hour drinking coffee, smoking, saying little, feeling each other with their eyes. Natasha smiled once. So did Lockington.

They left the restaurant and Lockington drove to the Flamingo Lounge. Natasha said, "Shall I come in?"

Lockington said, "No, I won't take long."

John Sebulsky was behind the bar, sniffing at a container

of coffee, making a face. He said, "The *Titanic* didn't really hit an iceberg, y'know."

Lockington said, "No, I didn't know."

Sebulsky said, "There was a Greek in the galley, making coffee. He spilled some, and it burned a sixty-foot hole in the bow."

Lockington said, "Well, I'll be damned!"

Sebulsky said, "It's too early for the Sugar sisters—they won't be here for an hour."

Lockington said, "Well, into each life some rain must fall." He ordered a double hooker of Martell's, downed it, and shook hands with Sebulsky. He said, "So long, John—it's been a pleasure."

Sebulsky said, "Back to Chicago?"

Lockington nodded. "For a while."

"Pecos Peggy make out okay?"

"Real good."

"Well, Lacey, if you're ever in town again, be sure to drop in."

"I'll do that."

Lockington left the Flamingo Lounge, turning left into Austintown, passing the Club Crossroads, swinging onto Interstate 80 a mile further on. The sun was bright, the sky was blue. Natasha Gorky lit two cigarettes, handing one to Lockington. He took it. He said, "Thanks." Chicago was probably still there, 425 miles dead west.

75

They were passing the rest stop just east of Akron on Interstate 80. Lockington jerked his head to his left. He said, "That's where Vince Calabrese shot Billy Mac Davis."

Natasha said, "Probably the only decent thing he ever accomplished. Lacey, let's get back to the beginning of this thing—I'll have explanations to make."

Lockington said, "The beginning was probably in the state of Mississippi, in late 'sixty-six—you said that Rufe was working that area then. That'd be when he got Bobbie Jo Pickens pregnant."

"He walked out on her?"

"I doubt that he knew that she was up the creek."

"If he didn't know, when did he find out?"

"About four years ago when he ran into Bobbie Jo at the Chicago Stadium where she was singing with Billy Mac Davis's political campaign. He recognized her, he made contact, and he learned that he was the father of a bouncing seventeen-year-old daughter. That may have bumped Rufe off the tracks."

"Conscience? I don't believe it."

"Well, there's so much good in the worst of us—Rufe had a conscience. It was calloused, but he had one. He became determined to make amends to the Pickens woman and to the daughter he'd never seen—it probably developed into an obsession."

"Where was the girl at that time?"

"Possibly in Mississippi with relatives, growing up, trying to emulate her mother, practicing to become a country singer. I'm not sure of that—I didn't ask her."

"It was Bobbie Jo who got Devereaux involved with LAON?"

"Yes, but I don't believe it was intentional—she probably introduced Rufe to Billy Mac Davis, and I'd imagine that they hit it off like a pair of cattle thieves. They were southern boys with similar leanings. In addition to that, Rufe needed money to set things right and Davis had a ton of it. Eventually they struck a deal—fifty grand a hit. Then, somewhere along the line, Rufe found out that he had cancer and from that point on it was Katie, bar the door—Rufe didn't give a damn. He knew his way around the shady fringes, he had a man to kill in Miami, and he decided to cut a fat hog in the ass. After he'd knocked off Wallace Vernon he drove across town and wasted a Mafia drug supplier named Juarez. He helped himself to a few kilos of cocaine. He owned a house in Leyden Township, a pop-off valve, good for any number of reasons including cooperative ladies—you know about that, of course."

"*Stop* it, Lacey—you're rubbing it in."

"Rufe drove the coke through from Miami and when

he'd dumped it at the place on North Onines Avenue, he was sitting on a potential of something in the vicinity of two million dollars."

"And he was running it to Youngstown a kilo at a time."

"Right. He'd fly to Chicago and come back with an attaché case full of cocaine. There's a ready market for it in the Youngstown area."

"And the Mafia was furious."

"To put it *mildly*—somebody was stealing their thunder, invading their marketplace, and selling Mafia cocaine. They went to work on it and they learned that the slug killing Juarez matched ballistically with the one killing Wallace Vernon."

"But how did the Mafia learn this?"

"How did the KGB get it?"

"Through a leak in the Miami police department."

"That's how the Mafia found out."

"But how did they single out *Devereaux*?"

"How did the KGB single him out?"

"Lacey, the KGB has three hundred thousand operatives in this country!"

"Uh-huh, well, the Mafia has fifty times that many sources of information—every tenth person you meet has Mafia connections of one sort or another. If they aren't genuine Mafioso, they know somebody who *is*. Killing Juarez was a serious offense—you just don't knock over a Mafia drug shipment and get away with it. The outfit turned all the dogs loose on this one!"

"All right, so they knew that Devereaux had killed Juarez and stolen their cocaine. Did they know that Devereaux was the Copperhead?"

"Of course—they knew it long before we did, but the

Mafia didn't give a damn about the Copperhead. The Mafia wanted the man who'd grabbed their coke. They knew it was Rufe, but they didn't know where Rufe was."

"And they believed that you did."

"Yes, but they were working from other angles—a Mafia enforcer named Bugsy Delvano back-tracked a basket of flowers that Bobbie Jo Pickens had sent to Rufe's phony CIA wake. That revealed a link between Bobbie Jo and Rufe. Delvano went to Bobbie Jo's apartment above the Club Howdy, and he beat her to death in an effort to learn Rufe's location. She held the line—all he got was blood on his hands. The same ape cornered me in the funeral home parking lot later that night. My partner cold-cocked him."

"The Mafia believed that you were an accomplice of Devereaux's?"

"Probably not, but they believed that Rufe had turned to me when the going got rough."

"Well, they must have known that Devereaux was somewhere in Ohio—they were waiting at O'Hare when he flew in from Cleveland."

"He could have flown from Minneapolis to Cleveland and then to O'Hare. And knowing that he was holed up somewhere in Ohio wouldn't have helped much. Ohio's the most densely populated state in the country."

"But how did they know that he was coming to O'Hare?"

"There might be a hole in the CIA."

"*Chawrt vuhzmee*, nobody's honest!"

"I had the cocaine, but I didn't *know* it. Rufe had given everybody the slip at Mike's Tavern—he'd taken a cab to his house on North Onines Avenue, he'd loaded up, he'd stopped near my apartment building and jammed the stuff behind the backseat of my car. Then he baited me to Youngstown with an empty matchbook and a thousand dollars. I was Rufe's delivery boy."

"The Mafia could have killed Devereaux when he was in Chicago. Why didn't they?"

"A matter of economics—there was a couple million dollars' worth of cocaine floating around. In Chicago, Rufe's luggage amounted to an attaché case—obviously he wasn't carrying the entire stolen shipment. The Mafia had it ass-backwards—it thought that the cocaine was in *Youngstown* and that he was bringing it to *Chicago*, when it was the other way around. It tried to kill Rufe but only after it was certain that it'd located the remainder of the stuff."

"Where did they think it was?"

"They believed that Peggy was storing it."

They rolled westward through a twenty-minute silence. Natasha's brow was furrowed. She was readying another barrage of questions, Lockington thought. Lockington was right. She asked, "Why did Billy Mac Davis try to kill you?"

"Davis thought that I was onto Rufe. Rufe was Davis's top gun—as the Copperhead he was invaluable. When Davis was sure that I was headed for Youngstown, he went for me."

"But if Devereaux and Davis were close, Davis would have known that Devereaux had sent for you."

"They weren't *that* close—Davis wouldn't have gone with the drug business. He'd have seen it as a focus of unwanted attention. No, Davis didn't know that Rufe wanted me to come to Youngstown."

"But Davis knew that Devereaux was alive, that his murder had been staged?"

"No doubt about that—Davis wouldn't have been

attempting to shield a man he believed to be dead."

"And then the Mafia killed Davis."

"Right—the Mafia was tagging me, figuring that I'd lead them to Rufe and to the cocaine shipment. If they'd lost me, the trail would have gone cold. Davis was interfering. Davis had to go."

"When did they think they'd located the cocaine?"

"Night before last. When Peggy picked me up to take me to Rufe, Mercurio and Calabrese followed us. She dropped me off and they trailed her back to the New Delhi. They saw her take the coke from my car, they added two and two and came up with thirteen. They planned to kill Rufe and me, then beat the facts out of Peggy when she returned to Rufe's—clean sweep."

"Where's that kilo of cocaine now?"

"Peggy had it—if she's smart she doesn't have it now."

"Do you think that the word got back to Chicago?"

"No, there wouldn't have been time. Mercurio and Calabrese are gone, courtesy of your friendly KGB."

"Don't knock the KGB, Lacey—it watched over you."

Lockington swapped subjects. "You reached Youngstown ahead of schedule."

"Yes, I was concerned because of the LAON contract on you. We made the trip at night—I phoned from an Austintown restaurant, not from Chicago. We followed you to the Flamingo Lounge, back to the New Delhi, to the Flamingo again, then to Hubbard and Warren. You were *busy!*"

"So was the KGB man who searched my motel room."

Her half-smile was sheepish. "Standard procedure—I didn't dare violate it. My men kept a protective eye on you that night. When Peggy picked you up they realized that a green Trans Am was on your trail. When she delivered you to Devereaux's place, they parked up the road to the west, staying close to you. When Peggy came back to the motel, the Trans Am was with her, but it returned to Devereaux's property before she did. It pulled into the drive, and after the gunfire my men pursued the Trans Am, eliminating its occupants."

"On your orders, of course."

"If your life was endangered, yes—on my orders."

Lockington felt icy fingers tickle his spinal column. She'd been very ho-hum about it. He said, "Look, just what was the KGB's stake in the game? Rufe had circulated word that he'd written a book. You appeared to be interested in that story, but you *weren't*."

Natasha shook her head. "His ploy was as obvious as the CIA's mock murder and wake. Devereaux thought that he'd be safe so long as he held the threat of a revealing manuscript. It was wishful thinking on his part, nothing more."

"From the very beginning, it was your assignment to kill him, wasn't it?"

"No, not from the very beginning—only from the time we realized that he was the Copperhead."

"That would have been after the killings in Miami."

"Yes. On instructions from LAON, Devereaux was murdering Communist sympathizers in this country. These people have been the backbone of the Soviet movement here—they're in every walk of life, particularly the media. They doctor the news, so that the news disseminated is slanted. Eighty-five percent of America's news distribution is Communist owned or controlled—press, radio, television."

"Misinformation."

"Yes, misinformation."

"The Communists aren't doing too badly on Capitol Hill, either—there's a couple hundred left-leaners up there."

Natasha was nodding. "The Soviet Union has a strong foothold in the United States but LAON and Devereaux were knocking a hole in the infrastructure."

"You couldn't kill Devereaux before you found him. I found him for you."

"You were our best bet—probably our *only* bet."

"I didn't spring the trap, but I put the noose around his neck."

"Regrets?"

"Of course."

"He had every intention of killing *you*, try to remember that."

"He was sick—try to remember *that!*"

"Lacey, a rabid dog is a rabid dog."

"Enough of this. Why was the CIA chasing Rufe?"

"The CIA was the only organization really taken in by his manuscript hoax—it actually believed that he'd written a damaging book. It knew that others were interested and it attempted to throw them off the scent by staging his assassination—it intended to hold matters in abeyance until it could determine how harmful Devereaux's writings might be, until it could round up all copies of the manuscript. Then the CIA would have killed him—*depend* on it. He was an agent gone bad and there's just one way to deal with that type in *any* branch of secret service."

Lockington said, "Yesterday evening, when you went to Room 5 to change for dinner—your men were there and you keyed them for this morning's action."

Natasha winked at him. "Yes, that would have been when you were keying the CIA men in Room 8."

They hammered along Interstate 80, the old Pontiac eating up the miles. In a few minutes Natasha said, "What was your clincher, Lacey—the names of those old baseball players?"

"That was it—you'd mentioned that the Copperhead had killed a Wallace Vernon from an apartment he'd rented under the name of Sam Sheckard. You said that he'd killed a man from an automobile that'd been rented by an Orval Overall, and that he'd knifed a man in a restaurant booth that he'd reserved under the name of Carl Lundgren. At that time these names were meaningless to me. Then I learned that the Club Crossroads had been bought by a man named Jack Taylor, that Peggy's red Porsche was owned by a Patrick Moran, and that the property on North Dunlap Avenue belonged to a Harry Steinfeldt and I *still* hadn't caught the brass ring, but I *should* have!"

"Why?"

"Because that's a standard baseball trivia question, one that I've asked and answered dozens of time—'Who was the fourth man in the Tinker to Evers to Chance Chicago Cubs infield?' The answer is *Harry Steinfeldt.*"

"I'm afraid that I'm not with you."

Lockington went on. "Then, when Rufe told me that he was using the pseudonym of Joseph Tinker, I had a hunch, and when I said that he should write a sequel to his book under the name of John J. Evers, he gave me a strange look. He passed over my remark but I got the impression that I'd hit a nerve."

Natasha said, "John J. Evers—the property on Western Reserve Road is owned by a John J. Evers! Devereaux thought that you'd cracked his cover—he *had* to kill you!"

"He'd have tried anyway—what the hell, fifty G's is fifty G's. An old baseball encyclopedia wrapped it up. The Copperhead was using the names of the 1906 Chicago Cubs—Sheckard, Overall, Lundgren—and so was Rufe—Pfiester, Schulte, Taylor, Moran, Steinfeldt. There comes a time when coincidences cease to be coincidences. The Copperhead and Rufe Devereaux were the same person—the nineteen-oh-six Chicago Cubs were Rufe's favorite baseball team!"

"A slender thread."

"Also, there was the fact that his instructions for receiving the manuscript had been too damned *explicit*—I was to be sitting in my car, waiting for Peggy's delivery at precisely six o'clock. Why did it have to be that way? Why couldn't she have brought it to my door and let me take off for Chicago when I was ready? He was setting me up."

"Do you think that Peggy knew that he'd try to kill you this morning?"

"No—she showed no surprise at my visit."

Another ten miles had fallen behind them when Natasha said, "Lacey, you're a good man."

Lockington said, "No, but once in a while I get lucky."

Natasha squeezed his arm. She said, "So do I."

They were west of Toledo, bearing down on the Indiana line.

76

It was eight o'clock on that evening. The heat was still in Chicago. He sat buried in the shadows of a Shamrock Pub rear booth, nipping at a double Martell's, looking back. Lacey Lockington spent a great deal of his time looking back, probably because he could find so few reasons for looking ahead—tomorrow had never been Lockington's favorite day.

He was taking inventory. He was living in a city that was coming down around his ears. He had $386 in his pocket. He had $721 in the bank. He owned a blue Pontiac Catalina that was due to explode sometime during the span of its next five hundred miles. He owned a private investigation agency that didn't have a client to its name. He'd fallen hopelessly in love with a woman who'd used him shamelessly, one he'd probably never see again. He'd cooperated in the execution of a man whose friendship he'd once valued. He was half-drunk. He needed a shave. He had a headache.

He watched a gross creature leave the Shamrock Pub bar. She lurched toward the ladies' room, passing Lockington's booth, stomping on his feet. Lockington groaned, gritting his teeth, seeing stars. The woman screeched, "You tried to *trip* me, you *swine!*" She belted Lockington alongside the head with a handbag that must have contained an anvil.

Lockington said, "Sorry." He meant every word of it.

Edna Garson came in. She sat at the bar and ordered a screwdriver, watching the door. Lockington raised his hand, waving to Edna. Edna didn't notice. Moose Katzenbach came in. He sat beside Edna at the bar. They embraced, chatting for a few minutes, laughing. Now he knew the identity of the blonde in Moose's booth at the Roundhouse. They hadn't wasted much time. Lockington watched them go out, holding hands. He shrugged. What the hell, he was glad for them. It felt good to be glad.

77

Lockington had been sleeping for three minutes, or perhaps it'd just *seemed* like three minutes—he wasn't sure. Lockington wasn't sure of a lot of things. In fact, he wasn't sure of more things than he was sure of, but there was one thing that he'd have bet his shirt on—*some*body was sitting on the edge of his bed. His .38 police special was in his shoulder holster where it should have been, but his shoulder holster was slung over the back of a chair in the kitchen where it *shouldn't* have been. Sometimes one mistake like that is all a man ever gets. In the darkness Natasha Gorky said, "I just happened to be in the neighborhood."

Lockington said, "Did I forget to lock my door?"

Natasha said, "No, it was locked. Why?"

Lockington said, "Just thought I'd ask."

Natasha said, "You know, it really wasn't as difficult as I thought it would be."

"Picking my lock?"

"No, convincing my superior that Devereaux really had

written a book."

Lockington sat up in bed. He turned on the nightstand lamp, found a pair of cigarettes, lit them, and gave one to Natasha. He said, "I thought that the KGB was laughing at that book yarn."

"It was, but it's stopped. I said that it was a very big book, and very well written. I said that Devereaux had told of the Athens matter."

"The Athens matter?"

"Yes—also the Belgrade business."

"The Belgrade business?"

"Uh-huh—Boris turned pale when I said that Devereaux had gotten into the Belgrade business."

"Boris?"

"Boris Kaputchev—he's in charge of Midwestern KGB affairs."

"You've been in bed with Boris Kaputchev?"

"He's my superior."

"That doesn't answer my question."

"Yes, it does. But that was before my retirement."

"Your retirement—when did you retire?"

Natasha took Lockington's wrist, tilting it against the light, peering at his watch. "Fifty-three minutes ago."

Lockington said, "Hell, it could be an hour—you can't trust that watch."

Natasha yawned. "Small matter—time's of no consequence when you're retired."

Lockington got out of bed, hitching up his pajama bottoms, walking toward the darkened living room, Natasha following him closely. In the living room he tripped, falling like a redwood. He said, "*Lights*, for Christ's sake!"

Natasha switched on a lamp. She said, "I don't believe I should have left it there."

Lockington sat up dazedly. "You don't believe you should have left *what where?*"

"My overnight bag—I don't believe I should have left it in the middle of the floor."

Lockington was shaking his head. He said, "At the risk of seeming presumptuous, I believe it is time that I learn just what the hell is going on here."

Natasha said, "Oh, yes—well, you see, this evening I went to see Boris Kaputchev. He was at work."

"Uh-huh, and where does Boris Kaputchev work?"

"He's night janitor in the Chicago CIA offices."

"Ah, yes—Boris has access to the Telex room?"

"Certainly—I met him there tonight. Noisy place."

"How did you get into the installation?"

"I told them that I was taking up a collection for charity."

"What charity?"

"They didn't ask, but I raised seventeen dollars."

"Nothing like airtight security. Back to Boris, please."

"We had a long talk—I told Boris that there are many copies of Devereaux's manuscript. Then I made certain inferences and stressed certain conditions."

"Certain conditions?"

"Yes, we were discussing my severance pay."

"The KGB gives *severance* pay?"

"It does now—in my case, one hundred thousand dollars."

Lockington didn't say anything.

Natasha said, "Plus the black Mercedes I've been driving—I've become accustomed to it, you see."

"I see."

"It's parked out front—my luggage is in it."

"But your overnight bag isn't."

"No, I brought it in because I didn't know what you might have in mind. I wasn't sure if you'd want to leave now or in the morning."

"Leave—for where?"

"I was thinking in terms of Youngstown, Ohio. It has trees—like Odessa."

Lockington got to his feet. He said, "It's now or in the morning?"

Natasha Gorky took his face between her hands, looking up at him with starry pale-blue eyes. She said, "Let's make it in the morning."

78

Their previous morning had been harrowing, their trip long, their evening eventful and revealing, the hours prior to their final Chicago dawn emotionally and physically exhausting. They'd slept. They hadn't gotten away in the morning, or in the afternoon. They'd gotten away at eight o'clock that night.

Natasha had driven south to the Eisenhower Expressway, swinging east to bore through the lower end of downtown Chicago, then south again. They'd just passed the 35th Street exit when Lockington said, "Would you pull over for just a moment?"

Natasha said, "Why—is something wrong?"

Lockington said, "Nothing that I can't fix."

She whipped the Mercedes onto the shoulder, stopping. Lockington got out, leaning against the car, looking back to the north. There she stood, the old whore—Chicago. She was silhouetted against the starless night sky, wearing her glittering diamond tiara of skyscraper lights, her long gray skirts of smog concealing her disease, her crimson sores, her seeping pustules. Lacey Lockington lifted his hand to her. He'd never come back, he knew that to be a fact. He just didn't love her anymore.

A southbound blue-and-white slowed to pull behind the Mercedes. A policeman shoved his head through the window. "Trouble, buddy?"

Lockington swiped at his eyes with the back of his hand, Chicago memories billowing over him. He said, "No problem, officer—I was just saying goodbye to Mrs. O'Leary."

The cop said, "Mrs. O'Leary?"

Lockington opened the door to the Mercedes. He nodded. "Yeah—Mrs. O'Leary—she owned a cow—"

DEATH WORE GLOVES

When Sister Rosetta's niece goes missing, the nun (whose favorite poison is anything bottle-bound and boozy) hires shifty P.I. Tut Willow to find dear Gladys. But as Tut pulls back the curtain on Gladys' checkered past, he also finds that someone doesn't want her found, and soon bodies begin to pile up. Is Sister Rosetta, lured by a twisted sense of family loyalty, behind the deaths of those out to harm her niece, or are Tut and Gladys just pawns in a much darker game?

Full of laugh-out-loud comedy and the darkest of intrigue, the author of *Death Wore Gloves* draws together femme fatales, a not-so-saintly nun, and a gumshoe willing to do anything to help an old flame.

KIRBY'S LAST CIRCUS

When the CIA chooses Birch Kirby, a mediocre detective with a personal life even less thrilling than his professional one, no one is more surprised by the selection than Birch himself. But the Agency needs someone for a secret mission, and Birch may be just the clown for the job. Going undercover as a circus performer, he travels to Grizzly Gulch to investigate the source of daily, un-decodeable secret messages that are being transmitted to the KGB. Birch interacts with wildly colorful characters while stumbling through performances as well as his assignment. With the clock ticking, Birch must hurry to take a right step toward bringing the curtain down on this very important case.

THE LACEY LOCKINGTON SERIES

THE FIFTH SCRIPT

Detective Lacey Lockington always gets the job done, but making the omelets of solved cases usually involves breaking a lot of eggs. So when Lacey gets suspended after tabloid columnist Stella Starbright names him as a "kill-crazy cop," he has to find new work as a private investigator. It's a step down, for sure, and one of his first cases is an unlikely one: former "Stella Starbrights" are turning up dead on the streets of Chicago, and the current one, the reputation ruiner herself, turns to an unlikely source for protection.

Going against his gut, Lacey agrees to keep tabs on Stella to keep her from sharing the grisly fate of her former namesakes. In the midst of all the madness, Lacey hunts the real killer, someone looking to silence gossip columnists for good. But can Lacey crack the case before another victim makes a different section of the newspapers?

Sex…violence…booze! This deadly mix will keep you on the edge of your seat in Ross Spencer's jaded-but-jaunty tale about a hardened cop with nothing but his reputation to lose.

THE FEDOROVICH FILE

The Cold War heats up when trouble comes knocking on the door of ex-cop turned Private Eye Lacey Lockington. Lacey is hot on the trail of Alexi Fedorovich after the high-ranking general publishes a controversial exposé detailing that Glasnost/Perestroika is a hoax. Federovich goes into hiding in the last place he suspects someone will look for him—somewhere in Youngstown, Ohio.

For someone who's pretty much seen and done it all, Lacey's unnerved when he starts dealing with Russian spies, Federal Agents, a man who doesn't want to be found, and an increasing body count of all his leads. Will Lacey, along with former KGB agent and live-in lover Natasha, get to the bottom of it all before Fedorovich finds himself on the wrong end of a firing squad?

THE CHANCE PURDUE SERIES

THE DADA CAPER

Chance Purdue may be better at a lot of things than he is at detecting, but he's the only man for the job when the FBI comes looking for someone to take on the Soviet-inspired DADA conspiracy.

Plus, he needs a paycheck. Chance gets off to a rough start as he's led on a merry chase through Chicago's underbelly and drawn into a case of deception that can only be solved with the help of a mysterious femme fatale who's as beautiful as she is cunning.

THE REGGIS ARMS CAPER

Try as he may, Chance Purdue can't seem to escape the world of private investigation. The now tavern owner returns to action to protect Princess Sonia of Kaleski, who claims to be the wife of an old Army buddy. Convinced he'll get to the bottom of things at his Army battalion's reunion, Chance indulges in the entertainment while leaving the more serious detective work to his new colleague, the scintillating Brandy Alexander. For Chance, the case provides more fun than intrigue, and yet its solution is a surprise for everyone involved.

THE STRANGER CITY CAPER

A quick and easy buck sounds good to Private Investigator Chance Purdue. But the paycheck seems to be a bit harder to earn when the job entails more than just looking into the a minor league baseball team in southern Illinois. His new client, the gangster Cool Lips Chericola, is definitely leaving out details. Enter Brandy Alexander, whose unexpected appearance in Stranger City, Illinois complicates things. Then throw in the Bobby Crackers' Blitzkrieg for Christ religious crusade, and you've got a super-charged powderkeg of a caper, with Chance holding both the match and the barrel.

THE ABU WAHAB CAPER

What happens when Chicago detective Chance Purdue is hired to protect a gambler with a target on his head? For starters, all hell breaks loose…

"Bet-a-Bunch" Dugan is being hunted by International DADA (Destroy America, Destroy America) conspirators, a terrorist organization out for control of the world's oil market. Dugan needs more than a little luck to walk away unscathed. He needs a Chance, and though he knows that half of Purdue's reputation is that of a guy you are aching to punch, the other half is that he's a dogged, if occasionally doomed, investigator.

No matter where Purdue's leads take him, though, he always seems to be one step behind DADA. As a hapless Chance watches DADA's deadly scheme move forward, a siren named Brandy Alexander enters the picture and things finally fall into place, or so Chance hopes…

THE RADISH RIVER CAPER

Private Investigator Chance Purdue and Brandy Alexander work in tandem on a case that finds them traveling to the Illinois town of Radish River. The CIA continues to need help putting a stop to the DADA (Destroy America, Destroy America) Conspiracy, a terrorist organization whose latest plot is completely under wraps, except that it promises immense destruction. Things prove difficult for Chance and Brandy as they do what they can to remain focused on the task at hand. But it's hard when distractions from football-playing gorillas, chariot races, copious booze—and especially each other—weave in and out of their lives and keep this case on the back burner.